DELIVERANCE OF
THE BLESSED

A B Endacott

Cover designed by Marcus Moltzer
Cover illustration by Nicole Sizer
Map illustration by Ellen Liu

This book is a work of fiction. Names, characters, places, and incidents either
are products of the author's imagination or are used fictitiously.
Any resemblance to actual persons,
living or dead, events, or locales is entirely coincidental.

ISBN 978-0-6487299-3-8

This work contains references to grief, oppression, and psychological mistreatment.

Books by the same author

The Second Country
Queendom of the Seven Lakes
King of the Seven Lakes

The Fourth Country
The Ruthless Land

The Third Country
Dark Intent
Dark Purpose
Dark Heart

Non Fiction (with Debut Books)
Mirror, Mirror

This book is dedicated in loving memory to my grandfather,

and to anybody struggling with the loss of someone they love.

"Do I seem mad to you? Well I am mad from not being able to shout what my heart demands.
There's a scream in my heart that's always rising up and I have to force it down."

-Frederico Garcia Lorca, Blood Wedding

ONE

Sunlight cascaded down from the high windows, coating the room in an ethereal haze. Kaylene's steps were cautious as she went deeper into the Hall of Mysteries. The air inside was cool due to the thick stone of the Sanctuary walls. Nerves churned through her. It was the first time in a long while that she had felt anything this intently. She ignored the array of exquisitely embellished plates, blunted weapons and rolled tapestries; they only registered in the periphery of her vision as she passed by them. She and her friends were here for only one thing. It was near. She could feel it.

The presence of her friends quelled her fluttering nerves. Leshan walked on her left, her jaw clenched so tightly it seemed certain teeth would break. Merika and Callam walked behind them; Callam's footfalls held the distinctive tap of someone who was overcoming trepidation with determination. It made sense – Luka was his brother, after all. Merika's footsteps were the most casual; she'd explored the Hall of Mysteries many times with disdain for any consequence she may face.

As with so much in the Sanctuary, none of the Blessed were explicitly prohibited from going into it, but it was clear that purposeless entrance was viewed as a form of superfluous curiosity. While they may not receive any specific punishment for being in the Hall, they certainly would be closely scrutinised, and all of Kaylene's desperate hopes required them to be paid as little attention as possible for the time being. Of course, if what they were trying to do was discovered, Kaylene was under no illusion that the Sanctuary would punish them – severely. They'd never be allowed to leave.

A Senior Blessed stepped from the shadows, making Kaylene jump. The crimson of her tightly fitted Sanctuary-garb seemed traitorously gentle in the afternoon light.

"What are you four doing here?" Her voice was thick with suspicion.

"Good afternoon," Kaylene said with perfected deference. She carefully kept fear from her face and far in the back of her mind. They had counted on nobody else being down here.

"And to you, child." Disapproval was definitely in her voice, as had been the heavy irony in her emphasis on the word "child". Kaylene and her friends were all into their adulthood. Their presence in the Sanctuary was an aberration.

Kaylene cringed inwardly. Some of the Senior Blessed were sympathetic to those who had not proved themselves sufficiently in control of themselves to be allowed to leave. Most weren't.

"Do you have a good reason for being in the Hall of Mysteries?" the Senior Blessed demanded.

"We had the afternoon free and wanted to accompany Merika here." Sweat collected under her arms and in the small of her back, pressed into her skin by the tightly-fitted style of clothes she was required to wear.

Merika stepped forward, an uncharacteristically ingratiating smile on her face. "There's an item here I need for my study –"

The Senior Blessed cut her off, clearly unimpressed. "This is not a place for playing with your friends. I would have thought the four of you were old enough to not require an escort."

It was ironic, Kaylene thought, that this woman had once been in a similar position to Kaylene and her friends, yet her animosity toward them was so unchecked. A bubble of anger at the Senior Blessed's hypocrisy began to swell in the back of her mind, pushing away the dark sadness that had shrouded her for so long.

The woman opened her mouth, doubtless to administer more rebukes, but her face went unnaturally still, the expression of malevolence into which it was contorted fixed into place.

Kaylene looked in shock at Callam. Of them all, only Leshan was less likely to breach the rules which encircled their lives. The reality of what they were doing – of everything they were risking to come here; their freedom, and even their safety – pricked at her. Callam's eyes were locked on the Senior Blessed; mindsmiths were rare, and what he was doing now was almost unheard of, due to the skill and difficulty it required.

"She wasn't going to let any of us stay," he said before Kaylene could ask her question.

"Can you hold her for long enough for us to look?" Merika asked. She was the most decisive of them, and always the first to act.

"You'd better start now," Callam said, the strain of speaking and holding the Senior Blessed in place evident in his voice.

The three scattered. The instructions were seared in their minds: a scroll of animal hide, old, with handles of green stone. Kaylene didn't even allow herself to consider the possibility that it may not be down here, or that they might not be able to locate it. Hers was not the only life that depended upon them finding the scroll.

Kaylene had been ready to end her life only the previous day – her birthday, although such occasions were not recognised within the Sanctuary. Kaylene had spent so many years behind its walls that she had forgotten which birthday it had been. She knew she had passed her twentieth year, but did not know how long ago that had been; she was amazed she still remembered the date of her birth. The salt air had stung her lips as she approached the cliff. She could hear the water crashing against the rocks below, the water that would carry her lifeless body away once she made the jump. A part of her wondered whether she possessed the courage to actually launch herself off the cliff. She imagined what it would feel like to fall through the air, to have the wind caress her as she flew down faster and faster until she hit the rocks below. There was something almost invigorating about the prospect of flight, even if it would be for only a few fleeting seconds. It was nice to think she would end her life feeling as though she were flying.

When she had reached the cliff's edge, her expectation that she would be afraid went unmet. She sat on the grass which tenaciously clung to the ground, staring at the expanse of sea. She traced the specks of white far out from shore that were ships making their way toward Curnith – the only way into the First Country. Where she was once fascinated by the distant lands those ships reached, lands she would never see, she found nothing. Instead, she just embraced the serenity of the moment. She would soon join Luka. She contemplated whispering a prayer to the many-faced god to guide her to a quick death but did not want to upset her sense of calm – of anticipation – by worrying about trivialities such as how long it would take her to die.

Her peace was disturbed by an old woman with skin tanned to a deep brown and wrinkles drawn on her face by a generous hand. The woman sat next to her with an unpardonable air of familiarity.

Kaylene stared at her, indignation intruding into the serenity that had settled over her. "Can I help you?"

The woman stared toward the horizon. "It's a long way down. Are you sure you want to get there by jumping?"

Kaylene's initial shock was quelled by logic; few people would come to the edge of a cliff for a protracted time simply to admire the view. It would have been easy to discern her intention.

"I have my reasons." Her reply was calm. The Sanctuary would have been proud of the control she was demonstrating.

"I'm sure you do," the woman said. "Perhaps I can help, though."

"Nobody can help me." Kaylene spoke with no anger, no misery, only certainty. Perhaps finally she had mastered herself. The irony that only when she had lost the desire to live free had she found the control that would have released her from the Sanctuary.

"You seem awfully certain. Do you really think you know everything about the world around you?"

There seemed a certain prescience to the question that gave Kaylene pause. She chose her words with caution. "I believe I know enough."

"Perhaps you should tell me your story, and see what I have to say," the woman suggested. "My name is Ay'ash."

Kaylene blinked in surprise. It was a name of one of the Old Ones, who claimed to be the original inhabitants of the land – whatever that meant. They were a reclusive lot, preferring to live in seclusion amid nature rather than in settlements. It was a fair preference given the treatment that had been inflicted upon their people.

"I also bear no great love for the Sanctuary," Ay'ash said.

That made sense. The Old Ones' beliefs and customs were not well known, nor were the powers they were rumoured to possess. There were suggestions that Ay'ash's people had some connection to the gods who had blessed Kaylene's people with their powers, but the Old Ones were tight-lipped and resisted any effort to force them to attend the Sanctuary. In response to their defiance, the Old Ones were permitted to only live within the

First Country's society under a barrage of restrictions so severe that it made life in the Sanctuary look lackadaisical.

Kaylene hesitated to reveal too much. The Old Ones were notorious for giving advice that later came back to haunt the person who had accepted it. But such tales were possibly more superstition than truth. The wizened old woman beside her radiated no air of malevolence. And Kaylene found herself wanting to speak of the pain that had wrapped itself around her and refused to let go. So she told Ay'ash about Luka, the unfairness of his death, the unbearable sense of loss that his absence left in her, and the fact that even her friends could not ease her misery. No, misery was too simple a word. She was shrouded in an inability to find any moment of joy in the endless moments that filled her day. Life had become stale in its sadness. Her story came to a halting end when she put into words her decision to come to the cliffs.

Ay'ash maintained her serene expression.

"That's one way of doing it," she said. "Or you could bring him back."

Kaylene trawled through the hall's packed shelves. The items were theoretically catalogued in accordance with a system, but she could discern no pattern. As her gaze skidded past a wooden bowl, she wondered if the Sanctuary truly believed these objects contained any power – Blessed or otherwise – or if they were simply items that could be neither categorised nor destroyed and thus were relegated to the Hall of Mysteries. Perhaps the amalgamation of seemingly useless and supposedly dangerous items was meant to deliberately confuse anyone seeking something of worth, leaving them unable to distinguish between what might be a truly potent item or a mere soup bowl.

"I think I've found it!" Leshan's voice echoed through the room, high with triumph and nerves.

"Hurry," Callam called. Strain hung heavily in the single word.

"Are you certain it's the scroll we need?" Merika's disembodied voice rolled across the cavernous space.

"Bright green handles, some sort of animal leather, rolled up. How many other items could look like that?"

"I won't be able to hold her for much longer." Callam's panic made his voice rise.

Kaylene shuffled as quickly as she could back to her friend and the immobile woman, pushing the limits of her restrictive clothes. Leshan was already there, the scroll for which Callam was risking so much clutched in her hand. It looked so small for something so vital to her hopes – to all their hopes.

"Is everybody where they were?" Callam asked.

"I think so," Kaylene said as Merika skidded into place.

The heavy wheeze of the woman's breath was the first sign that Callam had released his hold on her mind. Then she blinked as though surprised, looking carefully at the four before her. Her gaze roved over each of them in turn, suspicion making her eyes sparkle. Kaylene's heart sank. Her hand crept to her waist and the little knife she had secreted in her waistband. She had feared it would come to this. But as drastic action went from last resort to possibility, she felt a curious calm. There was nothing she would not do. The life of one bigoted woman seemed inconsequential against the enormity of her misery.

She had never killed anybody. She wondered if it would be difficult or messy. As the woman glared at them, conducting her silent evaluation, Kaylene looked for ways she could conceal the crime she had already committed in her mind. She would need something to mop up the blood. Provided they could move the body, she was certain she could call plants to pull the body deep into the earth where it would never be found. But in order to do the deed, she would have to be fast, make her blows count.

Callam coughed. The sound surprised Kaylene, its normalcy scattering the dark thoughts.

The woman gave them one final, especially unpleasant, glare. "Get out. This is no place for the likes of you. Even the young ones must have permission to be here."

Kaylene's fingers slipped away from the blade. The four friends arranged their faces into pictures of contrition and resentment and did as the Senior Blessed of Mysteries bade them. Only once they were out of earshot did they quietly confer among themselves about their success.

"Are you certain she won't remember a thing?" Kaylene caught Callam's gaze, wanting to be reassured by certainty in his features.

Instead, she glimpsed an expression on his face that bore a distinct resemblance to revulsion, but he moved his gaze away from her as he answered, so she couldn't be certain.

"I don't know, Kaya," he said. "I think so. If she remembers, it's because she thinks something was odd about us."

"Do you think she'll know you were holding the scroll?" Merika's tone was crisp and bossy as she addressed Leshan.

Leshan did not bristle at Merika's manner of address as Kaylene would have. Instead, she shook her head thoughtfully and pulled the scroll out of her bag. Taking the bag had been a risk, but they'd all agreed there was no other way they could hide the scroll, and Leshan was known across the Sanctuary for her obeisance. "I don't think so. It's quite small. Unless someone goes looking for it, I think we'll be safe."

Ay'ash had led her along a narrow path to a cave high in the cliff face. It opened up inside, its size and furnishings more like a rudimentary stone house than a cave.

Ay'ash motioned for Kaylene to sit on a colourful rug while she prepared tea. Kaylene accepted a rough ceramic vessel, the tea hot and swirling with flavours Kaylene could not identify.

The woman seated herself opposite Kaylene with an ease that belied her age.

Kaylene was not sure she believed Luka could be brought back, but the certainty exuded by the Old One had made her at least willing to extend the moments before her death long enough to hear the woman speak. The knowledge that she still had that option gave an odd sort of comfort – a promise that even if the ember of hope offered by the Old One's words were to be extinguished, the suffering it caused would be only short-lived.

"Do you really believe that I can bring him back?" she asked when it seemed the Old One was content to sip tea rather than talk.

The wave of a hand dismissed her disbelief in an almost scornful manner. "There are far more permanent things in this world than death."

"What do you mean?"

As Ay'ash began to speak, her voice, despite the creak imparted by untold years, took on a melodic quality that drew Kaylene in. The words themselves were lost amid the telling, imparting on Kaylene their general meaning.

The Old One spoke of a time when the world was more fluid, and barriers between realms did not exist. Ancient powers that could reshape the very fabric of the world flowed freely then, but then the divide between realms came, and people forgot about that part of history, and about exactly what those powers could do. Slivers of the truth had endured across history, woven into superstition and mythology about the power of a god to shape the world at will. These pieces of knowledge, she claimed, could be found, understood, and used like a god might use them, including movement between the arbitrary confines of death and life. Despite the fantasy of it all, Kaylene found herself believing this diminutive woman. The Old Ones were themselves all but fantasy, after all.

"I don't want to be a god," Kaylene said when the woman had finished. "I just want him back."

"There is a scroll of animal hide with handles of bright green stone in the Hall of Mysteries. Find it."

The four friends hid their jubilation until they were in Kaylene's room, the three girls piled on the narrow bed, Callam on the floor. Only then did their smiles blossom. Of them, Callam's was the least effusive, offset by a crease of worry on his forehead.

"Cal, is everything all right?" Kaylene asked.

He wrapped his arms around his knees, his blue eyes – so similar to his brother's – reflecting the worry on his brow. His gaze flicked away from hers and she wondered if he'd read her thoughts about killing the Senior Blessed. She braced for him to announce it to their friends, excuses on her tongue, even though they sounded feeble in her own mind. She wondered what Luka would have thought about her willingness to kill – he almost certainly would have been shocked, even disappointed. Or perhaps Callam had somehow heard her thoughts about her plan to end her life. When she'd initially told her friends of her encounter with Ay'ash, she had lied about the reason for being on the cliff, instead claiming she'd needed a moment to herself. Her friends had worried enough about her for the past months. She didn't want them converging around her now for fear she might try again. She wanted to be able to slip away – from them and this life – if Ay'ash had not spoken true.

Callam murmured, "I used my Blessing on another person."

The mood in the room changed as the seriousness of breaking so many of the Sanctuary's rules impressed itself on them, making the room seem claustrophobically small. Kaylene wondered if the others were worried about where the path they had begun to walk would end. The thought was quickly banished. The only thing that mattered, the only possible ending she could entertain, was one in which she held Luka alive and well. Everything else receded into a misty half-land of incoherence.

Merika gripped Callam's arm. Her sharp features were enhanced by the fierce set of her jaw.

"They keep us here claiming that we're not in sufficient control of our emotions. They treat us with disdain, and they expect us to remain obedient to them, respectful – no, reverential – to them." Her voice was tight with a resentment they all shared in different ways. It made her point all the more powerful. "There's nothing for you to be worried about other than whether or not we'll get caught, which we won't."

"But what if it's all for nothing?" Callam asked.

"Then we find another way," Kaylene said. Panic sought to claim her at the possibility. She felt Leshan's hand on her arm, reassuring, comforting, her friend instinctively understanding the grief that had bloomed inside Kaylene. She was grateful for her friend's comfort. Callam looked at her, his doubt obviously finding no quarter.

"That scroll will tell us how to bring him back from the dead," she told him, believing it with every part of her being. She had no other choice.

TWO

She dreamed she was with Luka. His arms were around her – she could even smell the scent which lay along his skin. They spoke, but she didn't pay attention to the words. The hum of his voice, the feel of his arms around her, even though a small part of her knew it wasn't possible for him to be there holding her, she let herself believe in the fiction her mind had created for as long as it would endure.

She woke alone. For a wondrous moment the last vestiges of the dream clung and she reached out. The emptiness of her narrow bed pressed upon her. The grief that engulfed her was familiar, but that made it no easier to bear. Her breath hitched. Her outstretched arm came to curl around herself as though she could hold the pieces of her broken heart together. Gradually, the burden of her sadness became bearable once more. Yet today she didn't have to debate with herself about whether or not she should get out of bed. Today, she had an ember of hope that pushed back against the darkness of her grief.

She dressed and made her way to the breakfast hall on the Sanctuary's lower floor. She was handed food by a girl of maybe fourteen who looked at her with open judgment.

Callam and Leshan were already sitting at the table the four friends normally occupied. Around them thronged other inhabitants of the Sanctuary – all much younger than Kaylene and her friends. She collected stares as she passed. Where once she had cared, or tried to find ways to prove herself unworthy of such disapproval, the loss of Luka had brought on an indifference to what others thought of her, but the desire to go totally unnoticed – to avoid all contact with people beyond her three friends. It was easy to make herself as small as possible, tucking her arms close into her body and ducking her head as though that meant the stares would miss her and she could pretend nobody else was there. The tightly-fitted top pinched against her shoulders, trying to force her to return to the rigid, straight-backed posture the clothes demanded of her.

Callam shuffled over as she approached and Lesha pushed a dish of sliced kerren fruit toward her; it normally went quickly, and Kaylene had come in late. She forced herself to smile – they were looking out for her.

Merika strode through the dining hall, her sharp features arrayed in a customarily unfriendly expression. Nobody dared look at her for too long and certainly not with any scorn or disdain. Her sharp tongue and willingness to unleash it on anyone meant people generally gave her a wide berth. Kaylene often wished she shared Merika's disinterest about what others thought of her protracted tenure at the Sanctuary.

The thought of their extended time at the Sanctuary made Kaylene glance over at Leshan. Beautiful Leshan with eyes the colour of sunrise and hair like sunbeams was the one whose continued presence here made the least sense. Kaylene had never seen Leshan angry, never seen her display the emotional excess for which they had all been detained rather than being let back into the outside world. Leshan was who the arrogant twelve and thirteen-year-olds would listen to with some respect and speak to with any apparent warmth. Luka had been like that, too. But now she had only Leshan.

"That scroll is useless," Merika said as she reached them. Her blunt proclamation had the other three looking around in panic to see who might have overheard. Fortunately, their status as pariahs meant everybody wanted to leave them alone.

Merika pursed her lips at her friends' caution, but sat down next to Leshan and lowered her voice anyway. "Does anybody know ancient languages? Because that's the only way we'll be able to even tell if the scroll says anything about raising the dead."

"You didn't find anything about the language written on the scroll?" Callam brushed the long fringe of hair, behind which he usually hid, out of his eyes to better regard Merika.

Merika made a show of slapping her forehead. "That's what I should have been doing rather than simply staring at the leather and waiting for it to make sense! Researching!" Her gaze softened and she made a gesture of apology to Callam. "Nothing that I could find gives any explanation on how to read the language – not even Kaya could decipher it. Anything I can find references the Old Ones' script and moves on without further explanation. It's almost as though someone went through every single text and removed that kind of information."

Kaylene felt as though weights were being placed on her body, making it almost impossible to remain upright. Without any way to translate the scroll, Luka would stay dead. The hope that had burned within her bright enough to make life seem bearable flickered, and the unendurable misery lurking in the shadows of her mind took a step forward.

Luka's death had fundamentally diminished the friends. The five had initially found solidarity in their shared status as outcasts. They became friends when they realised that they actually liked each other's company. While they all might have been deemed unbalanced in their emotional control, somehow the five together found an equilibrium. Luka's death had caused more than simple absence. It had thrown out that balance. Without his brother, Callam had become even more withdrawn, Leshan had become more fretful, Merika sharper, and Kaylene's entire world had fallen apart.

She could still remember the first time she had seen Luka, hair an eye-catching shade of mauve accenting eyes of soft blue, that shy smile sneaking across his face. She could remember him so clearly that it left an ache in her chest – the ache of where he should be, squeezed in next to her, looking conspiratorially up at Merika, offering a solution she might not have seen, pulling Callam out of his reluctance to be noticed and asking what he thought. Had he been there, Leshan would have smiled and said something unexpectedly funny, and Kaylene would have offered her own solutions. Luka's absence was everywhere, etched into the stone walls around them. And moments like this when it felt everyone was waiting for someone who wasn't present only served to reinforce the totality of his absence. Kaylene's desire to escape this constant, painful reminder gripped her yet again, and her thoughts returned to the cliff's edge.

Leshan broke the long, heavy silence. "Would your Old One be of any help, Kaya?"

Kaylene gnawed on her bottom lip as she considered. Blood, unexpected in its bright, salty taste, danced across the tip of her tongue. "I'm not sure. She said if we found the scroll it would give us everything we would need. If she knew that it was written in a language with no record, surely she would have told me."

"It's worth going to ask her, though, isn't it?" Callam said, raising his head with a quick, nervous gesture to meet her gaze. His eyes, blue like his brother's, sent another blow of sorrow through her.

She nodded and Callam's gaze flicked away from her eyes, down to her lips, then finally came to rest on the table's surface. She wondered if he could hear her thoughts, sense her grief at the loss of his brother. He had told them that he never pried into their minds. But she was not a mindsmith, and she had no idea if people's thoughts sometimes jumped out across the distance between people, especially if projected with enough force. It had always felt too rude to ask if that suspicion was true.

"It's a good idea," Merika said, her gaze still sharp, but without the intensity as when she had first arrived.

"I'll go today," Kaylene said. Hope resurfaced, and the bands of emptiness wrapped around her chest eased. The promise of action and the faint possibility of a solution was a raft to which she clung. "After we finish washing the Senior Blesseds' rugs," she added, allowing a groan to slip out.

Merika's pursed lips pushed tighter against one another at the reminder of the task set for them today. As they got older, the four friends were made to perform less and less pleasant chores. Kaylene remembered the days when she simply had been required to clean dishes. Washing the rugs of the senior members of the Sanctuary was a time-consuming and fiddly exercise that they were told was going to teach them patience. Kaylene was certain it was simply their punishment for not satisfactorily mastering themselves. As if such a thing were truly so easy. At least they were assigned the task together. Such tedium was always alleviated when shared with the others – it had always been that way, even with the dishes.

"Are you going to eat?" Kaylene asked Merika. She pushed the dish with the remaining kerren fruit toward her.

Her friend shook her head. "I ate while I was reading." It was prohibited to take food into the archives, but apparently that had not stopped Merika. Very little did.

"All right, let's go then," Leshan said with a sigh.

With a wave, Merika sent the crockery and cutlery flying across the room and onto the pile of dirty dishes. The display of her Blessing caused everybody to look at her in uncertain awe. Her smile was smug.

"You shouldn't do that," Leshan softly scolded as they walked out.

Merika gave her a look of cool indignation. "Why not? We are Blessed. We are given this power to use, not to learn how to stuff ourselves away so that only the barest embers of it are ever displayed."

Callam snorted but did not offer any comment.

"They're protecting us," Leshan said.

"No, they're restraining us," Merika countered.

As the four walked, Merika and Leshan fell into the comfortable rhythm of a familiar argument.

"Meri, you know what can happen if a Blessed does not know how to manage their emotions. The destruction that they can wreak—"

"We are blessed by the *many-faced god*, Lesha," Merika said with zeal refined over years of having this argument. "We're special, but we're treated as though our gifts are a shame on us. Perhaps we would better learn control if we were not told to hide who we are."

"I do not disagree that the ways of the Senior Blessed can seem harsh, but they are like us, Meri. What would they possibly have to gain from speaking about us – like themselves – in a way that describes us as dangerous if it weren't true?"

"Perhaps they've been told by so many that they should be ashamed of who they are – of their Blessing – that they're afraid of how they may be viewed if what they can truly accomplish is known," Merika retorted.

"What they can truly accomplish? Meri, you've been reading all night, I can tell by the circles under your eyes and the fact that you're speaking with someone else's words. We all know too well what damage can be done by a Blessed who has lost control of themselves."

Leshan's voice was gentle, but Kaylene still winced. Beside her, Callam's step hitched. She tried not to let the sense of loss bear her down. Even after all these months, it felt fresh each time.

"I've read every book in this divine-blessed place. I can see the truth behind the words of others when I come across it," Merika snapped.

Leshan, despite her sweet nature, had a way of knowing exactly what to say to rile Merika.

Kaylene and Callam remained silent as they walked through the halls of the Sanctuary, listening to the new combination of words put to the old argument between Leshan and Merika. They shared a glance of solidarity, comfortable in their shared spectatorship. The only thing missing was Luka, interjecting, taking the side of whoever he felt most deserving on the day. Kaylene was grateful neither Merika nor Leshan had explicitly mentioned what had happened to Luka, despite the reference to it. Merika had made a reasonable point, though. The Senior Blessed had a lot to answer for.

Merika and Leshan's argument petered out by the time they reached the chambers of the Senior Blessed. Such discussions were best not had within the earshot of the Sanctuary's overseers. Or indeed, many of its junior members. Callam knocked tentatively. Receiving no response, he opened the door. The room was the same size as Kaylene's and furnished with a similar lack of ornamentation. The absence of any personalisation or luxury was part of the Sanctuary's creed to eschew any emotional excess in pursuit of the greatest possible mastery of the self. Kaylene's room was also graced with a rug, but that was hers to clean. In theory, mastery of one's self-control as was seen in the Senior Blessed left little time for more practical matters, such as cleaning their rooms. Fortunately, there were enough of those who had yet to demonstrate their control to perform those duties.

Today the four had been tasked with cleaning the rugs of the Senior Blesseds' bedrooms. With mundane efficiency, they went along the corridor, collecting the rugs from the seventeen rooms. Whenever they went into the rooms of the Senior Blessed, Kaylene looked intently for tiny indications of the occupant's personality. There was always something; it just required a careful eye to find. In Senior Blessed Yaen's room, a jug of water and two cups suggested he frequently shared the evenings with someone. A much-read book of murder tales spoke to Senior Blessed Rael's affection for the genre. And the barrenness of Senior Blessed Maryam's room, in addition to the precise way her bed was made, spoke to her rigid devotion to the Sanctuary's ethos. Soon, all four friends had arms piled high with carpets, straining against their tight-fitted clothes to steady the loads. Halfway to the yard, Leshan spilled her bundle. The rugs tumbled to the ground with a series of thuds. A cloud of dust drifted into the air. Merika whisked them back into Leshan's arms with a quick gesture before Leshan could bend down to pick them up.

"Thank you," Leshan said.

Merika returned the thanks with a smirk. "I thought we were supposed to not use our Blessings."

Leshan's sigh was her only response.

It seemed Merika had made her point successfully though, for while they were supposed to wash the rugs by hand, they agreed that Merika should use her power over objects and Leshan her ability to control the elements to ensure that the task was done quickly. Callam, his mindsmith's gift useless, and Kaylene, her Blessing of control over the natural world similarly unhelpful here, stood to the side and idly listened to the debate as something more than observers but less than active participants.

"They claim we have no control over ourselves, but I can control my Blessing." Merika directed a carpet to drape itself over a line as she spoke. "And most people who can control objects can move only small things a short distance."

Kaylene wanted to rebuke her friend for her pride, but Merika's skill and control were indisputable. Most who had a similar Blessing could barely lift anything, let alone with control and purpose. Even though she wasn't supposed to, Merika practised using her Blessing, and it seemed to yield results, given what she could do.

"And Lesha, look at how she can make rain come from nothing. That's control beyond what most people can ever dream of. Or Callam, his ability to pluck people's thoughts from their head. And you, Kaya. I've never seen anyone do what you do with plants. Remember that day when you made the whole garden bloom?"

Merika's face glowed with the memory.

Kaylene certainly did remember. They'd been sitting in one of the Sanctuary's courtyards. It was a late summer afternoon. Her face tilted up to catch the rays of the sun, Kaylene had been barely listening to the others' conversation. She was more interested in the feel of Luka's arm against her leg. They hadn't yet become lovers, but the anticipation that something could and would transpire between them danced through her, intoxicating and invigorating with its promise. That day, in the bloom of summer, there seemed a humming connection between them that was nearing a crescendo.

Merika had asked her how many flowers she could make bloom at once.

She'd been more interested in the sight of Luka, a lock of wildly orange hair fallen across his blue eyes. The bass of his voice had curled around her chest and tugged as he'd repeated Merika's question.

With an effort of will, Kaylene turned to Merika. "I don't know."

"Make the flowers bloom," Merika said. Excitement radiated from her.

"What?"

"There are almost no flowers here. Make them bloom." Merika gestured to the garden beds. The bushes were bereft of flowers, as they usually were.

Kaylene raised an eyebrow at her friend. "I don't think I have that kind of power."

"How do you know?" Merika delivered her challenge with a smile that was annoyingly charming.

Kaylene relented. It was always easier to give in to Merika than to argue. "All right."

She'd tried before to find the words to describe what she experienced when she used her Blessing – often at Merika's insistent behest. But words felt inadequate. Kaylene was never not able to sense the presence of the natural world, even dimmed as it was when she was inside the thick stone walls of the Sanctuary. The best description she could offer of what she perceived was akin to looking out to the sea: it was comprised of many individual droplets but appeared to the eye as a whole. Yet if one dipped a hand in, the droplets could be seen in their uniqueness. While she was able to sense all the plants around her, she'd only manipulated one at a time. Yet Merika spoke true; Kaylene had never tried otherwise. She focused on her awareness of the surrounding court-yard – its growth confined by careful hands. She imagined her will as hands, moulding, shaping, coaxing the hidden blooms to emerge. She felt Luka's hand alight on her arm. The squeeze of his fingers suggested she had produced re-sults, and she opened her eyes to see that the flowers, which should have only been out during the rain-filled spring, were blooming alongside plants that only bloomed in the crisp coolness of autumn. Delight ran through her as a physical sensation; she'd never realised her Blessing could be so powerful or so beautiful.

Merika's excited laughter was a beautiful sound: pure joy. Exhilaration swept through Kaylene, evoked by the heady combination of her friend's ex-citement, the feeling of Luka's hand on her arm, and the joy of discovering she could do something this beautiful.

"Luka, can you change the colour of some of them?" she asked once she had recovered from her delight.

In reply, the flowers became a rainbow of colours from the most vibrant red to deepest blue.

Merika's delight in the discovery of the depths of their powers had been infectious.

"Lesha, Lesha, make it rain!" Merika's excitement was like that of a small child.

Leshan acquiesced with a good humour that defied her usual wariness of transgressing Sanctuary restrictions. A sprinkling of water so fine that it barely kissed the skin before dissipating made the air glitter as the droplets caught the sun. Kaylene thought she'd never felt so content, surrounded by her friends and the beauty they'd created. It was the kind of bone-deep happiness that stretched a moment into infinity, and she was overtaken by the hope that things would never change.

"Cal, can you make it so that we'll always remember this?" It was as though Merika had read Kaylene's mind and was suggesting the next best thing.

As he nodded, his hair fell across his eyes in the same manner as Luka's did.

Kaylene wasn't certain what exactly Callam had done, but she remembered that moment with a clarity that none of her other memories, warped by the prism of time and her own interpretation, possessed.

"Yes, Meri, of course I remember," she said eventually, dragging herself from the warmth of that memory and into the cold aches the present held. Merika's reminder made her realise that she really would do anything to get that back.

THREE

The wind pulled at her hair with vicious fingers, lashing strands of gold across her sight. On the cliff, the wind never abated.

With cautious steps, she navigated the narrow path to the mouth of Ay'ash's cave. The woman was sitting cross legged in the entrance, a serene expression on her face. She seemed unconcerned by the fact that she was only a breath from the sheer edge of the cliff and death below.

"Blessings upon you, Kaylene." Her voice, while soft, easily carried over the wind.

"We found the scroll," Kaylene said.

Ay'ash stood and led Kaylene into her cave, away from the wind and the crashing sea. She sat in front of the fire, and politeness dragged Kaylene to sit cross-legged on the floor, too. She noticed that no smoke from the fire filled the cave.

"Tea?" Ay'ash asked.

Kaylene nodded. The old woman deftly turned to set up a tripod above the flames, hang a pot off it, and throw a handful of ingredients into the pot that Kaylene would have sworn held no water only a moment previously.

"Why are you helping me?" Kaylene asked, trying to distract herself from a vague sense of unease which sought to claim her.

Ay'ash gave her a look that seemed suffused with amusement. "Why do you trust me?"

She had a point. Kaylene shifted, her eyes never straying from the other woman's. "Because I'm desperate."

"That's not a good reason to trust someone." Ay'ash strained water from the pot into two small clay mugs.

"It's a better reason than I've had in a while."

Kaylene accepted the drink and sipped, wary of burning her lips. Once again, she was unable to identify what flavoured the water. She wondered whether it had been wise to accept the offer of a drink, but the thought sidled away.

Ay'ash tilted her head as she regarded Kaylene, dark eyes bright with speculative intelligence. "How is life in the Sanctuary?" A knowing smirk tugged her lips upward.

Kaylene's eyes dropped to the surface of the water in her mug. Something about the woman's expression unsettled her. "It's as ever," she replied, choosing her words with care. "Children come in, are taught to control their emotions, and are then sent back home. Except for a few who do not master themselves." She did not need to point out that she was one of those few. Or indeed, what happened to those who could not control themselves at all.

She sipped her tea and looked again at Ay'ash. Kaylene was overtaken by the sense that Ay'ash was much older than she appeared.

"Why are you helping me? Surely you have some price?" Her whisper seemed deafening in the silence of the cave - even though the sea and wind had been so loud at the entrance.

Her question was met with a bottomless stare, and she felt the edges of her stomach churn. The silence stretched out so long that she was on the verge of speaking again simply to put some sound into the still air when Ay'ash spoke.

"I have many reasons for wanting to help you, all of them my own. But if it would make you feel more comfortable to provide payment, I'd like a memory. Tell me something of this Luka of yours."

Discomfort gave her pause, but the prospect of returning to her friends with the news of her failure, that all their efforts so far had been for nothing, was unbearable. She sorted through the recollections of the person she had loved more than anything else in the world, trying to determine what she would be willing to share.

"Something special," Ay'ash added, more command than comment.

Kaylene knew exactly what would suffice. "The first time we kissed, we'd known each other maybe a year and a half." It was with both a sense of unexpected delight and intrusion that she divulged this part of her and Luka's story. "I'd wondered what it would be like to kiss him for a long time. By then, people of our age had already started to go home, and I knew that I wasn't going to be sent home for a long time yet." She paused to collect herself. She always slipped in too much detail when telling stories, straying at times far from the narrative she was trying to recount. But Ay'ash was a good audience. She remained silent as Kaylene regathered her thoughts.

"We were doing chores – washing up after an evening meal. He was helping me lift a stack of plates and our fingers touched. I remember that I couldn't breathe. I was so fixed on the feeling of his skin against mine. Once the plates were set down, he intertwined his fingers through mine. I still couldn't believe it; I hardly dared look into his eyes – he'd changed their colour that day. I always loved the hue of his natural eye colour, although he changed it often, to suit his mood, he said. But my favourite was that blue.

"'Kaya, I have something to ask you,' he said. I thought it was something really serious, and I began to panic. His face was so still. Normally it was alive with this wonderful smile."

Kaylene paused again, almost overwhelmed with the force of her memory and the echo of the emotions it evoked – even ghosts of the emotion held potency. She could picture his face so clearly that it was impossible to believe he had been dead for so long already. The usual ever-present sense of quiet unfairness at how he had died receded to the background, banished by the warmth of the recollection.

She continued.

"So you can imagine my surprise when he said, 'Why have you never tried to kiss me?' I remember looking at him in shock, thinking I must have misheard. I told him, 'Because I didn't know if you wanted me to.' That moment, when I started to believe that he really did want to kiss me, but we hadn't yet, was exciting and terrifying and amazing all at the same time. He smiled, the tiniest smile. I only realised much later how afraid he was that I didn't feel the way he did. 'I want you to,' he said.

"I don't remember how long I took to understand what he had just said. It might have been a few minutes, it might have been barely a second. But once I did, I leaned forward and I kissed him. It was my first kiss, you know. It was probably clumsy and not very good, but his lips were warm against mine."

Kaylene halted, her voice rough with the memory. She looked at Ay'ash. The woman's eyes were half-closed as though she were savouring an exquisite taste and wanted to enjoy it with the fullness of her senses.

"Marvellous," she said eventually.

Kaylene felt near naked at the intimacy and detail with which she had recounted the story. Yet such thoughts were pushed aside by the fact that she also felt the phantom tingle of his lips against hers, could remember the way he had tasted on the tip of her tongue and the sweet ache that had made its way through her at their touch. It was good to relive that memory. She hadn't allowed herself to remember such things because they walked hand in hand with sadness so powerful that it made breathing near impossible.

"I know something of loving someone, and the way losing those we love can tear your world apart," Ay'ash said.

Kaylene considered the woman's words, feeling a lie or omission within there, but not certain where. "You'd really help me just out of sympathy?"

"Why did you love him?" Ay'ash asked, instead of replying to Kaylene's question.

Kaylene didn't have to think about her answer. "Because he made me better. He—" Her throat began to constrict, as though her body were trying to stop her from speaking the words lest they overwhelm her. She swallowed, feeling as though thorns had lodged themselves in her throat. "He made life worth living," she whispered.

When she was able to look at Ay'ash once more, she found the woman regarding her with an inscrutable expression.

"Do you really think I can't understand that? That I might not be moved enough to try to help others who have gone through this, where I can?"

"If you've lost someone that you've loved like that, why didn't you bring them back?" It wasn't that she didn't believe Ay'ash could help her – it was that she didn't want bitter disappointment to overwhelm her if Ay'ash was unable to help.

"Because to bring someone back from the Divine Realm requires more love than one person alone can possess. It was not the right time and I did not have the help or support of others as you do now. What one alone cannot accomplish, many who are strong and united in their love and intent can. You have friends who will help you. Alone, you would not be able to reach through the veil between the world we inhabit and the insubstantial realm. But with four of you, it should be possible."

Kaylene wondered when she'd told the Old One about her friends, but she was tired of interrogating the woman's motives. Allowing herself to remember Luka so deeply had left her exhausted, and her suspicion was replaced by grief as though she was feeling it again as though it were for the first time, driving the simple and overwhelming need to have him by her side once more. If this was what Ay'ash could offer her, she had no interest in looking for hidden reasons.

"Here." She held out the scroll to Ay'ash.

The woman took it, unrolled it, and returned it to Kaylene after only a brief glance. "It's certainly the correct scroll."

"So what does it say?"

Ay'ash shrugged. Something in the gesture had the flavour of sadism about it. "I don't know."

Kaylene felt incredulity swirling around her. "What?"

"The Old Ones are prohibited from being taught to read."

"So the scroll is useless. Why did you tell me to get it if nobody can read it?" Kaylene's frustration brought hot tears to her eyes.

"Because there is someone who can read it. His name is Thurien. He lives in Curnith and works as a clerk on the docks."

"How can I find this Thurien in Curnith? It's a big city." She heard the edge of her own desperation in her voice but didn't care.

"If you go to the harbour, you will see a building with a green door. If he tries to refuse you, tell him that I sent you."

Kaylene had grown up near the First Country's port city. The buildings near the docks were famous for being white. Any door painted green would be obvious.

"Thurien will be able to help you," Ay'ash said.

The ensuing quiet was total. Not even a trace of the sea and wind outside whispered through the space. It was as though the rest of the world had ceased to exist. The idea of being cut off from the world outside made a claustrophobic unease descend upon Kaylene. The silence, she realised, was not simply in her ears but also around her Blessing. She was aware of no nearby plants. No mould, no lichen, not even a seed that had long slipped down the cliff and nestled between rocks. That, more than the lack of noise, confirmed that this place and its inhabitant were deeply unnatural. Raising the dead went against nature; it seemed this was the place to start, but that didn't mean Kaylene wanted to be here for a second longer than was necessary. However, some impulse left her unwilling to show her discomfort, so she continued to sip the still-hot tea in large gulps, wincing as it scalded her throat.

"I should get back," she said once there was no liquid remaining. "They'll be wondering where I am."

Ay'ash smiled with knowing mockery in her expression. "I am impressed you came here unnoticed."

Kaylene handed back the mug, her thoughts on escape and the inarticulate discomfort she felt at the unnaturalness of the woman. The first time she had met Ay'ash, she had not noticed it because she had been too preoccupied by her decision to end her life, and then by the hope ignited by the prospect of bringing Luka back. But this time she felt that she had been toyed with, an object for some gratification. Yet even if she was being used by the woman for some perverse end, if she got Luka back she did not care.

For all its stringency in refusing to allow its inhabitants to leave before they had met the requirements of 'self mastery,' the Sanctuary otherwise allowed its wards to do more or less as they pleased. The pervading force that kept people adhering to specific routines and requests was the desire to leave as quickly as possible. That, and the enduring sense of shame at being Blessed, was an effective way to keep people cowed. For a long time, Kaylene had done everything asked of her – and everything inferred, too – out of a desire to return home and because she too was filled with the deep-rooted shame for being Blessed that had been nurtured by her ongoing failure to master herself. Perhaps her relationship with Luka and the deepening of her friendship with Callam, Merika, and Leshan were acts of undisciplined emotion, but she would have been happy to stay in the Sanctuary with them – with him – forever. The heavily implied rules of behaviour had become increasingly optional for her. Luka's death had left her unable to muster the care for rebellion or compliance. She followed routine because it was so well-worn that it required no emotion at all. No punitive measures would meet Kaylene for her recent absences – it was just another silently observed failure of her capacity to master herself. Were it known what she and the Old One discussed, perhaps there would have been a different response, but there was no sign of that. It was why she was not questioned about her absence across the morning when she returned in time for afternoon study.

In yet another pursuit of a disciplined self, the Sanctuary instructed its members to pick an area of study and pursue it to a high level. Blessed who were allowed to leave the Sanctuary often found employ as experts in their field of study. It made them a paradox: oft-sought, but treated with unease.

She entered the study room she and her friends habitually used, just off the grand archives on the Sanctuary's second floor. While nobody had a dedicated room, the force of habit and their well-known use of the room meant the other Blessed avoided it.

The other three were already there, heads obediently buried in books. Of course, for Merika it wasn't a veil of compliance but a genuine unquenchable thirst for knowledge that saw her devour as much information as she could. At Kaylene's entrance, the three heads lifted expectantly from the books over which they had been bowed to regard her.

"We have to go to Curnith," she announced, all but throwing her books on the sturdy wooden table.

Merika pulled a face. "Why?"

"Because Ay'ash couldn't read the scroll." Kaylene opened her books to the relevant pages with more-gentle motions.

"And someone in Curnith can?" Leshan asked. The calm of her low, melodic voice soothed the turbulent emotions that had roused themselves as Kaylene had walked back to the Sanctuary.

Kaylene nodded. She unwrapped a cloth surrounding a graphite stick and looked at the page she was midway through translating. Her chosen field was language, and over the years she had mastered the languages of the Godskissed Continent. The Fourth Country's rolling, drawn-out language had given her some trouble before she mastered it, but the Third and Second Country spoke practically the same language, more dialects of one another than separate tongues. She had now turned her attention to the speech of the barbarians who lived beyond the Godskissed Continent. With very little information about them other than what was gleaned through trade, untangling the language was a thorny task. With a reference point, she possibly could have deciphered the scroll herself, but if Merika couldn't find anything on the language of the Old Ones, then nobody could.

"So we need to get to Curnith," Merika repeated.

"I can say I want to take my family visitation," Kaylene said. Once a year, the Blessed were permitted to visit their families. Neither Kaylene nor her friends had chosen to take up that offer for several years. They'd all discovered that similar experiences awaited them in the places they'd once called home, made homogenous by time and prejudice: their families greeted them with poorly hidden shame and forgotten familiarity.

"You shouldn't go alone," Leshan said, her dawn-coloured eyes earnest.

"At this time of year, there are thieves on the roads. Ask to take me." Merika's demeanour was almost urgent, the words all but tumbling over one another due to the swiftness with which she spoke.

"Meri knows more than any of us about this kind of thing, it might be useful for her to go along." Callam spoke quickly, too, but from the obvious unease at being the focus of attention. Yet it did not detract from the fact that he had a point.

When nobody said anything further, it was clear that the friends had arrived at a consensus. The four put their heads down in a convincing display of studiousness and at least tried to return to their work.

As the time seeped past, Leshan pushed her books over next to Kaylene and slid along the bench so they were sitting closer together. "Are you all right?" she asked quietly.

"I think so," Kaylene replied. Callam and Merika could hear the conversation – the room was not large – but they offered the appearance of being absorbed in their own work. Her reply was not the entire truth. She could not shake the memory she had relived in the cave. With intractable stubbornness, her mind continued to evoke her first kiss with Luka in aching detail. Why she had chosen to recount that to Ay'ash she could not say, but now that she had unlocked the part of her mind into which the memories of Luka had been crammed, they were demanding their rightful space.

The memory poured through her of how sweet he had tasted, and how wonderful his mouth had felt against hers. She could not stop recalling the way he had been so hesitant, his lips barely touching hers until she had reached across and pulled him close. The fullness of the memory surrounded her, pain circling her chest at the loss of Luka as though fresh.

Callam shifted, breaking the totality of her remembrance and pain.

"Missing him?" Leshan guessed, her voice soft enough that the other two wouldn't be able to hear.

"I'm so afraid that at the end of all this we won't be able to bring him back," she confessed.

Her friend's hand slipped into hers. The comforting pressure of Leshan's fingers around hers somehow conveyed she was trying to take away Kaylene's worry and heartache.

"We'll do it, I promise," Leshan said, the quiet conviction of her words immeasurable. And the truly incredible thing was that Leshan's promise did take her mind off her worry and the exquisite torture of her remembering, for a while at least.

But that evening when she was alone, Kaylene could not keep the thoughts at bay any longer. She had spent months wondering what it would be like to kiss Luka before they finally did. She remembered the way she held her breath right before their lips touched. Then, in her solitude, she remembered what had come later, as they had explored each other, the fumbling, searching inquiries of touch and discovery. She relived the gasps of pleasure, the unexpected laughter, and she ached for Luka with unquenchable longing. That night, she dreamed of him again, but he stood on the periphery of the scene, a figure haunting her dream rather than part of it.

Kaylene woke alone and wiped tears from her cheeks. If the scroll did not fulfil what Ay'ash promised, the embrace of the waves and rocks at the bottom of the cliffs awaited. Kaylene found a dark comfort in that.

FOUR

The few occasions Kaylene had left the Sanctuary to visit her family were all characterised by a dreamlike awe evoked by the realisation of a whole world outside. Being outside the thick stone walls made her realise how outdated life behind them was. The cart provided to Kaylene and Merika was old and of the most basic style. The sleeker, more-modern carts and carriages they passed made her feel conspicuous in her drabness – the enclosed carriages were the worst; the Sanctuary's cart was tiny with only a small open tray in the back where they stowed their meagre luggage. However, even other open carts and wagons looked more comfortable – as though they'd been designed with an eye not only to the most basic function but to form as well, and as though the wood was smooth to touch because of a carefully applied finish rather than because it had been worn smooth. What made it worse was that the fashion of other travellers was notably different from the stiff, restrictive cut of the clothes designed to remind her to keep herself in control. The loose-fitting trousers and shirts, bound across the waist with a thick band of cloth, were designs she hadn't seen on her last trip outside the Sanctuary, too many years ago for her to count. Seeing them only made her hate the plain lines of the high necked, long-sleeved garb the Sanctuary required her to wear. The way the unBlesseds' clothes seemed to billow only made the inflexible material feel even more restrictive. She was certain that once they entered the thriving metropolis of Curnith, she would see even more daring designs.

Merika was a fabulous travelling companion. Even the barren terrain of the first two days of travel that separated the Sanctuary from any other settlement was made interesting by Merika. Her unslakable enthusiasm for learning everything she possibly could about the world was a beautiful thing. Kaylene had never known anyone as vivid as Merika. She conducted herself with an energy that translated into defiance of anyone or anything that might seek to diminish her. It infused everything she did, from refusing to yield ground to other vehicles whose consistent encroachment onto their side of the road suggested prejudice evoked by their easily recognisable garb, to haggling with the inn owners at night, her dark eyes daring them to charge a higher price or give a lesser room because they were Blessed. She had a wicked sense of humour, too, which she unleashed at every opportunity, reducing Kaylene to tears of laughter more than once. When they'd first become friends so many years ago, Merika's humour and cheeky insolence had manifested in a variety of inventive pranks that had caused them great amusement; Kaylene's favourite was when they'd soaped the floors and watched as everyone – including the pompous Senior Blessed – slid around. Childish, but uproariously amusing. Over the years, Merika's humour had evolved into sharp retorts and a broad range of jokes, from the witty to the crass.

Merika's resistance to any effort to contain her also found its expression in using her Blessing at every possible opportunity and encouraging Kaylene to do the same. On the road, when they paused for lunch, at Merika's instruction, Kaylene produced fruit and berries from flowers that would normally take weeks to bear. The girls plucked the food, sinking greedy teeth into the sweet flesh. In turn, Merika drove hands free, using her Blessing to adjust the reins of the hearat, the beasts of burden that pulled their cart.

Despite her initial worry about what others may think or say if they saw the two casually engaging in acts deemed so dangerous, Kaylene quickly began to share Merika's enjoyment in using every part of herself. She'd not realised how much effort she spent trying to block out her awareness of the plants surrounding her. As the days slid past, the freedom of being away from the Sanctuary and in Merika's company chipped away at the weight of the sadness that had accrued on her heart. She found herself smiling at times – and meaning it.

Yet despite the way the fun of travelling with Merika seemed to wipe away the tackiness of the malaise which had clung to her for so long, her second encounter with Ay'ash refused to dislodge itself from her thoughts. The discomfort the woman's presence had caused had ebbed in the way that most things did when viewed through the prism of memory, but the Old One's mocking eyes kept the taste of unease at the tip of her tongue whenever she recalled the woman's words about her friends' help.

"Meri, why are you doing this?" she asked on the third night in the hope that addressing the issue may go some way to dispelling her discomfort. "If we're discovered, I don't even know what they'll do to us."

They were lying on the bed they were sharing for that evening. Merika eased her hands behind her head, making Kaylene's head rock on the pillow. She did not seem visibly concerned by the possibility that some terrible retribution would be exacted for the rules they had broken and were intending to break. Those who transgressed too far were not seen for very much longer; they were treated even more harshly than runaways. Kaylene had witnessed the disappearance of only one troublemaker during her time at the Sanctuary, in her first year, after he'd repeatedly used his Blessing to sour the food in the stomachs of a number of the Sanctuary's inhabitants. There had been mass vomitings across a full month before the Senior Blessed discovered that he was the cause – Kaylene herself had been an unfortunate victim on two separate incidents. One day, the boy was gone with only the announcement that he had been the culprit and the Sanctuary would not tolerate anyone using their Blessing to harm another person. The Senior Blessed had never explicitly said what had happened to him, but the finality in the way Senior Blessed Maryam had spoken and the expression on her face offered little doubt as to the permanence of the way in which the boy had been dealt. It seemed extreme, but the very distinct scent of bile which had seemed to have sunk into the Sanctuary's walls, even for months after the boy's removal, had made the decision seem somehow less horrifying to a younger Kaylene for whom the scent evoked the desire to rush to the latrines and repeat the boy's handiwork. But such instances were few and far between. Most people just wanted to return to the outside world and shirked anything that even vaguely smelled like disobedience. The only other time someone had been disappeared was when Catice had had her fit. Again, Kaylene had found it hard to disagree with the brutal logic of the Senior Blessed, given the devastation the incident had wrought upon her, personally.

"Those old idiots at the Sanctuary are afraid of anything that looks even remotely like power. If they have the knowledge of how to reach into the realm beyond ours, why pretend it doesn't exist or can't be used? There's so much we don't know about our Blessings because they don't want to know. I mean, if Blessings were used to put up the barrier stopping us from crossing into the Third Country, we can do so much more than what we've been led to believe.

Who's to say we can't defy death, too?" Hot outrage entered her voice. "And Luka was the best of us. He shouldn't have died. Not in the way he did. And those fools hide away the means to right their wrongs?"

Unusually, Merika seemed lost for words, overcome by outrage.

Kaylene did not speak of this again with Merika, but the fire with which her friend had spoken kindled something within her. She'd never thought Luka's death should be viewed with outrage, yet Merika's words burrowed through her, uncovering a resentment she hadn't even realised lay sleeping within her. Suddenly, every thought about the Sanctuary was tainted with bitter rancour.

On the eighth day they entered Curnith. As they drove through the city's outskirts, the huge dyeing district made itself known by launching an assault on their noses, somehow made more repulsive by the heavy salt scent which hung in the air. Kaylene let out a sigh as the memory of her childhood home, inextricably intertwined with the sharp smell of the urine used to set dyes, asserted itself.

"Weren't you from a cloth dyer's family?" Merika asked as Kaylene audibly breathed through her mouth.

Kaylene nodded.

"So shouldn't you be used to this?"

"I always hated it." Kaylene took off her hat and waved it in front of her face in an unsuccessful effort to try and give herself some reprieve for the malodourous scent. "It stinks and you get colour stained onto your hands, even if you're careful. The whole thing is just revolting."

Merika had never suggested Kaylene might want to see her family. Of them all, Merika had never let a word slip about her past, and despite her otherwise-unquenchable need to know everything, she respected that her friends too may want to keep private their disappointments and anger with the families that had let them go. She'd never pried further when the others had mentioned their origins or spoken of the way their families had reacted badly when their Blessings had been discovered – including outright rejection, as Leshan once revealed what her wealthy family had done to her. Kaylene's thoughts went to visiting her family for a moment, but she found no desire to subject herself to the awkwardness that seeing them would invite.

"It's a well-regarded craft, though," Merika pointed out.

"Have you ever tried crushing snails for purple dye?" Kaylene said. "It's disgusting."

Thankfully, they quickly entered the outer districts of the port, beyond the dyeing district. Sure enough, the fashion of the people was different to those they had passed on the road. Kaylene glared with jealousy at the long skirts of the women and the artful revelation of their backs or décolletage by the elegant folds of their blouses. She felt the strict, high neck of her own collar with resentment.

Although she had lived near Curnith and had seen the harbour many times, she never failed to be amazed by the sight of the First Country's sole link to the outside world. The pass through the mountains that ringed the First Country had been blocked many generations ago. It was the only time in history that the Blessed had done something to dramatically affect the First Country. Time had obfuscated the exact reasons behind the barrier's erection. As far as Kaylene knew, there was ongoing debate about what was behind the decision to cut off the rest of the land – whether it was lingering fear born of the wars across the Godskissed Continent, or more basic prejudice.

Regardless, the port was a centre of activity, of otherness, and the rest of the world seemed crammed into the relatively small space of a single port. People wearing strange clothes and speaking in foreign languages moved about, exotic wares trundled through the streets on carts that strained to hold them. The exchange of coin, goods, and services flowed freely in a strangely coordinated, mesmerising dance. But the bustle and exotic showcase of the outside world was mere shadowplay in the face of the harbour itself. At sea level, below where Merika and Kaylene walked, was the circuit, the huge inner ring where the largest, highest-paying ships were docked. From there, the ships could access the warehouses along the circuit to more easily load or unload their cargo. An island in the middle of the circuit held the harbourmaster's seat. At all times, someone was inside the tall structure, observing the ships in the harbour as well as any vessels approaching the port. Leading out to the open sea was a corridor of columned stone that seemed impossibly built into the water. There, less-wealthy ships were berthed alongside ships of the First Country's navy. The navy ensured no ships entered the harbour without permission or came near any other part of the First Country's coast.

As they descended to the circuit, Kaylene looked back up at the main thoroughfare. It was lined by the shrines to the various aspects of the many-faced god. The quality or characteristic someone wished to be bestowed with would determine which shrine they attended. Kaylene had not been to any shrine in a long time.

The dock of Curnith was said to rival the palace of the Second Country, or the Third Country's capital, Oranis, in grandeur. She believed that. The first time she had been here as a child, when she'd been allowed to ride with her mother on a delivery, the area had seemed too beautiful, too magnificent not to be straight out of the tomes of legend. It had ignited in her a child's unbounded desire to work here, to board one of the ships and sail away, because the harbour seemed the splendid gates to the rest of the world and all its marvels. Seeing it through an adult's eyes, it was even more impressive, and she felt the echo of her youthful desire to work on one of the ships.

Unthinkingly, she turned to say as much to Luka. It was so natural for her to seek his view of the world and add it to her own that she had forgotten for one moment he did not stand beside her. The pain of that forgetting was unexpected, a sharp knife. She had not believed herself so treacherously forgetful.

As she waited for the pain to ebb, she turned her back on the sparkling sea and looked at the open-air oratorium where individuals could come on the anointed days and debate proposed policy and law. Even if she were permitted to leave the Sanctuary, Kaylene would never be allowed to take part in the debates, nor would she ever be allowed to vote on the matters of state as other citizens could. Being Blessed ruled her ineligible for such things. It was something she had given little consideration – life in the Sanctuary narrowed one's thoughts until that which was not of immediate relevance fled the mind – but as she looked at the high, curved walls, some of that anger awakened a few nights ago seeped into her thoughts.

Below, a crowd had gathered around one of the circuit berths to watch the unloading of a ship from the Fourth Country. The ship's origin was given away by the men disembarking. They were veiled from head to foot. Not a spare scrap of skin was visible. She felt a certain kinship with them, locked away as she was in the restrictive clothing of the Sanctuary.

She and Merika drew almost as many stares as the men from the Fourth Country. Blessed rarely left the Sanctuary before they had attained self-discipline, at which time they practically disappeared – told with a total lack of ceremony that they would be leaving and to pack a bag immediately. Upon meeting the criteria of self-mastery known only to the Senior Blessed, they were permitted to shed their distinctive garb and return to living amongst the unBlessed as though they were normal – in theory, at least.

Kayleen and Merika's Sanctuary clothes and the fact they were far older than most of the Sanctuary's Blessed marked them as a particular curiosity. Kayleen pretended to ignore the stares, telling herself that if she didn't see them, they wouldn't bother her. It was easier to do when rushing to keep up with Merika's confident stride as they searched for their destination.

The building with the green door was easy enough to find amidst its uniformly white neighbours, the colour of the door the only outstanding feature. Kaylene wondered how such divergence was allowed, but before she could say anything, Merika rapped on the door, no sign of any hesitation or uncertainty in the lines of how she held herself.

The door swung open. A man whose age it was impossible to even roughly guess at studied them, his eyes a striking violet. While he and Ay'ash bore no obvious similarities, something about him nevertheless reminded Kaylene of the Old One.

"Yes?"

"Are you Thurien?" Kaylene was overtaken with nerves and her voice came halfway between a croak and whisper.

"I could be." Those eyes swept over her with knife-sharp incisiveness, pinning her in place.

"Ay'ash told me to ask you for help?" Kaylene's nervousness made the statement into a question.

His eyes made one more critical pass over her, then he stepped aside so they could enter.

They found themselves in what looked like a clerk's office. It was well lit thanks to two large windows looking out onto the circuit. On the far wall was a door, and next to it a cabinet nondescript enough to be frequently used. On the other side was a small desk with two chairs in front of it. A cutting of flowers sat in a wooden holder; their freshness seemed out of place amidst the white-plastered stone walls. The room had the air of a reception area, yet the man sat behind the desk. He waited as the two friends pulled up chairs opposite him, his demeanour reminiscent of an expectant predator.

"We hoped you could help read a scroll for us," Merika said.

Kaylene glanced out the window rather than continue looking at this unsettling man. The building's location allowed a perfect view of the ship from the Fourth Country. A stout woman with flame-coloured hair was standing on the footpath, directing the activities.

The man held out his hand and Merika drew the scroll from her bag. His abrupt intake of breath had Kaylene swinging back around to look at him.

"In the hands of one who knows what this says, this can be a very dangerous piece of writing," Thurien said, turning the scroll over in his fingers.

Kaylene would have expected an extravagant spiel of caution, but he elaborated no further.

"Do you know what it says?" Merika's voice held a note somewhere between impatience and interest.

"I might."

"You're an Old One," Kaylene said quietly.

His smile broadened. "Old Ones aren't able to read their own script," he pointed out, putting the scroll carefully in front of him. The sardonic edge to his tone made it clear exactly what he thought of that prohibition.

"Why send me here if you don't know how to read it?" Kaylene asked. Both Thurien and Ay'ash inspired the feeling she was being used for entertainment. It felt as though she had walked into some kind of trap. Suddenly the foolishness of this whole plan impressed itself upon her – she and Merika were here at the instruction of a woman she'd met only twice and who radiated malevolence like an oncoming storm. The willingness to pay any price for even the chance Luka could be brought back seemed unpardonable now she realised that price may mean her friend's safety.

"Such rage." His voice was hungry. "Such a swirling torrent of emotion within you, ready to erupt at any moment. It is–" he paused, putting his elbows on the top of the desk and leaning toward her "–delicious."

The scroll flew from the desk in front of him into Merika's hands.

"Enough," she said, poorly constrained anger of her own giving the word a sharp bite.

Thurien laughed, sounding genuinely delighted. "My, my, the chaos that you have both brought in is quite refreshing. It makes an old man feel young again to see such passion."

"What do you want?" Kaylene snapped, fear giving her voice a brittle edge.

He regarded her once more with that intrusive stare. "Who would you reclaim from the Divine Realm?"

"His name is Luka," Merika said.

"And why are you so intent on tearing the world apart for him?"

Thurien's curiosity reminded Kaylene of a child lifting up a rock to examine the insects underneath it.

"He died because he was asked to do something that he should not have been," Merika said into Kaylene's silence. "We are owed a life and we want his."

Thurien turned to Kaylene. "And you loved him." It was not a question.

"More than anything."

He glanced out the window at the people from the Fourth Country, unloading their vessel. A slight young woman had joined the redhead. A long plait of dark hair trailed down her back.

"Do you know who they are?" Thurien asked.

Kaylene and Merika shook their heads.

"A family from the Fourth Country – or the remains of it. Are you familiar with what goes on there?"

Merika answered. "The powerful families invade each other, claiming their land and riches."

"Most in the First Country have little interest in the world beyond its borders. Shutting away the outside world tends to make it seem less real."

"I'm not like that. I want to know everything," Merika said.

Kaylene could see that despite her friend's wariness, she was intrigued by Thurien.

He laughed at some joke he did not deign to share. "The people you see there is all that is left of the Farwan family. For generations they were one of the Fourth Country's most powerful families. The woman with red hair, that is Tanita – the matriarch. Her daughter and heir, Lexana, stands next to her. They are here as exiles, having lost nearly everything."

"How do you know this?" Merika and Kaylene asked the question at almost exactly the same time. But while Kaylene's voice was laced with suspicion, Merika's was full of wonder.

Cool amusement touched his face. "I have my ways. I am a clerk, after all."

Kaylene fought and lost the battle to keep her eyebrows from rising. "What's going to happen to the foreigners?"

"Who can say how long they will stay here? Perhaps forever. Although I doubt it. They come from a land soaked in blood and vendettas. Once they have enough strength, coin, and willing fighters, they will go back. But the land to which they will return will be changed, as will they."

His words were punctuated by a shout from the docks outside. Tanita had evidently taken issue with the way a trunk was being unloaded. She strode toward the dock workers, waving her arms with each step. Lexana remained where she was, arms wrapped around herself, looking at the foreign port around her. The sense of loss her posture radiated did not obscure her obvious awe at the magnificent structure of the harbour.

"She's quite the mathematician, I believe," Thurien said, noticing Kaylene's observation of the foreign woman.

Kaylene dragged her eyes away from the exiles and back to the unsettling man on the other side of the desk. "Was that story intended to caution us that bringing Luka back from the realm beyond ours may bring back someone who has changed?" She was trying so hard to keep her temper in check. But she did not like the way he played with Merika and her. His manner was all too reminiscent of the Senior Blessed at the Sanctuary.

"Of course it is a warning. But it is also a caution that the person to whom you bring him back to may also be changed." He did not seem to be offended by the controlled hostility in her voice. Quite the contrary. "You know, it's wonderful speaking with people who actually think for themselves, who have fire in them." He clenched his fist to emphasise the point. A jewel in his ring caught the light, blinding Kaylene for the briefest of moments.

"What exactly would you do to bring back this Luka?" His attention was entirely focused on Kaylene.

She leaned forward. "I would tear apart the entire world."

He smiled. A predator's smile. "Then I will tell you how to do just that."

FIVE

"You know, we thought this scroll impossible to get back," Thurien remarked conversationally as he unrolled the object in question.

"Why?" Merika and Kaylene asked in unison.

"The Sanctuary has not been a place that welcomes our kind. And while most of those who reside within its walls have only the barest inkling of their powers, some of the Senior Blessed are actually quite capable of recognising and repelling an Old One. Besides, even if one of us could sneak into the Sanctuary itself, those who came before have left their mark in the walls. We would not get very far."

He divulged the information carelessly, not seeming to exhibit any concern that the two women might feel some loyalty to the place where they had lived for almost all of their lives.

Kaylene observed Merika's eyes grow bright with interest. "I didn't know any Blessed had done work on the Sanctuary itself."

He threw her a smile brimming with condescension, then turned his attention to the scroll. For several minutes, he said nothing, his finger moving lightly across the surface, an expression of rapt attention on his face. Then he looked up, clasped his hands together and rested his forearms on the desk. The silence of the room, the way the noise from the docks outside was totally removed, seemed to intensify as Kaylene found herself caught in Thurien's gaze.

"What you need to understand," he said, "is that we inhabited this land when your gods still walked on it. They might have created much, but they found this world, they did not make it."

"But the many-faced god did make us," Merika said, echoing the religious teachings they all knew.

He smiled that patronising, slightly cruel smile, keeping his attention fixed on Kaylene. "In a way. You may think that your belief in them in some way fuels your Blessings, but the truth is more complicated than that. They need you more than you need them. They hunger for the connection to this world that you offer. They are desperate to force open a door and step through."

He turned to Merika. "You know what the Third Country teaches about why your gods ceased to exist alongside mortals?"

She nodded. "Because they wanted a physical form, but could not. So they sought the power given to them by their believers, enough to make a body that could contain their power."

"Very well read indeed. The religions of the Third Country remember it reasonably well. But they are not quite correct. You are the result of their attempts to create a body that can withstand a god's power. You have the splinter of a god in you, put there before time was recorded and passed down through generations. It is this splinter that gives you your so-called Blessings, and that put up the barrier that prevents land travel between here and the Third Country. But this interference was not looked upon kindly. The gods were banished, and the wall between our realm and theirs was made impermeable."

"And is that where people go once they're dead?" Kaylene asked.

Thurien shrugged. "In a way. Certainly anyone who is Blessed could pass into the Divine Realm. That is why you can bring your Luka back."

"How?" Kaylene asked. The theological conversation was not why she was in this room with this unsettling man but if it got her the answer she needed, she would endure it.

"Hmm. One moment." He pulled out a sheet of linen paper and an ostentatious quill. Kaylene stared at the quill with the same jealous longing as she had at the clothes of the people of Curnith. The Sanctuary only allowed reed pens. There was a case to be made for the reed pen over a quill – they were more rigid and thus allowed unskilled hands to write with more ease, even if they also needed to be sharpened more frequently. But the reason the Sanctuary allowed no quills within its walls was because they were deemed too exorbitant, too much a display of ego, avarice, or excessiveness.

Thurien hummed to himself as he worked, appearing unaware of the two friends sitting opposite him. He occasionally scratched out a word, or pondered before writing something down. The only sound in the room was his hums and the scratch of his quill on the linen paper. He was finished quickly, checking back over what he had translated with a clerk's methodical approach. Then, he rolled the scroll back up, tested the ink on the page he had written to ensure it was dry, and pushed them both back to Merika and Kaylene.

As one, the two leaned forward to see what he had written. Almost certainly, it made more sense to Merika, but Kaylene was able to garner the general idea. She was certain Merika's mind was already dissecting the instructions, fitting them together with the pieces of knowledge she had hungrily sought and consumed over the years. Kaylene was more interested in the words themselves and what insights they may yield into unlocking the language on the scroll.

"Something's missing," Merika said, breaking through Kaylene's thoughts.

Thurien made a noise of affirmation.

The unease and frustration Kaylene had felt earlier rushed to push aside the alarm Merika's announcement had brought. "Why?"

He made an ambiguous gesture.

"There's a reference here to the stars," Merika said, putting her finger on the page. "Is it possible that this is wrong, or that their position in the sky depending on the time of year isn't accounted for?"

"Very good." Thurien's manner had all the markings of one of the Senior Blessed taking delight in making someone feel stupid. The realisation pressed against Kaylene's temples, squeezing out every emotion but for the rage she had always suppressed when faced with that demeanour.

The vase on the desk splintered as the flowers grew in a sudden spurt, and kept growing. The stems morphed, roots shooting out from the previously clean-cut ends, hungrily seeking soil. The tendrils snaked across the desk, their growth and movement the manifestation of Kaylene's suddenly unbridled anger. She barely noticed as Merika snatched the scroll and page of translation from the water creeping across the desk.

A snarl transformed Kaylene's face as she bared her teeth at Thurien. "I am not your plaything." Her arms gripped the side of the chair, nails digging into the fabric.

Thurien's smile was broad. "It seems the Sanctuary is doing a fine job of teaching you to control yourself."

Kaylene's response to his gibe came as the plants reached for him. Leaves and stems curled as though they would squeeze the very life from his body.

"Kaya." Merika's voice was sharp.

Her friend's words went unheard, drowned by the anger squeezing her temples, narrowing her senses to focus only on Thurien. The plant reached his hand. He didn't move. He observed it with a raised eyebrow and half-smile as it wrapped around his arm and snaked up toward his neck.

"Kaya!" Merika said more loudly.

When Kaylene did not respond, Merika, with a quick gesture, had Kaylene's clothes tightening against her, making it hard to breathe.

The plant around Thurien's arm put on a spurt of growth and reached his neck, but with her vision growing dark and chest burning, Kaylene could not sustain her rage. Abruptly, the plant slackened and Kaylene fell back in her chair, gasping for breath.

Merika maintained the hold for a few more seconds.

The dark spots slowly cleared from Kaylene's vision once her friend released her.

She glared at Thurien while she breathed deeply. He did not seem perturbed or angry. With a detached curiosity, he unwound the plant that had curled itself around him, putting it neatly to one side.

"That was very impressive," he commented.

"I'm sorry, she did not mean—" Merika was uncharacteristically apologetic. Perhaps it was her hunger for more information driving this contrition.

He cut her off with a wave of his hand. "You know, I really think you might have the ability to actually open a door to the Divine Realm." The expression on his face made Kaylene think that he had just consumed a filling and delicious meal. "My own apologies are in order. I'm afraid I was trying to provoke you."

Kaylene had finally caught her breath. The admission made the heat of her anger build once more, but she kept it in check – for now.

"Unfortunately, I do not know how to remedy this problem. That does not lie within my area of expertise. But what I have translated should be enough for you."

Kaylene knew dismissal when she heard it. She stood, her emotions a turbulent whirl. She wanted to remain, demand further explanation, but instinct told her the Old One would give them no more. The dismay at the incomplete information was not as strong as the need to be out of this small room and feel the sun and air on her skin. Merika stood too, her fingers possessively curled over the scroll and translation.

"Meeting you two was," Thurien smiled, "delightful." There was something else behind his words, something that Kaylene did not properly understand. It intensified her desire to leave. She strode to the door, waiting for her friend. She placed her fingers upon the handle. It was cold and unyielding against her skin. Merika stayed where she was, her posture and expression clearly conveying a desire to ask Thurien more. Kaylene made an impatient noise that pulled her friend across the room with obvious reluctance. The exchange was conducted under Thurien's gaze of detached amusement. He stood as Merika reached Kaylene's side. Perhaps it was a trick of distance, but he looked taller. The handle gave under her hand, although she would have sworn she exerted no extra pressure. The door swung open, and, foregoing any word of goodbye, Kaylene stepped into the bright sunshine and noise of the outside world with no small amount of gratitude.

Merika spoke as soon as the door had closed behind them. "He was fascinating."

"He knew more than he told us." Kaylene's unease at the encounter warred with hope that had emerged now that the sun was on her skin and wind played with her hair; he had given them information that would help bring back Luka.

Merika did not seem concerned by the man's unsettling demeanour. "Oh, he certainly knew more than he told us, but not more about how to get Luka back."

"How can you be sure?"

Merika shrugged in a way that suggested she also was not divulging everything.

Nearby, the Farwan family had finished unloading their ship. They were gathered together, all but the redheaded woman looking uncertainly about their new homeland. Kaylene's eye was drawn to the daughter with the long dark hair. She was fascinated by the conflicting emotions she observed in the girl. As if she sensed Kaylene's gaze upon her, the girl turned. She had huge dark eyes – Kaylene could see that even across the distance between them.

Merika spoke and Kaylene's attention was drawn away from the exiles.

"Are you all right?"

Kaylene regarded her friend with surprise. The question was unlike Merika; she did not pay much attention to sentiment or feelings; it was not in her nature.

"I'm fine. Sorry about in there, I didn't mean to get so angry."

"He was provoking you, and after everything..."

Merika was obviously at the end of her capacity for empathy.

Nevertheless, Kaylene appreciated her friend's effort.

"I still shouldn't have gotten angry. He had no idea what happened to Luka." Kaylene was more troubled by her behaviour than her reply let on. Not only was it entirely contrary to the Sanctuary's teachings, but it revealed an intensity to her emotions she hadn't realised existed. The way anger had overtaken her, using her body and her Blessing as a conduit for its expression, impressed upon her the relevance of what was said about the Blessed: they were dangerous and could not be allowed to roam free in the world if they allowed their feelings free rein. Her behaviour in Thurien's office had emphasised a fundamental lack of control. It reinforced that the Senior Blessed were right to refuse to allow her to leave.

Merika brushed aside Kaylene's concern. "He gave us what we needed, and that's the most important thing. Come on, let's find somewhere to stay the night."

The innkeeper had glared at them with suspicion and caution but ultimately did not give them any trouble. In their room, Merika pored over the translation of the scroll, excitement evident in the slight tremble of her fingers trembled as she smoothed out the two documents and the curve of her posture as she bowed over them. Kaylene kept her emotions leashed after the display of their potency that afternoon, but she too could not suppress excitement at the fact that they were closer to getting Luka back. Hope had begun to creep through her like a vine, and she did not want to remove it.

Merika took out a separate piece of paper and scribbled on it, muttering to herself. While her friend worked, Kaylene looked between the scroll and Thurien's translation. She wondered if she could learn something of the Old Ones' language from this translation. Kaylene had chosen language as her field of study more on a whim than for any real reason. Yet she had come to enjoy picking through grammar structures and idiomatic proclivities. They hinted at vastly different worlds not simply beyond the Sanctuary's walls but beyond the First Country. To perfect her understanding of the language, she had read as many books as the Sanctuary had and would bring in at her request. She'd read texts, trading agreements, manifests, and fiction. The assorted patchwork understanding of the rest of the world that the various texts had formed captured her imagination. Of late, her interest in the other parts of the Godskissed Continent had been muted by grief. But the first tendrils of curiosity had found their way to the surface, and she wondered if the language on the scroll gave away any clues about the world that had produced it.

Certainly, she could infer something of the grammar structure. There were similarities across all languages of the Godskissed Continent, and the Old Ones' tongue definitely seemed to share that. However, the grammar of the Old Ones seemed less complex.

"It's almost like it's more primitive," Kaylene murmured.

Merika raised her head from her fervent writing. "What?"

"The language of the scroll – it's like it's less complex than what we speak," Kaylene explained.

"Curious," Merika said, the word falling away as her mind considered the observation. She chewed the end of the reed pen absentmindedly.

Kaylene stood to ease an ache in her legs and walked to the window, a vague restlessness overtaking her. She wanted action. She wanted to bring Luka back now. Too much time without him had already elapsed. The passage of time brought with it the fear that she was beginning to forget the way he looked, the way he smelled, the feel of him. Already, she couldn't quite remember how much taller he was than her. It was a small detail, but that she could forget anything about him left the taste of cinders in her mouth. He had been the centre of her world. She knew every part of him, as he had her. That she might forget anything brought back the kind of panic she'd experienced as the aftershocks of Luka's death. It was Luka to whom she had turned when she was lost or uncertain. He was the person whose opinion she trusted most, whose fears she understood, and who saw and allayed her fears. Without him, half of her was missing, and she'd survived only thanks to the clarity of him in her mind. As that conjuration of him had begun to dissipate, she'd wanted to make herself disappear, too. It was what had led her to that cliff edge.

Trying to push aside the panic, Kaylene looked at the small tree in the inn's courtyard. The delicate orange of the blossoms caught the light of the setting sun as it scraped across the rooftop. Only a moment later, the sun slipped too low and the luminescence that had graced the tree was gone.

Kaylene watched with an outsider's curiosity as a trio of what she presumed to be friends entered the courtyard, big mugs in their hands. Their lack of reservation was so strange. She was torturing herself now. With a sigh, she turned back to Merika. "Do you know what we have to do?"

Her friend scratched her head. "Not all of it – I think I'll need to check a few things once we're back at the Sanctuary, but I have a rough idea."

Kaylene grasped at Merika's certainty. "Tell me."

Merika returned the end of her pen to her mouth as she looked over her notes. "We'll need to find a divide we can open. There's reference here to the symbolic act of opening. It's like..." She paused as she visibly struggled to compress her complex and technical thoughts into words simple enough to convey the concept to Kaylene. "It's like the Divine Realm is a shadow world to our own, but it doesn't quite align. You have to find a way to connect them properly – so, a door, or barrier, or something to open. Thurien said something about the barrier across the mountain pass – I think it might have been a hint that we can use it. We need to create a shape and act upon it with our Blessings. That should be enough to create the effect we need."

"And what, he'll just come out of this...doorway?" Kaylene left the window to come and look at Merika's notes. She shouldn't have bothered; they were even less clear than the translation Thurien had provided.

Merika shook her head, her teeth still working away at the reed pen.

Kaylene feared for its longevity.

"There's some comment about a choice – healing the body and drawing his essence back into it, or creating a body entirely anew."

Kaylene's eyes widened in repulsion at the prospect of recovering Luka's corpse and dragging it halfway across the country. After so many months, it would surely be rotten. Yet if that was what she needed to do to bring him back, she would do it. Fortunately, unlike the Second Country, the people of the First Country did not burn their dead.

"What do we need to do to create a body for him?"

Merika ground down on the reed pen. It broke with a loud snap. She pulled it from her mouth and stared at it with little surprise. She went through at least two a week, much to the admonition of the Senior Blessed. They claimed it demonstrated a lack of restraint on her part; she should be able to stop herself from doing it. Merika claimed that doing it helped her think and refused to make any effort to break the habit.

"Gods-cursed thing," Merika muttered, gathering the pieces of the ruined pen. "This wouldn't happen if they let me use a quill."

"You'd get bits of feather in your mouth."

Merika pulled a face before her attention was drawn straight back to the problem in front of her. She bent forward, her forehead wrinkled by a frown, and muttered indecipherably to herself.

Kaylene remained silent as she watched her clever friend work, hope spreading through her like a flower uncurling before the sun. Habit made her want to turn to Luka, to seek to share the barely restrained jubilation that she felt at the success that was so much closer now. It was so natural that she sought to share her thoughts with him, even after all these months. In moments like these, she was reminded just how unbalanced she was without him. She had not only lost a lover; she had lost her other half. Without him, it was as though she were looking at the world through only one eye. The constant war of emotions within her was exhausting; one gained advantage, held her, then something she saw or heard gave the other traction. She had no sense of solidity even within herself.

She whispered a prayer to the many-faced god, pleading with them to give her this, to ensure that the translation Thurien had provided was accurate, and that Merika could use it to find out what they had to do to bring Luka back.

SIX

As soon as they returned, Kaylene and Merika were summoned to Senior Blessed Maryam, who oversaw the day-to-day operations of the Sanctuary. She was a cold woman. She never offered a kind word, and she carried herself with an obvious impression of her own superiority. Kaylene had never liked her, and that dislike had only grown following the woman's apparent indifference to Luka's death. She'd been among the Senior Blessed who had come to tell Kaylene of Luka's death, but she'd let Rael, one of the kinder ones, speak. Kaylene always felt wariness around the woman now, fearing the arrival of some earth-shattering news.

As was custom, the travellers had to return extra money from what they'd been given and account for every coin spent. If it was deemed they'd spent more than was necessary, they would be punished. Senior Blessed Maryam's face retained its customary expressionless glare as the two handed over the receipts and provided an account of their journey. Merika and Kaylene had rehearsed their story the evening before their arrival, but under the woman's unblinking gaze, Kaylene felt certain the lie was obvious. The heaviness that had become her constant companion over the past few months descended upon her and settled atop her skin as she looked at the stone walls of the room.

"Merika, you may go," the Senior Blessed said once Merika had finished recounting their expenses.

Kaylene kept her face neutral as her friend left, but panic churned inside her.

"How did you find your family, Kaylene?"

Senior Blessed Maryam's question sent her heart fluttering. Never in her years at the Sanctuary had the woman asked such a question. It reeked of suspicion.

"Ah, fine."

"Really?" The woman looked at her with that unchanging expression.

"It's hard to say much more than that." She fought the temptation to break the woman's gaze or blink too much. Frantically, she cast her mind back to the last time she had actually seen her family. "They've changed. Grown up...grown old." She remembered the shock at seeing the thick streaks of grey in her parents' hair, the easy adulthood into which her siblings had grown. It was as though she was meeting strangers with familiar faces and manners rather than her flesh and blood.

"It happens when you stay away for too long," Senior Blessed Maryam said, her tone too flat to suggest whether she was observing or rebuking. "Family is one of the things that define us. The idea of not belonging there any longer is a hard one."

Kaylene's reply came without thought. "I think my grandfather's absence makes it hardest." Returning the first time after he'd died had been heartbreaking. She kept expecting to see him; the house itself was unchanged, so it made such little sense that he – one of its staple features – was not there, too. It was a loss she had not thought of for a long time. Luka's death had overshadowed every other sadness.

"It is a hard truth to face that being Blessed sets us apart from the rest of the world. Things such as returning to family are painful reminders of that."

The Senior Blessed's words hung in the air, some attached meaning seeming to linger just out of comprehension.

A beat of silence passed. The Senior Blessed sighed. "You may go."

Wonder at whether she had detected disappointment of some kind in the sigh was eclipsed by relief that it appeared her story had been believed. She went to find her friends.

"So we're back where we started." Callam's proclamation was unusually definite and held a certain glumness Kaylene could not help but echo.

Merika, despite scouring the library for information, had failed to procure any mathematical instruction on how to draw the shape she had described at the inn. She sat at their usual study table, her head in her hands.

"I don't know if the right information isn't in here, or if I'm just not skilled enough with numbers to understand this," she moaned, her voice muffled.

Had Kaylene not been battling to remain positive, she would have found her friend's despair amusing. Merika hated not knowing something.

Leshan looked up from the pile of books and tablets she had accumulated. Helplessness shone through her expression.

"I'm sure there's a way to find out what we need," she said unconvincingly.

"There is no way that I can know what we need," Merika replied, head still in her hands.

"Is there someone else who might know?" Leshan asked.

Merika snorted. "Yes, I'll just wander around the Sanctuary asking if anybody knows anything about mathematics. When they ask why, I'll say, 'Why, it's to raise our friend from the dead'. I'm sure anybody who can help will assist without any further questions or concerns."

Leshan persevered. "What about someone outside the Sanctuary?"

"I have no idea where to start searching for someone with that knowledge."

"Even if we found someone within the First Country who might be able to help us, they'd probably report us to the Sanctuary," Callam pointed out.

"There must be some way that we can find the answer," Kaylene said. Panic was beginning to overwhelm her. The hope to which she had clung so desperately was looking ever more tenuous. Familiar darkness threatened to press down upon her.

Callam flinched and put his hand to his head, as though it ached.

A deranged cackle from the greater library drew the four friends from their focus. Merika raised her head in a sharp movement, her features tight. The four exchanged a wary glance. Such abandon signalled something was wrong. The last time such a sound had been heard was the day Luka died.

Silence returned. The conversation resumed, although disquiet overlaid each word.

"We have almost everything else," Merika said. "What I've read confirms that we can use the barrier at the mountain pass to open a way to the Divine Realm. I know what to do to recreate a body for Luka, and I know that the vessel needs to be placed inside a shape that's determined by the stars' position, the nature of our Blessings, and Luka's age and size – but I don't know how to use those variables."

Her last words returned to the realm of angry despair. Merika flung herself to her feet and paced the length of the small room.

Kaylene felt helpless and stupid. She hated the feeling. If it had been possible, she would have slunk away unnoticed and found a corner in which to drown herself in tears.

The feeling reminded her of the first time Luka and she had properly spoken. She had been told yet again that she would not be permitted to leave the Sanctuary. Her grandfather was ailing, according to letters from home, and she wanted to be by his side for the rest of his days. She had gone to the furthest corner of a barely-visited courtyard and sobbed bitterly, even as a corner of her mind whispered that such a display of emotion was exactly the lack of restraint that kept her locked within the Sanctuary's walls.

Although it too was frowned upon, she had drawn the plants of the courtyard around her to shield her from the world. Yet her crying had been too loud and Luka heard as he passed by.

"Why are you crying?"

When she realised it was Luka talking to her, she nearly made the vines, flowers and tree roots cover her entirely. For the months he'd been at the Sanctuary with Callam, she'd watch him with covert fascination, wanting to talk with him but not knowing how. Friendships were difficult things to navigate in the Sanctuary.

"Go away," she choked out when it became clear he wasn't going to leave.

"I want to make sure you're all right."

"I'm fine." She pulled her knees to her chest even more tightly. She risked glancing up at him. Today his eyes were a sparkling green and his hair light blue. She later learned that he could change the shape of his features, too, but preferred not to, joking that he was worried he'd forget what he actually looked like.

"Do you like my choice of hair colour today? My brother says I look ridiculous." He spoke casually, as though the circumstances of their exchange weren't in any way unusual. It seemed a patronising approach.

"It's fine."

"You can make plants grow, can't you?"

She nodded. Her vexation grew, chewing up the overwhelming misery as it did so. She was disappointed. From afar he had been so intriguing, yet now he just seemed superior.

"Do you want to talk about it?" he asked.

She was conscious of how swollen her face felt. "I'm not going home yet."

"Ah." His face creased into understanding. "How long have you been here?" Normally it was an avoided question – it saved judgment and shame on all sides. But the way he asked made her happy to answer.

"Two years." It was around the time most people left. The last of the friends Kaylene had made had left two months earlier. Making new friends had been impossible and seemed unnecessary; she'd thought she would be leaving soon, too.

"You must miss your family. I'm lucky; my brother's here with me."

"I know," she said shyly.

"Kaylene, isn't it?"

She was surprised but glad he knew who she was. "You're Luka, aren't you?"

He flashed a sweet smile. "I quite like it here," he said. Then he obviously remembered the source of her distress. "But I've not been here so long." Apology hung in his voice.

"Why do you like it?" She'd never heard anybody express fondness for the Sanctuary unless they'd been plucked from dire poverty. Even then, the admission was grudging and flavoured with shame. Luka's comment held neither characteristic.

"It's peaceful. They bring in texts on any subject we want to study, and this building is beautiful."

She remembered with vivid clarity how incredulous she'd been at his last comment. But that was Luka, able to see beauty everywhere, able to find calm amid the most tempestuous of moods.

"Do you know any hidden places?" he asked.

"What?"

"You know, places most people don't know about. In two years you must have found some." He held out his hand in request that she show him, and suddenly, she was glad she wasn't leaving just yet.

The present intruded on Kaylene's recollections as another cackle punctured the quiet. As always, the memory of Luka smothered her with sadness. She wanted to cry, but an emptiness within her big enough to swallow the world made the act of crying seem pointless. She glanced around at her friends. All had fallen completely still and were watching her. Callam met her gaze, his face unusually pale.

Kaylene was about to ask him if he was all right when Merika slammed her hands down on the tabletop. The crack made everybody jump.

"I can't believe that there's no solution," she snapped, more to herself than anyone else.

"You said Thurien was playing with you. Is it possible he gave you a hint?" Leshan said.

"I'm sure of it," Merika said, her frustration seeping through her posture.

"What exactly did he say?" Leshan asked.

"I don't know, Lesha! It was over two weeks ago. I can't remember every word."

"Wait," Callam said.

Merika's eyes narrowed as she swung her gaze to him. "Don't you dare go messing about in my head, Cal."

"Too late," he said with a small smile of apology.

She hissed through her teeth at the intrusion.

Kaylene could understand her unwillingness to allow Callam to trawl in her thoughts, but Merika's opposition was unexpected in its vehemence, especially given what his help was likely to achieve. Besides, Callam was the most gentle person she knew – even more so than Luka. He would not walk through the mind of another person for his own amusement.

"I didn't look at anything. I just pulled out the memory," he said. "I promise," he added emphatically when Merika glared at him.

"Don't ever go into my head again without asking," she snarled.

"Do you remember anything that might help?" Kaylene asked, frustrated at her friend's reaction.

"A moment, I'm—"

Another cackle from the archive's main hall cut her off.

The four exchanged wary glances. The silence that filled the space after the intrusion of the noise was brittle. Merika opened her mouth to speak again but the laughter resumed. This time, it did not stop. With unspoken accord, the friends left the room. The only thing worse than seeing whatever mania was behind the sound was imagining it.

The boy was perhaps sixteen years of age – already older than was normal in the Sanctuary. Blessed were gathered in a rough circle around the boy where he sat on the floor of the archive, laughter crawling through him in spasms. It was as terrifying as it was mesmerising. Shivers ran along Kaylene as she watched the boy rock back and forth, his arms wrapped about himself. Leshan's hand found hers, the tightness of her grip keeping Kaylene in the moment rather than becoming lost in the horror of memory. On Leshan's other side, Callam hissed like he was in pain.

The sound of agonised birdcalls filtered into the room. Kaylene glanced toward the sound. The distress in the bird sounds sent her skin rippling. A howl came from one of the Sanctuary's hearat. Kaylene glanced toward the boy, understanding. His Blessing must be an affinity with animals.

A crack against one of the high windows made everybody jump.

A girl who could not have been more than twelve went over to the window with a boldness that Kaylene could not help but admire.

"What was it?" another girl called out.

"A bird. It flew straight into the window and killed itself." The reply was immediately proceeded by another crack that reverberated throughout the area.

"Someone get a Senior Blessed!"

The cry came from within the huddle of children watching in impotent horror.

Merika moved her hands and several heavy books flew toward the boy.

"Stop, Meri, what are you doing?" Leshan's voice thrummed with indignant confusion.

"If I hit him, he'll probably faint," Merika replied. "We need to do something before every bird in the area suicides against the windows."

Her point was emphasised by another heart-stopping howl.

"You can't simply throw books at him." Leshan kept her voice low but intense. "You might kill him."

"So?" With a small gesture, Merika sent the books soaring to the roof above the boy.

"Wait," Callam said. Normally so quiet, the authority in his voice made Merika pause.

As she watched Callam and realised what he was about to do, it felt as though she'd had ice-cold water thrown over her. Shock that he would – that he could – use his Blessing to calm the boy made her breaths come in heaving gasps. She wanted to look away, but her gaze was glued to Callam. His own stare was locked on the boy, but his expression was vacant. The lines etched in the skin from nose to mouth said that whatever he was doing, he was fighting through extreme pain to do it. The howling laughter continued for a few more moments, punctuated by sickening thuds and howls, then abruptly, the boy fell quiet. Kaylene hardly dared look, but when she did, he was sitting placidly, a dazed expression making his features slack.

A timid stillness entered the archive. Most of the children were unaware what had made the boy stop; their fear and uncertainty saturated the air.

Kaylene could bear it no more. She wrenched her hand free from Leshan's and fled, passing a Senior Blessed who was running toward the archive. When she reached her room, Kaylene flung herself onto the bed and began to sob, rage and bitterness making her throat raw.

Cautious steps and the lightest pressure beside her did not interrupt her outpouring of grief. A part of her considered trying to speak, but she knew she could not form the words around the cries that tore from her throat.

Leshan waited.

Finally, Kaylene raised her head. She had no tears left. Her throat felt completely dry.

"Open," Leshan commanded, her beautiful low voice soothing.

Obediently, Kaylene opened her mouth.

Her friend summoned sweet, fresh rain just above her open lips, and the water slid down her parched throat.

The rain dissipated and Kaylene swallowed, her throat still sore but no longer unbearably swollen from her cries.

"I know," Leshan said softly before Kaylene could say anything. The empathy in her voice was heartbreaking. Her eyes were huge, the pink and orange of a dawning sun glimmering with reassuring warmth.

"He died for nothing," Kaylene said. She was amazed by the evenness in her voice. She had expected herself to succumb once more to violent tears. Yet the breath she drew was steady. Slowly, she felt for the rage woken on her trip to Curnith. She had thought it had been drowned, but it burned steadily.

"If they'd just have asked Callam—" She clenched her fists. "Why did they ask Luka?"

Leshan's sorrow was undisguised. "He was the kindest."

"But he should never have been asked to try to calm that girl down," Kaylene said.

And just like that, she returned to the day he died.

Luka's affinity for soothing people, for making them feel better even when in the throes of the most vile, violent emotion, was well known. From the day he found her crying in the garden, Kaylene had seen Luka make even the most distraught of people smile. It was not a Blessing, simply something about his nature. She loved him for it.

The day he died had started like any other. But then screams had begun, reaching every corner of the Sanctuary.

Kaylene and Luka had been lazing together in the courtyard. He was sitting. She was lying on the grass. Her head was cradled in his lap, and she was looking at the sky. The clouds were crossing the expanse of blue with a certain impudence, coalescing into a multitude of shapes. It was a perfect day on which to do nothing but sit with someone you loved. Kaylene had thought there was no way she could imagine herself happier.

The screams had disrupted them from the reverie into which they had both slipped. Kaylene sat up with a start, nearly cracking her forehead against Luka's chin. His hand came to her arm, half comfort, half a gesture to ensure she was all right. Her hand covered his in reply. There was a unity, a balance in the way they moved around each other that spoke of the years that had passed in which they had been closer to one entity than two separate people.

"What do you think it could be?" Kaylene asked.

His hair was the same gold as hers that day. The sunlight glinted off it, and she remembered that it had been hard to see his face properly. His shrug was what she remembered more than the expression on his face.

Running footsteps were a staccato noise punctuating the screams. A young girl, obviously terrified half out of her skin, came into the courtyard.

"Luka," she gasped.

"Yes?" He sat up straighter, although his hands remained on Kaylene's arm.

"They want your help. Catice is having some sort of fit, and they don't know how to calm her."

"Of course." Luka stood up and reached down to help Kaylene to her feet.

The last glimpse of him had been the delicate line of his cheekbone. She couldn't remember her thought when she looked at the fragile beauty of his face.

He hadn't even kissed her goodbye, so arrogant had they both been in the certainty of his return.

SEVEN

When they came to tell her, she had been contentedly translating a letter from the Second Country; easy work that made money for the Sanctuary. The knowledge cultivated by the people who resided within its walls brought in more than enough to maintain the building. Merika was sitting with her, saying something that had left her in a fit of laughter. What Merika had been saying she could not remember, no matter how hard she tried. It seemed profane that she had been laughing even as Luka's body lay cooling.

"Kaylene." It hadn't been the fact she'd been called that arrested her attention – although she'd thought it strange that Senior Blessed Rael was speaking when Senior Blessed Maryam was also there. What had truly given her pause was the way in which Senior Blessed Rael spoke. None of the Senior Blessed spoke with such timidity, such uncertainty. It made her immediately wary.

"Yes?" she asked.

"Come with us, please." Again, Kaylene was struck by the tentativeness within the command.

"Why?" Kaylene stood, but folded her arms across her chest.

"We would like to speak with you." Senior Blessed Rael gestured to the two Senior Blessed who flanked him.

"Why?" She repeated the question, unease skittering across the surface of her obstinacy.

"Something very sad has happened."

Reliving it, Kaylene remembered not even contemplating that something had happened to Luka. She assumed that one of her parents or siblings had been struck by tragedy – her grandfather had died nearly seven years previously. There was an echo of the manner in which she had been informed of his passing in the way they were looking at her now.

With a sigh, she relented as she had always known she would, asking Merika to mind her work. Rael led her into one of the kitchen courtyards; the other two Senior Blessed melted away as they stepped into the open air. The fact that it was just the two of them should have told her something was incredibly wrong, but she hadn't given it too much thought. Neat rows of vegetables peeked through the brown earth. Nobody else was present. That was when she really should have started to worry, but instead, Kaylene was shrouded in confusion about why she was being taken there to be informed of something that likely wasn't going to affect her life within the Sanctuary.

"Sit." The authority of Rael's command was undermined by the waver in his voice.

That was when Kaylene realised. "Luka," she breathed, cold horror crawling across her skin.

"He was speaking with Catice and she wouldn't listen. Her Blessing is the ability to heal. Or, to injure. She—" Rael bit off the end of his sentence, either searching for the right word or catching himself before going into detail that might be too much for Kaylene to bear.

"Is it serious?" Kaylene focused on the practicality of the problem rather than the fear screaming from the back of her mind. "Will he be disfigured? He can change the appearance of things, so surely he'll be able to hide any scarring."

"I'm so sorry. He's dead."

Kaylene stared at the older man for several seconds. His words seemed nonsense, surely incorrect or misheard.

"Kaylene?" Rael said softly when she did not reply.

It seemed she had understood correctly, but he surely must be mistaken. "No." Her voice was firm. "He's not dead."

"I was there, Kaylene." Rael made no effort to stop the tears filling his eyes.

"You didn't check. He can't be dead."

"He is. I'm sorry."

For one more moment, Kaylene was silent. She felt as though the world had stopped being real and instead she was hearing a story told about her rather than having this happen to her. Then, the implications of what he'd just said slammed into her like ice water and she felt too heavy, too awkward, too constrained by the limitations of the flesh and blood that housed her. She screamed, a long agonising scream that ripped through the air. Her arms came to curl around her torso, as though she could keep herself from tearing apart.

The garden around her began to grow at a fantastic rate. Vines slithered across the soil, reaching and wrapping around pillars. Flower buds formed, then bloomed, then died without bearing fruit. Stalks speared toward the sky, reaching the height of the courtyard roof. Then, as Kaylene still screamed, every single plant withered and died, leaving behind a yellow, brittle forest.

Her display of power had unnerved the Senior Blessed. Rael had taken a step back as two others had rushed forward from the doorways in which they'd been hidden. Occasionally she wondered what would have happened had she directed the plants in the garden toward the Blessed who stood there while her world fell apart.

She wondered that now as she sat on the hard bed in her cold, stone room. Would she have torn them apart with nothing but plants and the force of her grief? Could she have torn down the courtyard? Or the Sanctuary itself?

Leshan was still next to her, watching her with profound sadness etched into her sunrise-coloured eyes. Kaylene swallowed, pushing the memories back down. She knew if she did not stop reliving that day, she would likely go mad and end up like the boy in the archive or the girl who had killed Luka. Catice had disappeared from the Sanctuary once her fit subsided. Kaylene did not know exactly what happened to her; the Senior Blessed had made no announcement as they had with the rebellious boy in Kaylene's first year. The entirety of the Sanctuary knew of Catice's fit and the terrible consequence it had caused. Yet everybody had a clear idea as to how the Senior Blessed had dealt with her. From the moment Kaylene had arrived in the Sanctuary, she'd been told by numerous older Blessed of rare instances when someone would have some kind of fit. The Senior Blessed always dealt with them – permanently. Such instability saw others hurt and that was not something they could sanction. These events were thought more a whispered tale to frighten the newly arrived than truth. It was the reason for the nonchalance with which Luka and Kaylene had treated the request to help soothe Catice. That the girl's mind had snapped so wholly seemed a tragedy almost without precedent. And yet.

"They should have asked Cal." The mindless grief and rage that had overtaken Kaylene were washed away, replaced by a more reflective anger.

"Perhaps they didn't think Callam could actually calm someone in a fit of hysteria."

Kaylene remembered the expression of pain on Callam's face as he'd worked his Blessing on the boy. But Kaylene did not want to give any quarter to the Sanctuary. "They still shouldn't have asked Luka if she was like that."

Either agreeing, or not seeing a point in contradicting her, Leshan remained silent.

Kaylene leaned back against the wall. The stone was cool even in the depths of the humid summers of the First Country. Now, in early spring, the surface held a chill that seeped into Kaylene's skin.

"We're told the many-faced god takes us into the Divine Realm after death, but that's so vague and terrifying. Luka was here one day, and then suddenly he was gone, and it didn't make sense to me then, and it doesn't make sense to me now. How can an entire person be here, be alive, able to feel pain and fear and happiness and then suddenly...not be? It's not fair, it doesn't make sense, and the idea that he's in the embrace of the many-faced god is so insubstantial that it's a worthless platitude to cover up this collective terror that there is nothing beyond this life – that everything we do here has no meaning, is of no consequence, that the act of loving someone, of being loved – it does not endure, it all means nothing." The words tumbled out of her, faster and faster.

"I can't understand that he was here – tangible and warm and alive, and then—" her voice hitched, but she pushed through "—and then I was told I'd never get to see him again, never get to hold his hand or hear his smile.

"It's not fair and it doesn't make sense and I just...I can't accept it. Maybe it's stupid of me, but I believe Ay'ash when she said I can get him back because it is the first bit of sense I've heard since that day when he was simply gone – that it can be undone. Because his death was a mistake, and we're taught to fix our mistakes, not just move on from them."

Her throat once more felt raw. It was as though the pain of what she'd felt every day for so long, in being put into words, had seared her as it left that dark place where it had nestled between her heart and gut and been given both more and less solidity.

"I'm starting to forget him, Lesha." The clear image of Luka was becoming indistinct. More and more she recalled fragments of the angle of his face or the twist of his smile rather than what he looked like standing in front of her.

The impermanence of even memory frightened her in ways she couldn't articulate.

"You could never forget him."

"What if we can't get him back?" she whispered.

"The only way we can't get him back is if we stop trying. And if we stop trying, I'm afraid of what that will do to you."

Her friend's confession was unexpectedly tender.

"I'm so lucky that you care for me so."

Leshan's smile was tiny. Sad. "You're family to me."

The moment was interrupted by a knock at the door. Merika did not wait for a response, but rather than barging in as was her customary way, she opened the door gently. Kaylene could see Callam hovering behind.

"Cal said it was all right to come in," Merika said, her voice unusually quiet.

Kaylene felt decidedly undeserving of their friendship.

"What happened to the boy?" She felt bad not knowing his name, but after so many years at the Sanctuary, it seemed pointless to learn the names of the younger Blessed who came and left so quickly. Especially given the way most of them regarded Kaylene and her friends with a mixture of scorn and apprehension.

"He's asleep," Callam said as he and Merika crowded into the room.

"What caused it?" Leshan asked.

Merika looked to Callam expectantly. Clearly, she'd asked and received no answer.

He shifted, obviously uncomfortable with the full attention of them all. He spoke quietly and quickly. "I don't know. It wasn't really able to stop and think. But..."

"But?" Merika prompted, her voice just shy of sharp.

"It was like there was another identity in his mind."

"Did it say something?"

"Thoughts aren't like words on a page, Meri." Callam's voice became uncharacteristically irate.

"What happened to the animals?" Leshan asked, her voice full of sadness.

"Dead, I think," Merika said.

"What would drive them to kill themselves?" Leshan said.

"Maybe he called them, or maybe he made them feel pain."

Callam's eyes met Kaylene's and she wondered yet again if he was reading her thoughts.

"I don't think it's that simple," she mumbled, feeling heat rise to her face under his gaze. Re-living those horrible moments had cut open the wound they'd caused. The pain, the sense of weight that came with every breath, returned, and the promise of relief offered by the cliffs and water was the only thing that eased some of the heaviness that made everything impossibly difficult.

Merika's voice cut through Kaylene's thoughts and the silence in the room.

"I think I might know how we can get the measurement."

Kaylene sat up. The bed bounced at the roughness of the movement. "Really?" Unbridled desperation infused her voice.

Merika nodded. "If nobody from the First Country can or will help us, what about someone from outside the First Country?"

"How are we supposed to get on a ship? Nobody will ever let a Blessed on a ship without about a thousand permissions."

Merika shook her head. "We don't have to leave. They've come to us."

Kaylene's eyes widened as comprehension arrived. "The refugees," she said. The horror of the afternoon receded as wild, terrible hope exploded within Kaylene's chest.

"Remember, Thurien said that the daughter was some kind of genius when it came to equations?"

"Do you think that she will help us?"

Merika smirked. Obviously she had come up with a plan. "We can always persuade her." She threw a glance at Callam.

"Do you really think that you can do that?" Worry clouded Leshan's tone.

Merika didn't wait for Callam to answer. "Of course he can. After what he did in the archive, I'm certain."

It was typical Merika, to see something like the unsettling incident and finding inspiration in it. While there was something a little callous about it, Kaylene admired her friend's ability to work everything in service to her goals.

"Cal, are you comfortable with this?" Leshan asked, looking intently at the slender young man who had pressed himself against the wall as though he wanted to be overlooked.

His mouth tightened and he nodded, a determination in his features that Kaylene had never seen before.

"I'll go with him." The words left her lips before she'd even thought them through.

Merika opened her mouth to voice an objection but Callam, obviously anticipating her resistance or covertly reading her thoughts, spoke first. "I want Kaylene to come with me."

Merika said nothing, dissatisfaction written across her expression.

"Kaylene's more likely to be allowed out a second time," Leshan pointed out. "She's the one who was Luka's love. If Cal says he wants to pay final tribute to his brother and bring Kaya, they'll be more likely to be lenient. Besides, she's also the only one of us who speaks the Fourth Country's language. That may prove useful."

Merika's sharp inhale made clear that she was frustrated her plan was being changed, but she did not object.

Kaylene wondered if she should be leaving the Sanctuary, despite her definite statement that she'd accompany Callam. The incident with the boy in the grand archive seemed to confirm everything the Senior Blessed said about the danger the Blessed posed. After her own outburst in Thurien's office, she was more convinced than ever that she did not deserve to leave the Sanctuary permanently. She looked up, ready to tell Merika she wouldn't go, but her gaze landed on Callam first. He was looking directly at her. Challenge was in his expression, and she found it so mesmerising that her intended words evaporated.

In the days leading up to their departure, Kaylene worried increasingly about travelling for over a week with Callam. While shared grief over Luka had offered them a certain understanding, it had not given her any greater insight into the brother of the man she had loved with her whole heart. Her concerns only deepened when Merika told her that the exiles had settled in the Skyfire region in the heartland of the country, which would nearly three weeks to travel to and from. She was so overcome by worry that she'd barely wondered how exactly Merika had managed to uncover this information.

It was likely to be a very silent trip. She'd always found Callam reserved, always been mildly uncomfortable around him, really. While she was hardly loquacious, Callam made her seem downright outgoing. Over the years, she'd been disabused of the assumption that he was chronically shy, but his preference to not take a central part in conversation left her unsure how she should interact with him at the best of times.

Luka had always spoken to his brother, drawing him out of wherever his thoughts dwelled. Now, being around Callam only reminded her of his brother's absence, from the shocking way they resembled one another, to the silence that now emanated from him.

It didn't help that she felt he could hear more of her thoughts than he claimed. If that was the case, then he'd have to know she thought he should have died instead of Luka.

The willingness of the Senior Blessed to allow Kaylene and Callam to pay final tribute to Luka surprised her. She wondered if her newfound resentment toward them was fair – allowing her to leave the Sanctuary twice in such a short time seemed more than reasonable, almost caring. If only they knew her true purpose.

On the day the set off, Kaylene and Callam were halfway through the barren lands that encircled the Sanctuary when a spring thunderstorm beset them. Kaylene, wondering if this was some kind of omen from the many-faced god about how the rest of this trip would be, miserably wished Leshan were there to clear the area around them and keep them dry. Leshan also would have offered a comment about the downpour that may have altered Kaylene's resolute misery about it. Callam sat in silence as she guided the hearat off the road and under the lacklustre shelter of some trees. With an absentminded thought, she directed the trees' canopy to thicken and better keep the water from them. The Senior Blessed may have frowned on it, but they were not here, soaking wet.

They dismounted from the cart and stood in the lee side of the cart for the meagre extra shelter it offered.

"I can hear your discomfort." He did not look at her as he spoke but rather at the ground, which was swiftly becoming mud.

"Sorry," she said, awkwardness causing her to link her hands and then unclasp them several times.

"It's all right. It's at least a change." His voice was softer, more melodic than Luka's, but Kaylene could hear a similarity to it that made her heart skip a beat.

He continued, "Most people are uncomfortable around me because they know I'm a mindsmith. At least with you it's because of Luka."

"Meri and Lesha aren't uncomfortable with you because of your Blessing." Kaylene realised she was neatly avoiding addressing his comment.

The curve of his smile was all she could see of his face. His hair, falling over his features as he looked down, hid the rest of his expression. "Of course they are."

She scoffed.

"They aren't as bad as some of the others, but they both have thoughts they don't want me to know," he said. "Meri's better at keeping me out."

Kaylene remained silent in her discomfort. It was unlike Callam to be so direct.

"Every time I touch your mind, it's almost too much for me to bear," he said quietly. "You're so sad." He was adamantly drawing circles in the mud with his foot. The dip quickly filled with water.

"I'm sorry." Kaylene wished she had more to offer him than words.

"It's all right." He gave a little shrug. "You can't help it."

His casual absolution left her with a deep sense of shame. She had been too caught up in her own grief and misery to consider how that might affect her friends. Even though Luka had died, she still had them, and she had never paused even for a moment to be grateful for that.

"I feel bad too, you know," he said. "Do you think I don't know it should have been me? He's my brother and he died doing something I could have done."

A blush stole its way along her cheeks. Again, she had nothing to say in the face of her own shame.

"Meri and Lesha might be doing this in part for you, but I'm doing this for him. He was all I had when we were growing up on the farm. Our parents were so ashamed to have two sons who were Blessed, but he never seemed to let that affect how he felt about himself – or me. I want him back because he's my brother, and he was mine before he was yours." Callam did not seem angry. He was merely opening his thoughts to her in the way that hers were open to him. She appreciated the insight.

"Meri's excited about the challenge as much as she is about bringing Luka back," Kaylene said. She did not resent Merika for that. "And Lesha just wants everyone to be happy."

"Leshan wants you to be happy," Callam corrected her.

She'd not really considered her friends' motives for helping her in this. It hadn't seemed important beyond the fact that they were. The selfishness imposed by her grief and single-minded focus was unpleasant to realise.

"Lesha would do anything for those she loves," Kaylene agreed.

He fell silent and seemed to be concentrating entirely on digging shapes with his feet.

"Do you dislike me?" she asked eventually, voicing the question that had always hovered on the edge of her mind. The way he had spoken about Luka just then certainly had made her wonder if he resented the time she had taken away from the brothers.

Callam finally raised his head and looked at her directly. His features were so similar to his brother's yet still his own. His face was longer, his lips fuller and more pouted. "I've always liked you."

"Why are you so reserved around me, then?"

His gaze was even; his eyes never strayed from hers. She'd never realised what a deep shade of blue they were.

"Because I make you sad." He made to get back on the cart. "I think the rain's letting up." His manner was offhanded, but Kaylene wondered what he was really thinking.

EIGHT

The rain seemed to have cleansed the land, making everything brighter, clearer. Being away from the Sanctuary and the new routine quickly established across the days helped Kaylene relax; after a couple of days on the road, she realised with surprise the bands that had coiled around her chest for so long had loosened their grip. The beauty of the landscape made her worries about spending so much time with Callam melt away. She was glad for his silence – it allowed her to drink in the sights without distraction. On the third day, they crossed into the skyfire region, colloquially known as the Flame County, where skyfire trees were in early bloom. The trees grew in abundance here, and their orange-red, multi-petalled flowers carpeted the place where the treetops met sky in ersatz flame.

The road became busier as they went further into the midlands. People flocked to witness the spectacle of the unfurling flowers filling the landscape with the illusion of fire. For a few weeks each year, people thronged to the skyfire region, filling the inns that provided vantage points of the spectacular trees along the plateau. Kaylene had never seen the trees in bloom; she'd only ever read descriptions and seen the occasional drawing. In fact, she had never even been to this region of the First Country. Despite the seriousness of their mission, she could not quell her excitement at being able to see this for herself.

Being outside, near the trees and grass rather than the barren stone walls of the Sanctuary, she felt herself blossoming, as though she was shucking off the worst of her sadness as hope, nurtured by the open land and fine weather, took hold of her. It was a magnificent sensation.

"What's it like, being a mindsmith?" she asked Callam as midday approached. It had always felt like prying before, but she felt now in the open air with the backdrop of beautiful trees that it was no longer an intrusive question. "Surely you'd hear so many nasty thoughts."

"The first thing I learned was how to stop myself from hearing too much. I really don't overhear people's thoughts unless they're particularly strong. But sometimes it's really nice. It was nice being around you and Luka. Lonely sometimes, but nice. The way you two felt for one another, the way you thought about one another. Being near it was like lying in the sun."

The matter-of-fact way in which he told her brought a smile to her face, even as sadness pricked at her. "That's a lovely way to look at it."

"I think I'd go mad if I didn't see things that way. I do hear a lot of awful things. I mean, I don't go looking into other people's minds, but sometimes I can't help but overhear. When I was little and first started to be able to read people's thoughts, I heard so many awful things, and I couldn't control it properly. It's the way with any mindsmith. In the same way that you simply listen out for what people are saying around you, I did that but with people's thoughts. Sometimes I had trouble distinguishing between what people said and what they thought. It was hard."

He looked away from her and fixed his gaze on the skyfire trees, evidently uncomfortable at speaking so much. Certainly, Kaylene had rarely heard him say as many words at the one time.

"Is it better in the Sanctuary?"

He nodded, but did not turn his head. "They teach self-control in the Sanctuary. Most people there might be children, but they control their minds well."

Kaylene wondered if Callam actually wanted to leave the Sanctuary. The peace he had found there would certainly be a compelling reason to remain.

His laugh was more like a heavy exhalation. She knew he had heard her thought. "It's much nicer out here – the sun seems to shine...differently than in the Sanctuary. But I don't mind being there."

She shifted, surprised with the ease that he had understood her exact thoughts. "I thought you didn't pry into other people's minds."

"It's unusually easy with you, especially if we're this close." His eyes remained locked on the flame-like flowers.

"Why?"

"Your mind is like Luka's. I knew him so well that I couldn't stop myself from hearing his thoughts. They had a familiar...sound. When you and he first became close, you were like everybody else. If I wanted to read you, I had to try. But your mind changed. I don't know how to describe it other than you fitted to him and he to you. Now I have to try to not listen to you."

"So—" she swallowed as the realisation engulfed her "—when I came and told you about the scroll..."

"Yes, I knew that you'd initially planned to end your life."

"Why didn't you say anything to the others?"

He glanced at her, something like guilt on his face. "I didn't know how to tell them. It seemed so personal, like it was the only choice you still had about your life. And then you decided against it. You got...less sad. So it didn't seem I needed to tell Meri and Lesha. But I should have. I...I'm too much of a coward. I didn't want to discuss it or answer the questions about why I could hear your thoughts."

Here, in the countryside, thoughts of suicide seemed so far away. She could remember that she wanted to end her life, and if she allowed her thoughts to dwell on the Sanctuary, the echo of that impulse stirred deep within her, but she couldn't envisage actually stepping off the cliff. She couldn't imagine *truly* wanting to push away from the solid ground.

"It isn't your job to save me," she said eventually.

Heat entered his voice, surprising her with its intensity. "Of course it is. That's what friends should do for one another – look after each other, pull each other back from their worst places. And I didn't know what I could say that would help you. Just because I know your thoughts doesn't mean I know how to change them."

"There's more than one way to save someone," Kaylene said quietly.

She knew the revelation that he had almost free access to her thoughts should have made her uncomfortable, but it didn't. She trusted him with her thoughts.

"I'm sorry you hear it all."

Finally, he looked back at her.

"It's all right." He shuffled to make himself more comfortable on the hard wooden bench. "If we get Luka back, it will be better."

According to Merika's information, the Farwan family had taken over a modest inn in the heart of the Flame County. How foreigners had managed to acquire the appropriate dispensations to own property let alone operate a business within the First Country, Kaylene did not know. The First Country's tendency toward seclusion fostered what many might call xenophobic policies.

Yet the Farwans were apparently the proprietors of the inn at which Callam and Kaylene arrived after ten days of travel, and business seemed to be flourishing. The building was small but immaculate. The walls had either been recently painted or cleaned with an unforgiving eye. A beautiful skyfire tree sat in the middle of the courtyard, the golden-red buds glowing against the white of the walls. It sang in Kaylene's mind with a distinct vibrancy. The two-storey building was in the style of the region – efficient lines with little ornamentation. The square windows were spaced at regular intervals; no dirt or cracks were visible in any of the frames.

A hostler came to meet them. He took the reins from Kaylene and helped both her and Callam down from the cart. He was well dressed and polite, although his eyes flicked to the distinctive clothing of the Sanctuary, he made no comment.

They were shown into the inn's salon. The little room, separate from the eating area, was filled with a pleasant smell: sweet, but without the headiness of certain floral scents, undercut by a sharp note that prevented it from being overwhelming. While the furnishings were all standard for the First Country, something about their arrangement was unusual. Kaylene was unaccustomed to little tables being placed between chairs. Equally, the second set of curtains across the salon's windows – sheer enough to let in the light but filtering it so that the room had a pleasant haze rather than catching the fullness of the afternoon sun – was something she had never seen. Despite the oddity, it was by far the nicest inn that Kaylene had ever visited. Although, she had only been to a handful of inns, most of them in the past few weeks. Before she had been sent to the Sanctuary she had never gone outside the immediate vicinity of Curnith. Her first stay in an inn had been on the way to the Sanctuary. As a scrawny eleven-year-old she had thought that the wool-stuffed bed was the most exciting thing she had ever seen, despite the trepidation she had felt at being sent to the Sanctuary. At the time, she had thought she would be there at most a year and see her family soon enough. How wrong she had been.

Callam nudged her leg with the toe of his boot. It disrupted her musing and she realised that he must have heard her thoughts again. The twisted expression on his face made her realise that the bitter tenor to her reminiscing must have had quite an unpleasant edge to him.

"Sorry."

He offered her a small smile. "Don't worry about it."

A serving girl came in. She, too, was well presented and well mannered. Like the hostler, her eyes flicked uneasily across Kaylene and Callam's clothes but she said nothing about it, and her voice was cheerful.

"Are you two looking for a room? We're quite full, but I believe we may have one left."

"Actually, we'd like to see Lexana," Kaylene said.

"Is there any particular reason? I can't imagine Lady Lexana has any business with the Sanctuary," the girl asked in that impenetrably polite manner.

"We understand that she has a talent with numbers and were hoping she might be able to help us."

"Ah. Well, I'm afraid Lady Lexana is away; I can't say when she will be back."

Kaylene threw a glance at Callam who indicated with a small flick of his fingers that he was already at work within the girl's mind. As Kaylene turned back to look at the serving girl, she saw her expression go slack.

"Lexana is here," Callam said. "The girl will get her," he added, sounding distracted as he sorted through the serving girl's mind.

Within a few moments, the girl left. Kaylene was impressed by the extent of Callam's power. Mindsmiths were a paradox in that they were highly sought –in exception to the case of most Blessed, for their Blessing. However they were also viewed with wariness, even by those wealthy enough to employ them. Nevertheless, Callam's control over his Blessing was unusually strong, even for a mindsmith.

Only a minute later, Tanita Farwan appeared, recognisable by her distinctive red locks. Her mouth was a tight line, suspicion and hardness written across her face.

Kaylene felt the beginnings of panic within her.

Tanita did not bother with any perfunctory pleasantries. "I hear you are asking after my daughter." She spoke Iteran with only a slight accent.

Kaylene nodded, her mouth dry in the face of this woman's bluntness. Something about her left no doubt she would be ruthless if and when necessary.

"Why?" Intelligence and anger shone within the older woman's sharp eyes. Too late, Kaylene realised the enormity of what they were attempting to do. This was a woman who had been humiliated in her own land. For someone that intimidating, humiliation would not sit well. It made her dangerous. In panic, Kaylene glanced at Callam. The fluttering panic in her stomach bloomed when she saw his puzzled frown.

Tanita stared with overt hostility at Callam.

"You would dare?"

The wide blue pools Callam's eyes had become said enough for Kaylene to realise the depth of trouble they had invited upon themselves. Somehow, Tanita Farwan knew he had tried to manipulate her thoughts.

"What do you want?" Tanita snapped. Her ire made her accent thicken, elongating her vowels.

Kaylene shrunk back, but rather than evade notice, it drew the fearsome woman's gaze to her.

"We need her help." The admission burst from Kaylene in the tongue of the Fourth Country, surprising even herself that she was able to form words.

The older woman's eyebrows rose. She switched to Quaren too, her arms folded across her chest as she spoke. "And how exactly can my daughter help you?"

"We've heard that she is good with numbers, and we have a problem we hope she can solve."

Kaylene suffered the woman's glare for what felt like a thousand years. Then, Tanita broke off her stare to instruct a discreetly hovering serving boy to fetch her daughter. She sat down, her expression still hard. However, Kaylene now felt she was being appraised rather than intimidated.

At a gesture from the woman, she and Callam sat.

"You are from the Sanctuary?" Tanita asked.

Kaylene nodded.

"But only he—" Tanita's gaze flicked to Callam, who was staring steadfastly at his feet "—is able to manipulate minds."

Kaylene nodded again. "My Blessing is different."

The foreigner's hands came together, fingers interlaced in a meditative gesture. "What can you do?"

"I have a way with plants."

Callam finally raised his head to look at the older woman. Kaylene presumed he had been following the conversation through her mind.

"Do you have a Blessing?" he asked in Iteran, obvious curiosity overwhelming his natural shyness.

Tanita's gaze moved back to him. From the way she was staring at Callam, Kaylene thought that she was about to yell at him. She answered with a curt shake of her head, easily moving back to Iteran.

"You could not touch me because I have been provided protection against your kind. At home, we have people with their own, what do you call it – Blessing – and they can protect against such things, for the right price."

Kaylene thought it generous they had been offered any explanation of how Tanita had detected Callam in her head. She wondered about the woman's motives.

Any further discussion was, thankfully, prevented by the arrival of Lexana. She glanced around the room with huge dark eyes. She had delicate features, but Kaylene would not have called her pretty. Yet those eyes were mesmerising. Her hair hung free around her face in a sheet of shadow, making her seem somehow smaller than she'd appeared on the docks.

"You called?" Lexana asked in the speech of the Fourth Country. The deference to her mother's request seemed to be contradicted by the stilted manner in which she addressed her mother.

"Yes." Her mother did not offer further explanation.

Lexana hovered for a moment with obvious uncertainty, then sat in a chair next to her mother.

"These two are from the Sanctuary." Tanita did not pause to give her daughter time to recall what the Sanctuary was, but Lexana seemed to know exactly what it was. For foreigners, they'd certainly done their study.

Lexana frowned as she looked at Kaylene and Callam. "I thought most people in the Sanctuary were children."

Kaylene fought the impulse to blush. "Most, not all."

Lexana started, obviously not having expected Kaylene could understand the quick exchange with her mother. A vague look of embarrassment crossed her features at the oversight.

Tanita said to her daughter in their tongue, "They were hoping that you might be able to solve a mathematics problem they have."

Now, Lexana did look surprised. "Do you have the problem here?"

Callam handed over the parchment which Merika had filled with writing. "We need to know how long to make it down to the nearest finger," he said.

Kaylene translated.

Confusion clouded Lexana's features, then cleared. "Ah, I forget that you have a different measuring system."

"Will that be a problem?" Kaylene asked.

Lexana had already bowed her head to the paper. At Kaylene's question, she glanced up distractedly. "Hmm? No, it won't," she said before returning her focus to the equation. Those eyes that had stared at Kaylene with such nervousness had attained new focus. She chewed on her lip in contemplation, the slightest smile lifting her cheek.

"Can you do it?" Tanita asked her daughter.

Lexana held up a hand to indicate she was still working. In the same gesture, she swept hair away from her face, pushing it back across her shoulder. In Kaylene's opinion, she looked prettier like that.

After a long moment, Lexana looked up. "Yes," she told her mother.

Her focus turned to Kaylene and Callam. The expression on her face drew a similarity between herself and her mother. Despite her seeming vulnerability, there was iron in this girl.

"What is this for?"

Kaylene chose her words carefully. "It's complicated. We're looking to create a door of sorts."

The girl frowned, obviously aware that she was being given only a small piece of the truth.

Kaylene hesitated, uncertain how much the girl knew of the way Blessings ran through the First Country. By all accounts, the other countries of the Godskissed Continent did not really have a complete or full acceptance of such things. Most who were gifted with the echoes of a god's power hid their Blessing rather than nurture it. Although, she recalled that the Fourth Country was apparently more aware of this facet of existence. Nevertheless, some instinct left her feeling that Lexana would not appreciate being given only half the truth.

"We are looking to open a portal into the Divine Realm."

The girl's expression transformed into one of surprise. "You can do that?"

"Well, we think we can."

"Why?"

Kaylene noted Tanita watching the exchange intently. "We want to find someone."

"Bring someone back, you mean," Lexana said.

Reluctantly, Kaylene nodded. She did not want to speak of bringing people back from the dead. It made her sound either some kind of lunatic or someone who had made a discovery for which a great many people might kill. Yet she had no choice but to answer truthfully. She had very little doubt that Tanita – and Lexana, for that matter – would spot a lie. If she wanted the information that Lexana could give them, she would have to take the risk of telling the truth.

The look exchanged between mother and daughter puzzled Kaylene until she properly scrutinised Lexana's face. There she saw a certain kinship in the shadow of some great loss. Callam, evidently hearing her thoughts, stiffened in his chair. She did not need to read his thoughts to know he too was worried about the price this girl may ask in exchange for her assistance.

"Are you certain that it will work?" Lexana asked.

"Lexa." There was a note of caution in Tanita's voice.

Her daughter's face tightened, making her look far older than a girl just out of her childhood. She did not acknowledge that her mother had spoken. Her eyes remained unwaveringly on Kaylene.

"I can only hope," Kaylene said honestly.

Lexana swallowed, her eyes seeming to grow even larger. Her self-control was otherwise excellent. "I can do it."

Tanita leaned forward, her eyes that of a dealer. "We will need something in exchange, though."

"Mother." Now it was Lexana's turn to give warning. As her daughter had, Tanita ignored the rebuke.

Kaylene felt her stomach clench. She wondered if it would be possible to bring back whoever it was Lexana had lost. She hoped that if they revealed that it might not be achievable, the girl would still help them.

"As you would probably know, there is a village nearby – Carrow. The local administrator is a member of the Carrow family and bears a particular grudge against me. I bought this inn from his cousin after the woman encountered some financial trouble. I have every permit I need from the central government, but unfortunately, I need a permission to be certified as an official firebloom-watching location." Her irritation at the esoteric rule was obvious in the clipped way she spoke.

"I don't know what we can do to try to persuade him," Kaylene said. "Is there anything else we can maybe do instead?"

"Nonsense, of course you can persuade him." Tanita nodded to Callam. Her face was uncompromising. Despite her daughter's disagreement, it was clear this was the price for Lexana's help.

Kaylene glanced at Callam. It would be up to him to manipulate the man's mind, after all.

He did not hesitate. "I'll do it."

NINE

They stayed at the Farwan inn that evening.

Most unusually, the inn had a wash house. Kaylene indulged herself and found the money well spent, feeling much refreshed when she joined Callam for dinner.

Tanita invited them to join her and her family in taking their evening meal. The offer surprised Kaylene, but after a few minutes of conversation, she realised that the woman now viewed them as business partners and was extending them the relevant courtesies.

The food was odd: regional vegetables thinly sliced, stacked on top of each other, and covered with cream and cheese. Kaylene had not eaten such food before, but she was certain the addition of strong spices was not traditional. Not that she didn't enjoy the meal – it was simply strange when compared to the stew of mixed vegetables usually served at the Sanctuary or the grilled and baked fish dishes that flavoured the memory of her childhood.

They sat at a long table in a space obviously reserved for the Farwan family in the dining room: Kaylene, Callam, Tanita, Lexana, two boys who were at the beginning of their adolescence, and three eerily silent men. Even the boys were more subdued than was normal for their age.

"How are you finding life in the First Country?" Kaylene asked, unsure what other conversation she could offer these people.

Tanita considered the question before answering. It seemed she was a woman who rarely did anything without consideration. "I have had many dealings with the First Country over the years. But living here offers a very different perspective."

Kaylene ducked her head in acknowledgment, but mused that it was not actually an answer. Callam, sitting opposite her, caught her eye and smirked, hearing the thought and obviously agreeing.

"And you, Lexana?" Kaylene asked.

The Farwan heiress pursed her lips. "It is peaceful here," she said softly.

Remembering that the Fourth Country was a land with constant conflict between the families of power seeking to unseat one another, Kaylene could easily understand how Lexana thought the First Country a tranquil haven.

"Do you agree with my daughter's assessment?" Tanita asked, sharp brown eyes evidently seeing disagreement in Kaylene's face.

Kaylene gave a shrug that she hoped was ambiguous. "I know very little about the peacefulness of our land, Lady Farwan. The Sanctuary does not offer much information about our politics."

Callam chimed in, earning a surprised look from the Farwan women. "As you probably know, our country runs according to the people's consensus. Any who are so interested can come to the debate and vote on new laws, and those who sit in positions of government are chosen every year. That certainly means every man or woman has the chance to be heard and, as such, confers a certain equality on everyone, leading to peace. But it also has its drawbacks."

Kaylene translated for Lexana's benefit, surprised by the amount he spoke and the breadth of his knowledge. He threw a look of amusement at her, evidently hearing that thought, too. She resolved that she would have to be more careful with her thoughts. That, too, received acknowledgment in the form of a little laugh.

"I am curious – where did you learn to speak our language so well?" Tanita asked. "As you yourself noted of the Sanctuary, those within its walls are quite secluded from the world outside."

"All within the Sanctuary are encouraged to pursue a field. It is said to assist us in achieving control over ourselves."

"Control over yourselves?" Lexana enquired, an eyebrow raised in curiosity.

Kaylene looked down at her plate, uncertain exactly how to explain.

Callam spoke instead. "The Sanctuary was created to ensure that anyone in the First Country who is Blessed is not a danger to themselves or others – mainly others." He gave a wry smile that held the tenor of a dark private joke between them.

Kaylene translated, biting back her own smile.

"The best way to ensure that we are not dangerous is to teach us to control our emotions and keep them from controlling us," he said.

Kaylene searched for the best way to phrase the sentence, the complexity of the grammar distracting her from looking at their hosts' faces. When she looked up, Lexana wore an undisguised expression of confusion.

"And what if you fail to learn this control?" Lexana asked.

Callam opened his mouth to speak, but Kaylene said what he would have. "We are not permitted to leave."

Lexana stared at Kaylene for several seconds, frowning. Then she gave a decisive sniff. "Well, that's stupid."

Kaylene looked at Callam and the two of them burst into peals of laughter. Through her mirth, Kaylene saw Tanita scowling at her daughter, obviously aware of what Callam and Kaylene's age signified. But Kaylene did not find Lexana's comment to be insensitive in the slightest.

She liked the foreign girl, despite – or perhaps because of – the enigmatic shifts between extreme shyness and forthright certainty.

After dinner, Kaylene left Callam to his own devices and went up to the roof of the inn to watch the day fade. The roof was set up to be a viewing area for visitors to take in the skyfire trees. With the absence of a licence, patrons could not be directed to it. Kaylene was the only guest to have found it thanks to curiosity-driven exploration. She did not let the closed door bother her, and chose a bench against a wall. The solitude was enjoyable.

When the door opened, she prepared to excuse her presence.

Lexana waved away the beginnings of her apology and sat on the bench next to her.

"Sorry, am I bothering you?" she asked, the thought evidently occurring to her belatedly.

Kaylene shook her head. "I've never seen sunset over the skyfire trees," she said. "I don't think I ever thought I would," she confessed after a pause.

The foreigner sighed. "I didn't even know such a sight existed in the First Country. Yet it's perhaps more beautiful than any of the landscapes my home has to offer."

Despite her words, the wistful note in her voice was unmistakable.

"You miss your home?" Kaylene asked.

The question was considered carefully before an answer was forthcoming. "There is very little left for me back home." Lexana took a deliberate breath before she continued. "Yet, it is home. This beautiful, peaceful country is not home. Perhaps in time, though, it will become so."

"Do you really think the First Country is so wonderful?"

Lexana turned to her. "Don't you?"

Kaylene shrugged. "I've lived most of my life in the Sanctuary. I don't really know enough to say, other than what I've read or been told."

Lexana frowned. "Doesn't that bother you?"

Kaylene shrugged again. "It's not really something I've thought about."

Lexana turned away, seemingly content to look out across the flat land. A breeze stirred the late spring evening, softly waving the branches of the skyfire trees. The final golden rays cutting through the clear air to shine on the treetops created the illusion that a fire raced across the sky as the breeze stirred the blooms. Kaylene wondered how the trees produced flowers that were so different in colour – even on the same branch.

"May I ask you a question, Lexana?"

"Call me, Lexa, please."

Taking that as an assent, Kaylene continued. "When we told you what we are trying to do, why didn't you...well, I mean, most people have someone that they lost who they would want back. Do you want that?"

Her words were met with a pause.

"I'd be lying if I said there wasn't at least one person who I wanted to see again, if simply for my own peace of mind. But to bring someone back from beyond is more than I think I would want. That sort of working scares me." She did not speak with any judgment; it was merely the kind of frank admission for which Kaylene liked her.

"But you're willing to help us?"

"Yes." Lexana paused. "I'm sorry that my mother is making you go to the magistrate in exchange for my help."

Kaylene waved the apology away. "I understand. It's business."

"That's gracious of you. I wish she'd just let me help you – that not everything was about business for her."

Kaylene contemplated this as she returned her focus to the landscape. "It's so beautiful," she murmured. As had happened in Curnith, she went to tell Luka her observation of the way the name "skyfire" suggested something far more tumultuous than the sight in front of her. To her mind, the glow of the trees seemed like a fire that had burned down after many hours, something comfortable, in front of which you were happy to curl up and doze, head resting on the chest of the person who you loved most in the world. Catching her mistake, she pressed her lips together and squeezed her eyes shut to hold back tears.

When she opened her eyes, she found Lexana looking at her.

"Who are you trying to bring back?"

Kaylene liked the sound of the girl's voice. It had a clarity that reminded her of the very first birdcall on a still morning.

"He was Callam's brother."

"And what was he to you?"

Kaylene forced the whisper out through a throat that threatened to close up completely. "Everything."

The understanding in Lexana's face almost brought her to tears, but Kaylene refused to let herself cry in front of a near stranger.

Lexana leaned back against the wall. "Ah."

"You've not asked if we could do that for you," Kaylene said quietly.

"No, I haven't."

"But there is someone you lost. Someone you thought of." She'd seen it in the girl's face across the dinner table.

"It's complicated."

She sensed a whole story behind those words. "Do you miss them?"

"More than you'd imagine. He saved my life. He...opened my eyes to many things. But he also betrayed me."

"Oh."

"Like I said, complicated."

"Do you want to see him again?"

"Of course. He died...suddenly. So much was unsaid, unanswered. I have so many questions for him, so much I want to know, if he'd tell me. But I've learned that life moves forward, even when you think it can't possibly do so. The world continues, indifferent to our joy and sorrow. To bring him back wouldn't necessarily give me the answers I want. I have to let him go and let my life adjust."

Kaylene could think of nothing more awful than letting Luka go or of her life adjusting to the point where his absence was normal. The mere prospect awoke fire-winged insects in her stomach.

Perhaps sensing her anxiety, Lexa spoke, her voice kind. "But that's my truth. It's a lot easier to say than to live. What you told us over dinner of this Sanctuary of yours – life there…it sounds as though someone special would make it bearable."

Kaylene did not glance at her. She was preoccupied with winning the struggle against falling entirely apart. Through eyes filled with tears, she focused on the landscape. The oranges, golds, and reds became a palette of colour in her blurred vision. Even then, it was beautiful, and the beauty of what lay before her seemed so unfair when the pain of Luka's absence felt as though it were tearing her apart from the inside.

"I hope you get him back." Lexana's voice beside her was filled with soft emphasis.

Kaylene swallowed back her sobs. "Thank you," she whispered.

Callam was in their room when she returned. The last vestiges of light coming through the window lit the room in a dim glow. He was sitting cross-legged on the bed, his eyes closed.

"Are you all right?" he asked, without opening his eyes.

"I'm fine," Kaylene said hoarsely.

His snort indicated his disagreement.

"Could you hear me, even up on the roof?" She hadn't gone there to give herself a reprieve from knowing Callam could hear every thought passing through her mind, but it certainly had occurred to her that she could allow her thoughts to move freely up there. The possibility that he could hear her from so far away was unsettling.

He shook his head. "But I can hear you now."

"I don't like having you in my head," she exclaimed, her recently-stirred anguish finding a satisfying outlet in ire at Callam. It also conveniently eclipsed the guilt that had sprung up at knowing he would have heard her disquiet at him having access to her thoughts.

He shrugged and opened his eyes, which reminded her so painfully of his brother. He flinched as he heard that thought.

"I don't much like being in your head." That he could speak so calmly seemed impossible.

"Well, try harder to stay out of it," Kaylene snapped.

Had she spoken to Luka with such a venomous sting, he would have looked at her like a wounded animal awaiting a killing blow. But Callam's face remained impassive.

"Have you considered that the reason you're so desperate to bring back Luka has nothing to do with him at all?" The calmness with which he asked his question had the same effect as his brother's hurt would have – it threw Kaylene from the cresting wave of her anger.

"What?"

"Obviously you miss him, but perhaps he made life in the Sanctuary bearable. Have you thought that this is less about him and more about the fact that you can't bear life in the Sanctuary without him?"

Callam tilted his head as he asked the question. It was a mannerism he did not share with his brother.

"There's no difference between life in the Sanctuary without Luka and life without Luka."

"Of course there is. The Sanctuary keeps us prisoner. But if you're imprisoned with someone who makes you happy, you don't notice it."

"How can you possibly make such a claim?" Kaylene's anger returned quickly. The fact that his words held an echo of what Lexa had said on the roof shook her more than she would have liked.

"I've been in your head, Kaya." Callam's own anger appeared in the sharp bite of his voice. "And because of it, I know you."

Kaylene stared at him. More tears forced their way to her eyes, and looking at Callam through them made her see Luka. "You don't know me, you just listen to me."

"And I hear all the things you don't want yourself to hear," he snapped. His patience, it seemed, was at an end. He stood in a fluid motion and strode across to face her. "Just because you don't want to hear the truth about what you think or feel doesn't mean I can ignore it."

She rarely remembered how much taller than her Callam was. The way he shied away from everybody's gaze made him seem a full head shorter than he was. Now, though, he towered over her, his anger holding him up. The ragged heave of his breath revealed just how upset he was. She forced herself to look up into his summer-blue eyes.

"Focusing on Luka means you don't have to focus on how horrible life in the Sanctuary actually is," Callam accused. "That's why the rest of us are going along with this insane quest. Because we're all desperate to forget that the Sanctuary is a prison that none of us is ever likely to escape. You know as well as I do that if we ran away, they'd hunt us down. So to try and forget that, we play this silly game to try to bring him back. Have you thought about what you'll do if this doesn't work, which it probably won't?"

She presumed it was the sudden hot spike to her anger that made him take a step back, but it could simply have been the look in her eyes. For a moment it looked as though he wanted to take back everything that he had said, but his mouth firmed into a line of resolve and he walked past her and out the door, closing it with the gentlest of pulls behind him, somehow so much worse than had he slammed it.

Kaylene remained where she stood for a few seconds, shock immobilising her. Then she carefully made her way over to the bed where Callam had been sitting. Their exchange had lasted only for a few moments, yet it felt as though it had gulfed hours. She unlaced her boots and kicked them off, then lay down. The smooth plasterwork of the ceiling stared back at her as she tried very hard to push the confrontation from her mind. She wasn't certain what was more shocking: the fact that Callam had gotten angry or what he had said.

She asked herself if there could be truth to his claim that her determination to bring Luka back was because life within the Sanctuary was so desolate. To suggest that Luka was simply someone who had made her unending time there bearable seemed to belittle what had existed between them. Kaylene had always thought that her and Luka's relationship was the sort of love about which epic tales were written. But perhaps it was merely a love like any other, and the purpose that it served was to make a life of restriction and imprisonment bearable. If that was true, then what was she really doing trying to bring Luka back?

The door opened slowly and Callam came back into the room. She turned her head to look at him. She didn't say anything – she didn't trust herself to say anything.

The look of contrition on Callam's face was enough to compel her to rush over to him. He held his arms wide and she gladly sank into his embrace.

"I'm sorry." His voice was muffled against her hair.

"So am I," she said into his chest, squeezing her arms more tightly around him. It was easy to do – Callam was sapling-slender.

When they finally released one another, the fatigue not only of the day's events but from the months of torturous emotions weighed heavily on her. She wanted to speak further about the heated words they'd flung at each other, but fatigue obscured the way to open such a discussion, so she remained silent, and he did not choose to comment on it.

"Come on, let's get some sleep," Callam said. "We have to uphold our bargain with Tanita Farwan tomorrow."

TEN

The morning was free from haze and the illusory fire of the skyfire blossoms nodded in the wind as Kaylene and Callam drove their cart to the township of Carrow. The argument of the previous evening had not led to any lingering acrimony. If anything, she noticed a distinctly more relaxed tenor to their exchanges. In the same way that the land after heavy rain had a clean quality, it felt as though their own tempest had cleared away something Kaylene hadn't even realised had been muddying things between them.

Breakfast had been bread fresh from the oven of the Farwan inn. The thick slices were still warm, and even more delicious when dipped into the accompanying bowl of cream flavoured with some of the spices Kaylene had found so unusual in the previous evening's meal. Tanita was directing the production and service of breakfast when Kaylene and Callam entered the dining room. She looked as though she had been up for several hours, yet moved with an energetic exuberance that seemed to defy fatigue's attempts to claim her. She personally handed the bowl of dipping cream to Kaylene, a smile on her face.

"This is traditional breakfast in the Fourth Country."

Something about eating flavoured cream for breakfast seemed utterly decadent, but that made it all the more satisfying.

Kaylene felt contentment spread through her as the cart rattled along. Her stomach was comfortably full and she was looking at a sight that was the subject of a great many works of art and stories. While the sensation only lasted for the space of a breath, it perturbed Kaylene. She had not thought such contentment possible without Luka by her side. She knew Callam heard the thought, although he made no outward sign of it. At length, she decided to speak aloud those treacherous sentiments.

"I thought Luka and I were special, like the kind of love that is written about in that ballard, The Twins of Curnith, but you were right, what you said last night."

The admission hurt less than she expected.

Callam shook his head. "Those stories weren't epics because of who the people were, but what they did for one another. Kaya, you've defied the rules of the Sanctuary and travelled halfway across the First Country to try to bring him back from beyond death. That sounds like an epic story to me."

"It doesn't make what you said less true."

In the silence that followed, she conjured a world of responses from Callam, none of them reassuring.

"Do you think it means you loved him less, if he made life in the Sanctuary bearable?" he asked eventually.

"You tell me," she said, wanting him to give her answers to the questions that eroded her certainty.

He chuckled. "If you don't know, I don't know, Kaya."

She contemplated not answering, but found herself wanting to face these questions – and wanting to go over them with Callam. "I think it means that even if we get him back, I can't go back to life in the Sanctuary like it was before."

"Do you really think we can go back to life in the Sanctuary at all if we succeed?"

She looked at the blush of red blooms across the skyline. He had asked the question she'd been avoiding. It was probably why he'd asked it.

"I was ready to end my life. Thinking that far in advance now..." She sought the words to paste on to amorphous thoughts so as to tramp them, give them some definable shape. "It feels like I've been moving through a horrible dream for so long that the reaction of the Senior Blessed and what may happen if this goes wrong...it all seems unreal."

"And now you feel like you're waking up?"

She kept her eyes on those magnificent trees. "Yes."

"And?"

"I don't know. But this is the only way forward that I can see."

"Look, I said what I said last night because I wanted to hurt you. You were so angry at me, and that was—" He cast about for a different set of words. "It's hard, being able to hear everybody's thoughts, and it's hard not being able to help hearing yours. But I can promise that I'd always want to hear your thoughts. The way you love Luka is so strong; most people never feel that way about anyone. Certainly nobody's ever felt that way about me."

She glanced over at him, surprised by the depth of the sorrow she heard in his voice. "Is there someone you want to love you like that?"

"Not really." Because Callam was driving the cart today, his eyes were fixed on the road. A slight tightening of his jaw gave away the lie, but she did not push him on it.

The journey to Carrow took only an hour. The sun shone hot and bright as they approached the town and Kaylene looked with envy at the people they passed: the drivers of carts and wagons, and those walking along the road, their arms laden with items. Kaylene was mystified by the tightly-packed bundles of the pale pink plant piled high in many of the wagons they passed. She tried to figure out what they could be without any success. Then her attention was claimed by the people shepherding herds of woolly grembits along the side of the road with astounding casualness, never once having one of their pack stray, even a little. Almost all the people wore clothes that left their arms bare and billowed freely in the breeze that offered respite from the heat of the late spring sun. By contrast, she could feel sweat coalescing under the stiff, restrictive material she wore.

They passed fields tended by strong-looking men and women, their skin ebonised after years of labouring in the sun. Kaylene stared unselfconsciously. She wondered what made them so disciplined that they worked in the confines of the neat rows rather than cutting across the flat, open landscape as they willed.

Underneath the sun and open sky, something of which Kaylene had been only vaguely aware became undeniable: her awareness of the myriad of green life around her, from the expanse of crops to the tiny weeds and grasses encroaching on the road. Their presence had been tickling at the edge of her perception for days, becoming gradually more complex and insistent. Now, when she turned her focus to it, she could distinguish the spread and nuance of the plants' energy. If she concentrated, she could feel each individual blade of grass.

She wondered what had amplified her Blessing like this, finding an unexpected enjoyment in this new scope; it felt as though she was stretching out long-cramped legs. She'd never considered the limits of her Blessing; she'd spent so long trying to use it in the smallest of ways that the prospect that practise and focus might allow her to do amazing things had never occurred to her, aside from that one moment in the courtyard under Merika's bossy direction.

A nearby skyfire tree, hidden by its fellows beside the road, caught her attention. It hadn't bloomed fully, the petals yet to emerge from the meagre scattering of buds along its branches. She knew this although she could barely see the tree. The thrill of her reach raced across her. Curious, she willed buds to form across the rest of the tree, and then, in her mind, she pictured them appearing. A gasp escaped her lips as she saw the sudden bloom of colour.

Callam made an appreciative noise beside her.

Kaylene could not keep the smile from her face. She'd always thought her Blessing a curse, something in which she should find shame. But it was hard to reconcile the beauty of a tree being brought to bloom with the prejudice and self-loathing that she had been instructed to paint on to her own skin because of something with which she'd been born. The thought, now planted in her mind, could not be dismissed.

"Are you sure that's wise?" Callam asked.

She ignored his caution. It was just like that day in the courtyard all those years ago as when she had brought as many buds as the trees could bear. She reached out to more trees lining the avenue into the town. Suddenly, they were driving underneath a canopy of blossoming fire. The light filtering through the thick blossoms overlaid everyone under the trees with a warm orange glow. People looked up in surprise; a few cringed away from the sudden incredible growth of blossoms. Kaylene could not care that she had displayed her Blessing so publicly. Delighted laughter spilled from her at the beauty she had created.

"Kaya." Callam's intermingled frustration and affection was plain in his voice.

"I really don't care," she said. She was proud of what she had done. The road leading into Carrow was now a visual feast, and that, as far as Kaylene was concerned, was nothing for which she should feel ashamed. Her Blessing might bring danger, but it could also bring beauty, and in that moment, she absolutely could not find a way to care who might know it was her doing.

He laughed in response, the sound unbridled. That fuelled her delight even further. Never had she seen Callam as free from restraint as she had over the past few days. This aspect to who he was – the emergence of quick humour and appreciation for boldness – was Callam, but different, as though he was somehow more vibrant, more like a solid person rather than a shadow of herself, Merika, and Leshan. She pulled the thought back quickly, but Callam had heard it. He did not seem upset. In fact, amusement shone through his eyes.

"You know, you're different, too. You're more certain. Gods, you really think I'm like a shadow to you three?"

She deliberately slowed her thoughts, tilting her head up to look at the carpet of colour above. "That's inaccurate. You aren't our shadow, but you don't really protest if something bothers you."

"You let Meri boss you around, too," he said.

She inclined her head, not bothering to verbally acknowledge the point. He would have heard the thought, anyway.

"She'd be delighted by this," Kaylene said.

His smile shone through his voice. "Of course."

They fell silent as they entered the town. She gazed about with open wonder at the style of buildings she'd never seen before with the huge windows that nearly took up entire walls, or the ornate embellishments carved onto the wooden windowsills and doors. Carrow was the metropolitan hub of the skyfire region. The region's inns bought supplies from its markets; the Farwan inn had two gerril to supply milk, but the flour for its bread would have come from the Carrow market, as would many of the vegetables and fruits it served.

The buildings were shorter than those in Curnith, and the harbour town's renowned white stone was nowhere to be seen. Instead, many buildings were made from timber, and others were built with a reddish brick that gave the streets a warm feel.

As they turned onto a main road, businesses and official offices dominated. Kaylene stared at the huge circular walls of the region's oratorium. The high, smooth walls held a certain authority that continued to draw Kaylene's eye back to them.

"Where are we supposed to find this local magistrate?" she asked.

Callam shrugged, concentrating on navigating the busy street. He hissed in panic as a child ran across the road, closely followed by a frazzled adult.

"Pull the cart over," Kaylene told him.

He did as she instructed.

She dismounted, grateful for the respite offered to her backside.

Callam's laugh was one of sympathetic agreement.

"What are you doing?" he called as she stood, the plan in her head evidently vague enough for him to not understand what she had in mind.

She waved in a gesture she hoped would indicate he should wait with patience and trust. His laugh was a clear sound that made her smile.

She returned a few minutes later. His eyebrows were raised as she climbed back onto the cart, wincing as her poor tortured backside was once again forced onto the hard wooden seat.

"You just asked someone for directions?" he said incredulously.

"Well, what else were we supposed to do?"

He considered her question, then apparently came up with no better solution, looking away in overt defeat. It was her turn to laugh.

He did not ask her to repeat the directions she had been given, instead guiding the carriage to the left.

"Why are you going this way?" Kaylene asked.

"Because that's where you were told to go," Callam replied.

"No it wasn't."

"Yes it was."

"I was the one who was actually told where to go," Kaylene said, her indignation rising.

"You're misremembering it."

"I'm not."

"I can read your thoughts. Do you really believe that I'm wrong?"

"I know what I was told," she insisted.

"So do I."

Kaylene folded her arms across her chest. "I am certain that you are entirely incorrect."

He did not reply as concentration at negotiating the busy streets stole across his face.

Kaylene sighed, resignation settling over her.

Soon enough, it was clear he had misread the directions from Kaylene's mind, and they were hopelessly lost. The streets had narrowed, more trees populated the roadside, and it looked as though they were in an area devoted more to habitation than commerce. She could not suppress her smugness. Callam made an inarticulate noise that sounded as though it was a mix of frustration, embarrassment, and even amusement.

"So you pulled it straight from my head?" The challenge in her voice was lessened by the amusement she could not quite conceal.

"You misremembered it," he accused.

Their bickering continued for a few minutes and ended with Callam descending from the cart and asking a passer-by for directions.

He returned with a blush spreading across his cheeks that spoke more effectively than any words.

"Where should we go?" she asked, fighting a grin of triumph.

He did not answer but instead steered the carriage back the way they had come, to where Kaylene had first sought directions.

She made no effort to contain her grin as Callam directed the carriage right instead of the left he had insisted they take. She said nothing, knowing that her thoughts were intruding into Callam's head more loudly than if she had shouted. The embarrassment on his face was delightful reward.

Eventually they passed through the other side of the town and turned onto the driveway of a large estate. Kaylene presumed this was Carrow family land. While all official positions were appointed through election and thus open, in theory, to anyone, it was well known that having wealth and land made election more likely.

Skyfire trees lined the driveway, and the beautifully manicured lawns that stretched beyond them looked as though they had never been defiled by the tread of feet. Flower beds filled with the spiky purple crengion flowers wove through the lawns in delicate patterns. The choice to only have flowers in one colour interested Kaylene. She thought it more lovely than had the architect used several colours.

The best word for the building was elegant. Columns of grey stone punctuated the long flowing lines of the red-brick building. Windows at regular intervals would offer a delightful view of the lawns she and Callam were now passing. The drive ended in a circular turnaround with a fountain at its centre. Water jetted in a graceful arc from the throat of a fish into a basin held by a naked youth of indeterminate sex, and then trickled into the base of the fountain. Kaylene had never seen such luxury and she felt an overwhelming urge to run away at the sight of all this wealth. Beside her, Callam made a noise that sounded as though he agreed. But Kaylene pushed away the urge, reminding herself that this was all for Luka, and if she ran they would never get him back.

Callam pulled the cart to a halt and a serving woman came out to greet them. The shine of her boots was enough to nearly blind Kaylene, yet it did not entirely distract from the fine weave of her tan blouse. If the servants wore such exquisite clothes, Kaylene wondered what the master of the house wore.

"Are we expecting you?" the woman asked in a tone of polite suspicion.

Kaylene shook her head, rendered mute by awe.

"We were hoping to speak to Magistrate Carrow," Callam said, sounding unfathomably composed.

Kaylene felt a wreck of nerves and insufficiency.

The woman did not bother to disguise the way her glance lingered on their garb. "Is this on Sanctuary business?"

"Of a kind," Callam replied.

Without another word, she retreated between the columns of the front entrance.

"She will let us in," Callam said, iron certainty in his voice.

Sure enough, the woman returned moments later. "If you please, follow me."

Callam and Kaylene dismounted, Callam handing the reins to another servant who had trailed after the woman.

As they walked between the columns, Kaylene craned to look at the ceiling of the entranceway, high above. The stucco was shaped into a dizzying pattern of concentric squares, some painted with blacks and dark blues. The grandeur of decorating a ceiling struck her, as did the pointless beauty of it. Somehow, she found that even more intimidating than the rest of the property, and it was with extraordinary trepidation that she followed the serving woman to meet the magistrate.

ELEVEN

They walked along beautiful parquet floors that made each footstep an echoing snap. Kaylene was fascinated by the opulence of the way the polished timber pieces were placed not only to form the pattern, but in such a way that the colour of the different pieces matched. She barely glanced anywhere else.

They were shown into a lavish room set up for relaxed conversation and comfort. Kaylene was immediately struck by how spectacularly luxurious the couches and chairs looked. The brocaded blue fabric looked far too fine to have someone sit on it, although the curve of the cushions suggested it would be inordinately comfortable to do so. Magistrate Carrow turned from the view of the front lawn offered by the huge, clear windows as they were announced.

His appearance was a counterpoint to the expectations set by the magnificent, elegant house. He was on the shorter side of average and a little plump. A small, brown beard framed his mouth; it was as neatly trimmed as the lawns outside. Eyes the colour of the crengion flowers looked at them with an unexpectedly open expression.

"Welcome." His greeting was exuberant and filled with a genuine warmth that surprised Kaylene. He surveyed them, obviously curious, but made no comment about their age or what that must mean about their status within the Sanctuary. "Are you in need of any refreshments?"

A servant came in balancing a huge tray laden with fruit and pastries, fear written across his face that one of the items precariously near the edge would fall off. His relief once the tray was placed on the table without incident almost made Kaylene break into a fit of hysterical giggles.

Callam plucked an iceberry from the opulent arrangement. He made a noise of approval as he chewed.

"Now, what might the Sanctuary seek from me?" The magistrate poured himself a measure of golden liquid into a glass – an actual drinking glass.

Kaylene stared at it in amazement.

The magistrate saw her stare and smiled. He picked up a second from a neatly ordered line. The array represented a small fortune. He poured more of the liquid into it and proffered it to Kaylene.

When she did not immediately take it, he made a little gesture of encouragement. With enormous trepidation, she crossed the distance and took the glass. Her fingers curled around the stem and she nearly dropped the glass in shock at the smooth, cool material against her skin.

The magistrate smiled as he watched her reaction. "You've never drunk from a glass before?"

She shook her head.

Near trembling, Kaylene sat in a chair, her other hand coming to cradle the flute, desperately afraid of dropping and breaking it. She glanced at the magistrate's face. His expression was gentle.

"I grew up drinking from glass," he said thoughtfully. "It's refreshing to see a first reaction to it."

She looked down, almost losing herself in the golden liquid. The man's kindness caught her by surprise. Cautiously, she took one hand off the flute so she could run it along the fabric of the couch on which she sat. The sensation of it underneath her fingertips was sublime; smooth, tightly woven. It felt like indulgence.

Magistrate Carrow bade Callam sit. "Are you certain I cannot offer you a drink?"

Callam complied with the request and shook his head. "I'd be too worried I'd break it," he confessed, causing the magistrate to erupt into laughter.

He took a seat of his own and looked intently at Kaylene and Callam. "Perhaps we should eventually come to the purpose of your visit to me?"

Kaylene glanced at Callam, but he seemed uncertain of what he should say.

Curiosity had overtaken the man's expression. He looked from Kaylene to Callam, waiting for a reply. She took a sip of the drink he'd given her in order to ease the sandy-dryness in her throat. It was the most delicate flavour that had ever graced her tongue; robust with the taste of the fruit from which it was made, but refined into a single, glorious note that held infinite complexities without any of them detracting from the complete flavour. She closed her eyes to savour it all the better.

When she opened them, she saw the magistrate staring at her, his eyes bright with intelligence. With an uncomfortable start, Kaylene realised that he knew they were not there on business relating to the Sanctuary. Her eyes slid back to Callam and she wondered why he had not reached into the magistrate's mind.

Another moment of silence passed, then Kaylene could not stand it any longer. "We aren't exactly here in the name of the Sanctuary."

The magistrate leaned back into his chair, looking unsurprised. He left another uncomfortable space into which Kaylene felt once again compelled to speak. "We're actually here to ask a favour of you."

He arched a single eyebrow. Suddenly his face, which had seemed so pleasantly rotund upon their entry, had a far sharper cast. Still he said nothing.

"On our way, we happened to stay at an inn run by foreigners. The Farwan family. And we got to chatting with the owner. She said that they did not have the necessary certification for her inn to be a firebloom-watching location."

"She was most generous to us," Kaylene continued. The words felt too large in her mouth. "And we hoped to repay her kindness."

The magistrate crossed one leg over the other. "Unlike some, I have no qualm against the Sanctuary or those who live within it. However, the First Country keeps itself separate to the rest of the Godskissed Continent for good reason."

"Magistrate Carrow—" Kaylene began, casting a pleading look to Callam. He stared ahead with a blank look she did not have sufficient time to decipher before the magistrate spoke.

"Please, call me Ardyn."

She looked at him in surprise. The mix of his unexpected courtesy to them and his xenophobia was something she never would have expected.

"Why aren't you uncomfortable with us being from the Sanctuary?" She glanced uncertainly back to Callam to find him still motionless. She fought against the fear that surged inside her.

He shrugged. "Why be afraid of thunder when it sounds above?"

"Because you might be outside in the midst of a storm," Kaylene replied, trying to quell her terror and discern what needed to be said to extricate them from the sudden danger which Callam's stillness signalled.

He chuckled, not unpleasantly. "It helps when you have shelter. Although, if we dispense with this metaphor, perhaps it makes a bit more sense for me to explain to you that your friend will be fine presently. I presume he is a mindsmith?"

Kaylene nodded as shock worked through her. Now, Callam's immobility made sense. The world of trouble they'd just invited was unfathomably large.

"I've a protection in my mind that temporarily immobilises anyone who seeks to work their way into my mind," the magistrate explained.

Kaylene looked down at the delicate glass vessel in her hand. A blush worked its way across her cheek and down her throat.

"I'm sorry," she whispered. She truly was, too. He'd been nothing but kind. Whatever punishment came, they deserved.

"I must confess, when I heard that two older members of the Sanctuary were here to visit me, I immediately stopped what I was doing. I was curious to know what exactly you wanted. Knowing you are here to ask me to grant the Farwan inn a certification did surprise me." His voice was quite gentle, devoid of ire.

She looked up.

A half-smile played about his face.

"You're not angry?"

"Well, maybe a little," he said. "But the Sanctuary breeds more complexity than most ever consider. If you are requesting something so unusual, you would have a good reason."

"Will you grant it?" Hope that they'd be successful, that they would bring back Luka and the world would finally be less cruel and terrifying, flared in front of her, tantalisingly close.

"Why are you so interested in their certification?"

Kaylene knew that to deviate far from the truth would be unwise. He gave the impression of knowing a lie when it was offered.

"I need a favour from the Farwan daughter."

"I assume you will not tell me what this favour is?"

She nodded.

"And if I grant this, they will give you what you need?"

She nodded again.

Kaylene watched the consideration on the magistrate's face, hardly daring to hope. He brought a hand to his jaw and rubbed his thumb along the line of his beard.

Finally, he appeared to arrive at a decision. "I will do this for you. I still do not believe that a foreigner should have this permit, but I am a soft-hearted fool, despite what others may say. However—" he held up a finger to forestall the thanks that Kaylene was about to profusely voice "—I will one day perhaps request a favour from you in exchange for this."

Kaylene wondered what exactly he may ask of her. "Why would you help me in exchange for a simple favour?"

Beside her, Callam suddenly stirred, inhaling with sharpness that made her jump.

"You're a mindsmith," Callam said, sounding both awed and afraid.

Kaylee looked at the magistrate, her eyes wide.

"Few who are not mindsmiths themselves would be able to discern such."

Callam's eyes slid away from the man's scrutiny.

"How do you hold a position of office?" Kaylene asked, her curiosity overwhelming her surprise. She didn't really follow politics – not having a vote and the Sanctuary's seclusion had diminished her interest — but she assumed Blessed weren't allowed to hold positions of power.

His smile gained a sad edge. "There is a curious loophole in the law that means Blessed are not allowed to vote in any matter of state, but they are not prohibited from being elected to any office."

Kaylene was incredulous. "And the people of Carrow voted for a Blessed?"

The sad note to his smile grew. "One of the privileges of being born to wealth is that a Blessed child can be kept from the knowledge of others."

Kaylee glanced back to Callam, who had lowered his eyes to intently regard the platter of food. She wondered what thoughts were going through his head. He did not show any acknowledgment of her curiosity.

"How long were you at the Sanctuary?" she asked.

"Not very long. Apparently I found self-mastery quite quickly." A flash of wry humour traversed his face. He looked back to Callam. "Come now, young man, don't feel bad. It's all in good fun."

Callam finally looked the magistrate in the eye. "I'm sorry."

The magistrate laughed heartily. "Ardyn, please. And no need to apologise. You weren't to know I was a mindsmith, too." He certainly sounded as though he held no ill will toward Callam's intrusion.

Ardyn took a sip and leaned back in his chair. "I take it you have never been to the Flame County?"

They both shook their heads.

His smile was gentle, and the almost calculating keenness to his expression vanished. "You're in for a treat. Lucky you've come at the right time of year, although the peak of the blooms won't happen for another two weeks this year."

Kaylene and Callam were content to allow Ardyn's enthusiasm to drive the conversation and they listened as he spoke on about the specifics of the region and its importance to the First Country. Subject matter that could have been dry, he made interesting with his obvious passion, and Kaylene found herself leaning forward with interest to hear what he had to say, almost forgetting to sip the exquisite liquor in her flute. She was particularly interested in Ardyn's explanation about the skyfire region's other economic base – the lysellum plant, which was turned into the drug forget-me-not – it seemed that was the crop in the wagons she had puzzled over as they drove in. His lip curled with disdain when he spoke of the voracious quantities in which the Fourth Country consumed it, although Kaylene wondered how he could not see why certain people's circumstances might mean they wanted to slip away from the weight of their torturous emotions. At that thought, Callam glanced at her. That she was not bothered he knew about her plan to end her life still surprised her. Since she'd found out he knew, she'd felt less alone than she had in a long time. It made her feel understood, and that had driven away many of those thoughts about ending her own life. It was strange to realise how quickly she had become accustomed to looking for his reactions to her thoughts. He acknowledged that thought with a slight curve of his mouth.

"It's so generous of you to spend so much time speaking with us," Kaylene said when she realised just how long they'd been sitting and talking with Ardyn. The afternoon was already almost wholly gone. She'd barely noticed the time passing, so interested had she been in the glimpses of the rest of the world that Ardyn had offered them.

He sighed and gifted her with another of his sad smiles. "I know what it is to be trapped within the Sanctuary, wondering what is passing me by in the world outside. And it is good to speak with people who know what it means to be Blessed."

Suddenly, Kaylene saw not a Blessed man with the incredible luck to be wealthy, but someone who was terribly lonely, perhaps assisted by wealth, but secluded from the rest of the world by it, too. She felt a great pity for him, hiding his Blessing while trying to serve the people who lived in the town named after his family.

"It's kind of you. Only recently, I've realised how much of the world I haven't seen. Even your house, it's so magnificent," Kaylene said.

There was a world of complexity behind Ardyn's smile. "Unfortunately I can't show you around the region but I can give you a tour of the house, if you'd like?" There was a boyish cast to the question.

"Didn't we interrupt your work?" Kaylene asked.

"It can be done later," Ardyn said. "Anyway, I need to sign the paper for the foreigners. You may as well accompany me to the bureau."

He sprang to his feet with a dexterity belied by his plump frame.

Ardyn led them through several outlandishly large rooms. The array of items in each room was dizzying to Kaylene who was used to the Sanctuary's sparseness. She wondered how one person could have a use for so many things.

Callam laughed as he caught her thought, hiding the laughter behind his hand.

"Are there others in your family who have been Blessed?" she asked Ardyn as she stared at a wall covered with lacquered paintings of the Carrow family. Some smiled, some frowned, some simply looked bored. Each must have deliberately chosen their facial expression – a curious insight into them. Ardyn's portrait of his younger self beamed with open honesty.

"Not that I can tell. I am—" he sighed "—an anomaly."

"Are your children Blessed?"

"I have no children. My mother and I decided it would be better to ensure I do not propagate a line of Blessed. A cousin of mine will take all of this upon my death." He waved a hand to indicate the room, and house beyond.

"Don't you want children?" Kaylene was amazed that he would so willingly give up having a child of his own.

"It's never been something I've desperately wanted, no. Although, my companion, Damyan, and I often house the poor children of Carrow in the height of winter and summer. He's very good with them. We could always adopt someone who would of course be my heir, but it feels too unfair a burden on them, to ask them to keep my Blessing a secret – or to keep it from them. Watching how he is with them, sometimes I regret the decision, but I know it is for the best."

Sorrow for Ardyn wound its way through Kaylene. Because she had never been faced with the prospect of life outside the Sanctuary, she had not considered how the confines of the Sanctuary would follow her were she to be released. It would be a terrible thing, she reflected, to be free from the oppressive walls of the Sanctuary and yet still be so limited in living. She wondered how much of the decision to not adopt an heir came from the fear of that un-Blessed child one day rejecting Ardyn for his Blessing.

She glanced at Callam and they shared a sad smile. Evidently he agreed.

Ardyn led them into his bureau – furnished and outfitted for his position as magistrate. He explained that he had preferred to meet them in one of the informal sitting rooms rather than in the more functional office. Kaylene thought that if that sitting room had been informal, then she had not the imagination to envisage what formal would be. The large, beautifully decorated room with huge windows and exquisite furnishings made her aware of the sparseness and modesty that had drenched so much of her life. Only Ardyn's manner had made her feel even a little relaxed.

The wood panelling made Ardyn's bureau feel smaller than it actually was. Cabinets made from the same wood lined one wall. Ardyn went to one and rifled through several compartments as he muttered to himself.

"Ah!" He pulling out a piece of linen paper. Words were stamped on it.

Ardyn crossed to a large desk and picked up a quill. He remained standing as he filled in the blank spaces on the page. His handwriting bore the neat lettering the Sanctuary required of its students, despite the fact that he used a quill.

"This should be all in order for the Farwan inn," Ardyn said cheerfully, holding the paper carefully as the ink dried. He took one final businesslike, evaluative look at the page, then rolled it up with efficient movements and passed it to Kaylene.

"Would you care to stay for the evening?" he asked.

Kaylene shared a look with Callam, who spoke for her.

"Thank you, but we should be getting back to the Sanctuary as soon as possible."

Ardyn looked disappointed but did not press the issue. He called to an attendant waiting discreetly outside the bureau and ordered Kaylene and Callam's cart be prepared. The man obediently trotted off. Kaylene wondered if the man had any inkling that the magistrate was Blessed and how he would behave if he did know.

The magistrate's comfortable chatter continued as he led them back to the entrance, pausing often to show them an object or ornament he thought may interest them, or a room which they hadn't previously seen. It made the relatively short walk take quite a long time.

When they walked out into the late-afternoon sunlight, Ardyn turned to Kaylene. "Might I ask a favour of you? Another favour?"

She looked at him warily, but nodded.

"I have heard that the trees on one of the main roads leading into Carrow experienced a sudden bloom."

Kaylene looked at him in surprise. "How did you hear that? We only passed through the road a short while ago."

"Little transpires in this part of the world of which I am unaware. People like to talk."

She raised her chin defiantly. "I am not ashamed of what I did."

"You misunderstand." Ardyn raised a hand of apology. "I was wondering—" he paused, looking uncertain "—could you do something similar here?"

"Really?" Use – or appreciation – of a Blessing just wasn't considered something done by upstanding people.

The push and pull between bias and delight was obvious in Ardyn's expression, but delight won. "The idea of someone using their Blessing for no reason other than to make something beautiful – it's lovely. I would like to see that very much."

Before he had finished speaking, she was nodding. Wonder crept through her at the idea that the defiant impulse to use her Blessing to create something beautiful had ignited in someone else the idea that Blessings might not be something only to be viewed with secrecy and shame. It felt good to realise she'd done that.

She closed her eyes and reached out her perception to the lawns. Seeds long dormant in the soil, the ones that had been planted but for some trick of fate had never grown, pulsed in her awareness. She breathed out, sending her will to the multitude of seeds. She breathed in and brought them all to sprout and bloom in a riot of colour that eclipsed the homogeneous green of the grass. The flowers were intermingled. Variety and shade fought for space, but there was a curious harmony to their coexistence. The elegance of the flower beds with crengions blooming in only one colour had been startling in its reserve, but this was beauty expressed in abandon. Kaylene could hardly believe that this feast of colour on which their eyes gorged had been prepared by her alone.

She glanced at Callam. His and Ardyn's faces were bathed in the multi-coloured light of the field, wonder pasted across their features. She heard a sniff and looked more closely at Ardyn. He was weeping.

"It's beautiful."

As though she was stepping through a dream, Kaylene crossed the swept dirt of the driveway and approached the lawn of flowers. Up close she could see their profusion. She bent and extended a cautious hand into the crush of petals. Sure enough, the flowers grew together as thickly as a carpet, offering enough resistance that she really had to push her hand through them. The crunch of footsteps signalled Callam and Ardyn joining her.

"This is magnificent, Kaya." Callam's voice was soft with awe.

The flow inside her strengthened. The Kaya of six months ago would never have been bold enough to bring that row of trees to bloom or to imagine she could craft something as spectacular as what lay before her. The person who'd created this spectacle was someone new. Certainly, she'd done a similar thing before, but under duress from Merika. This person brought trees to bloom and fields to colour, and wondered at the trepidation with which she had viewed the part of her that could create such beauty. Yet that was the truth of her country – someone like her had to hide something intrinsic to who she was in every facet of life to be accepted.

"Thank you," Ardyn said.

Kaylene surprised them both by flinging her arms around his neck.

He returned the embrace. It was a proper hug – the kind between friends.

The light dipped, as though a curtain had been drawn across the sky. The sun was nearing the horizon. "Gods, I didn't realise how late it was getting. I'm so sorry for keeping you all afternoon," Ardyn exclaimed, releasing her. "Will you be all right to find your way back?"

Kaylene was unable to stop herself from throwing a smirk in Callam's direction. He was resolutely staring away from her.

They made their farewells, with Ardyn reminding Kaylene that she still owed him a favour, and she promising to fulfil it whenever he asked. She wondered if he ever would take her up on the promise – or if she'd ever see him again.

"He certainly wasn't what I expected," Callam said as he steered the hearat down the driveway.

Kaylene said nothing. She was preoccupied with her thoughts. An inarticulate sadness at the loneliness she had glimpsed in Ardyn warred with elation at the fact that they were one step closer to getting Luka back. Once again, she dared to allow herself to believe they would be able to bring him back. Yet that thought was tempered by the question of what sort of life they would lead once she had returned him to her side.

TWELVE

Once more they found themselves sharing a large, wool-stuffed mattress in the Farwan inn. Callam and Kaylene were exhausted and Kaylene was grateful that both Tanita and Lexa had been occupied with an urgent matter and unable to see them when they returned just in time to catch the end of the dinner service. They had waited for an hour or so, but neither woman had returned, so they retired, leaving word with one of the staff to pass on news of their success when either Tanita or her daughter came back.

Sleep should have placed them both in its thrall, but Kaylene found herself unable to still her thoughts long enough to be able to slip into dreams.

"Stop thinking so loudly," Callam said from the far side of the bed.

"Sorry. I can't stop thinking about Ardyn."

"I know."

She smiled as she shuffled over to the centre of the mattress so she could speak softly. "It seems so unreal that someone like him is Blessed."

"Maybe to you. He immobilised me pretty effectively when I tried to read him."

"Was it bad?"

Callam's sounded thoughtful as he answered. "It was frightening. I've never thought I couldn't protect my own mind. It wasn't even that he was better than me; I just wasn't expecting it."

"Do you think he hates his time in the Sanctuary?"

Callam turned so he was looking at her. "It's not all bad at the Sanctuary. Remember when we told the incoming Blessed that they had to run five spares before breakfast every morning?"

Kaylene laughed. "Gods yes, how many years ago was that?"

"Four, I think. That was one of our better ideas."

She remembered the giddy delight they had taken in the horrified faces of those children. Perhaps it had been a cruel prank to play on the incoming Blessed, many of whom were already sufficiently afraid of being at the Sanctuary, but its execution had been so flawless that Kaylene couldn't feel bad no matter how hard she tried.

In the dark she couldn't see the colour of Callam's eyes, only the outline of his features. In that moment, he bore such little resemblance to Luka that it was no resemblance at all.

The last time she had been this close to someone she had been with Luka, but then they had been wound around one another, embracing with unquenchable desire and familiar tenderness. Kaylene missed being touched in such a way. She had not really allowed herself to miss such banal things as physical intimacy, but that deprivation was there, tugging with insistent hands at her body. She was glad the dark concealed her blush as she realised Callam would be able to hear her ruminating on her desire and the fact that it was their proximity that provoked it.

He laughed, but the sound was gentle, understanding. "Don't worry, I won't tell if you won't."

The intimacy of the way he spoke danced unexpectedly across her skin. She liked that. She liked that he'd marvelled in the beauty her Blessing could create. She liked that he didn't speak if he had nothing to say. She liked that he, despite having access to her thoughts, kept them – and his own – largely to himself. She liked that he'd allowed her in.

She woke intertwined with him. His arms encircled her and she was pressed against him so tightly that there was no space between them. Her lips rested against his neck. His pulse pounded against her mouth. For a moment, she did not realise where and with whom she was and instinct had her lazily tilting her head up to find the line of his jaw and from there, track along to his lips. Her kiss woke him and his arms tightened about her as he returned her kiss and pulled her on top of him. The dance of his tongue against hers was unfamiliar, and it was that which brought Kaylene fully to wakefulness. She pulled back abruptly and rolled off him, heat that was only in part due to her mortification coursing through her.

"Kaya—" Callam began as he sat up, but she cut him off with a wave.

"Please, don't worry about it." Her voice was hoarse with embarrassment and, yes, arousal.

"But—"

"Cal, I really don't want to talk about it." She kept her gaze determinedly at the space just above his head.

He fell silent.

"I'm going to go to get some food." She rolled out of bed, grabbed her outer clothes and hurriedly put them on in a way that showed Callam as little as possible of her undergarments.

Tanita was in the dining room on the ground floor, supervising the breakfast service with her meticulous eye. As Kaylene entered, she came over to her.

"I'm sorry we missed you last night." She offered no further explanation, but to Kaylene, she bore slight signs of fatigue.

"It's no problem," Kaylene said. She wondered whether what had transpired between her and Callam would have occurred had they met with Tanita and her daughter the previous evening. At the memory of the way his lips had felt against hers, a thrill ran through her. She told herself angrily that it was merely a physical reaction and to focus on the intimidating woman in front of her.

"I must say, I'm quite impressed you managed to extract the certification from him," Tanita said.

Kaylene endured the scrutiny with a shrug and a smile. "Between Callam and I, we know how to get what we need." Her voice held a lightness she did not feel.

"Well, once you've eaten and Callam is down, you should both come to see Lexana."

A jab of shame coursed through her as she remembered that she was here to bring back Callam's brother – the person she loved.

"Callam may still be sleeping," she said awkwardly.

Tanita raised an eyebrow and looked pointedly past Kaylene's shoulder at Callam, who had just descended into the breakfast room.

Kaylene swung back to Tanita. "I suppose we'll both meet Lexa, once we've eaten."

Callam did not sit next to her as they ate but instead struck up conversation with some travellers from the other side of the country. Kaylene sat by herself, covertly observing Callam's conversation, and wondered where the shy young man who barely spoke had gone. Away from the Sanctuary's high walls, he had become someone totally different. He was still far from outgoing, but the almost painful introversion had disappeared. In its place was a shy charm. Humour peeked through his demeanour like glimmers of sunlight behind clouds. She liked this version of Callam a great deal, and she liked this version of herself around this version of him, too.

Evidently hearing this thought, he glanced at her, but she dropped her gaze before their eyes could meet and bent her thoughts so they were only about the food in front of her.

When she was done, she handed her plate back and followed Tanita's directions to find Lexa. Callam followed a few moments later.

Lexa was in a little administrative room checking through a large ledger. Her proclivity for numbers was obvious in the speed with which her reed pen moved along the lines. At their entrance, she looked up and smiled.

"I heard you got the permit." Like her mother, she offered no explanation for what had required them the previous night, and Kaylene suspected it would remain one of life's little unsolved mysteries.

Kaylene held out the document that she had run up to the room to fetch.

Lexa unrolled the parchment. She surveyed it with a frown. "I'm slowly learning your language," she said with a little laugh. "I can't believe you speak Quaren fluently."

"And Tritarth and Secondus," Callam chimed in.

Kaylene blushed at the pride in his voice.

Lexa's eyebrows rose. "So many! Does everyone in the Sanctuary speak all the Godskissed Continent's languages?"

"No," Kaylene said. "We each choose an area of study. Mine's language."

The foreign girl fixed Kaylene with the kind of appraising stare she seemed to have inherited from her mother. "What made you choose languages?"

Kaylene paused. "They take me somewhere else."

Lexa's dark eyes held hers a moment longer and Kaylene felt an understanding pass between her and the other girl.

"I know that feeling," Lexa said softly. She broke eye contact and turned her attention to the document, her demeanour once again pure business. "From what I can tell this seems to be in order."

"It is," Kaylene assured her as Lexa read over it once more.

Lexa placed the parchment aside and rummaged around the table. When she found what she sought she let out an "ah" of victory. "I have done the calculations that you requested – down to the last finger."

Kaylene took the paper and looked at the neat lines of numbers. Maths was one language that made little sense to her, but she was sure Merika would find coherence in the figures.

"Thank you."

"It was an interesting break from accounts," Lexa said.

"We appreciate it nevertheless," Callam added.

Kaylene avoided even glancing at him.

Lexa favoured him with a smile. "I must confess, I will be curious to know if this works."

"We can only hope." Kaylene felt a stab of guilt at what had transpired between her and Callam. They were here to bring Luka back. One half-asleep kiss could easily be pushed aside to be practically forgotten. The sharp intake of his breath let her know that he had heard her thought, and she chided herself for her carelessness.

"I should just say..." Lexa began, but halted, obviously still deliberating whether or not this was a thought she should share. When neither Callam nor Kaylene sought to speak, she continued. "This work, it requires a lot of energy. It's dangerous. When you do it please be careful." There was an earnestness to her that was unexpectedly endearing.

Kaylene felt she'd made a true friend and regretted that she would likely never see the girl again. "I promise."

Lexa nodded gravely. "I hope we meet again." She came around the desk to embrace Kaylene.

Kaylene returned the gesture, startled but touched.

They set off soon after, heading back to the Sanctuary along the way they'd come. But while the landscape seemed almost the same, so much felt different. Where previously the modest vehicle with just enough room behind the driver's seat to accommodate a travel bag had seemed small but comfortable, Kaylene now felt thrown against Callam far too frequently. She was acutely aware of the way her leg pressed into his when they took a curve. She could not help but feel the heat from his body traversing the small space between them. She even swore she could smell the sweat on his skin.

What made it all the worse was she couldn't deny that she had liked the feel of him under her. She had liked the way he had kissed her, and despite her best efforts, she could not keep from remembering with aching clarity those few moments before she had realised where and with whom she was. Worse still, as she tried to keep those thoughts from entering her head, they returned with redoubled insistence, and she knew that beside her, Callam was hearing everything as though she was narrating it all aloud to him. It was mortifying.

"Kaya, this morning." The words bust out of him, rending the silence between them.

Kaylene looked uncomfortably as far in the opposite direction from him as possible.

"It was a mistake, neither of us was properly awake, you didn't know it was me, and I didn't know it was you." She spoke quickly, trying to get all of the words out so that she didn't have to continue to speak about this any longer.

"But that's just it. I knew it was you." There was a desperate strength in his voice. He was nearly shouting.

She turned back to look at him, surprised by the strength of his emotion.

"I love my brother and would do nothing to hurt him. His love for you is so complete that it burns to feel." Callam spoke with determined emphasis. "And when you two are together, you and he are changed, you become part of one another."

His voice had returned to its usual cadence, although it was rough with emotion – the emotion he was trying to share with her, or the fear of baring himself to her, Kaylene could not guess.

"I told you I could hear his thoughts, regardless of whether I tried or not. And that because of how you were...intertwined, I began to hear yours, too. But I didn't explain what that meant. To have another person's thoughts always in your head – it's sometimes hard to know what's yours and what's theirs.

"I feel...complicated things for you, Kaya. I don't know if those feelings are mine, or Luka's, or even yours. This morning, I knew it was you. I'm sorry, I should have stopped you, but..." He trailed off abruptly and said no more.

Kaylene thought she might cry. "Why tell me?" she whispered. She needn't have spoken. He would have heard the thought anyway.

"So that you understand why I keep a distance."

She wanted to take issue with his logic, but she couldn't begrudge him – even from keeping it from her in the first place. So she said nothing and allowed the silence to settle between them.

The day wore on and she cast her gaze out along the country rather than allow Callam to fill any part of her vision. As they drew ever closer to the Sanctuary, she felt a sense of heaviness take root somewhere in the pit of her stomach; a sense of oppression and constraint closed around her with each span they came closer to the place that had been her home for so many years she had lost count.

Yet she still could not find it within her to utterly despise life there as Merika did. Within the walls of the Sanctuary were so many good memories, many of them featuring Luka, that it was more a home to her than the place where she had spent the first years of her life.

She could not find it within herself to hate the place where she and Luka had come together, where the safety and certainty that came with loving and being loved had enfolded her, making every sad or bad moment bearable. Callam had been right: she and Luka had been totally enmeshed – more than one person but slightly less than two. It had only intensified the physical connection between them.

She still vividly recalled the first time she and Luka had properly explored one another's bodies. There had been no finesse in the movements of their hands or hips, yet there had been a certain ecstasy in the discovery. It had been raining. The muted light had made the moment seem even more private, somehow outside of time, every second elongated into infinity and yet passing by so quickly that all Kaylene could remember was the sound of Luka's breath and how the mere cadence of his inhalations and exhalations said more than he ever could in words.

She had marvelled at his body, the feel of his ribs underneath her fingers, the unexpected growth of hair in the centre of his chest. Equally, she had delighted in the way his hands had skipped along her hips to rest along the space between her behind and the small of her back. It felt so natural. Rather than feeling as though they were entering new territory, she felt she was traversing a familiar land that had somehow become buried in the recesses of her memory.

With a start, she arose from the memory that had engulfed her without her even noticing. Embarrassment burned through her as she realised Callam would have heard every part of that memory, including the physical thrill that had accompanied it. His cheeks reddened in affirmation.

"Sorry," she mumbled, feeling her own blush.

Callam did not reply.

The awkward stiltedness persisted during the next days of travel.

Kaylene did not know what else she could say to Callam that would assuage the uncomfortable tension between them. They requested separate rooms when they stopped for the evening, and the subsequent nights, too, delving further than they should have into the money allowed to them by the Sanctuary for the journey. Kaylene could not care whether or not they would face recrimination for the amount they spent, overcome as she was by the desire to acquire even a little reprieve from being in Callam's presence.

Only in the evenings did she allow herself to think about what he had confessed to her. During the days when she sat next to him she had become practised in keeping her thoughts firmly on trivialities. In the evenings, her mind lingered on the cut-off memory of his mouth and hands. Carefully, she examined the guilt and its coexistence alongside desire and she sought to understand exactly what it meant. Despite her ruminations, she could not understand the different rooms in her heart. It was almost like there were two Kaylenes: one who loved Luka, who liked life in the Sanctuary with him, and the other who enjoyed using her Blessing, defying the ways she been taught to constrain herself, and who kept wondering what it would be like to kiss Callam again.

On the last evening, as they ate their dinner, Callam sought to breach the void of silence that had only grown between them. Kaylene would have preferred to take her meal back to her room and eat it in the security of knowing that the thoughts passing through her mind would remain hers alone, but the semblance of normalcy needed to be maintained. Any odd behaviour on their part would be noticed, commented upon, even reported. Neither wanted to draw any extra attention or comment.

"I'm sorry."

She looked up from the spice-coated fried vegetables with which she'd been trying to occupy her whole focus.

"About what I said. I shouldn't have told you."

The rigidity with which, for so many days, she had kept herself separate from Callam softened. She did not want to be like this with him. She just hadn't known how else she was supposed to be with him.

"It's all right. I'm sorry about what happened."

She was not careful enough with her thoughts and by the slight narrowing of his eyes she knew that he had heard the truth; she hadn't been entirely sorry about what had transpired between them on that morning. That knowledge pushed her clumsily on.

"You say that Luka and I were more akin to one person than two, but before you I'm laid bare. You can hear my every thought. It's in a way more intimate than even being with Luka."

He gave her a tiny sad smile. "I know."

"Of course you do. And mostly, I like that. It's hard to know how I should be with you, Cal." She hated her inability to put voice to emotions that defied clear, specific words.

He heard that, too, and reached out to cover her hand with his in a gesture that conveyed that he understood far more elegantly than any words.

She gave up on words and instead allowed her thoughts to flow, making no effort to resolve the chaotic jumble of ideas or the disparate strands that churned and crashed together. Fragments of confusion over her assumption that she could be happy only if Luka was by her side overlapped with the understanding she'd nurtured about her Blessing being something to fear and of which to be ashamed. The sense that she'd somehow got everything wrong was a constant background to this, and the undercurrent of something more powerful than sorrow and self-loathing tugged at her, even as she was unable to name it.

There was such intimacy to allowing her mind to be free while looking into Callam's eyes. A heat built within her that made her skin tingle and left her achingly aware of the feel of his skin against hers where he held her hand.

That thought, too, he heard, and the sudden darkening of his eyes spoke to his answering desire. But with a shuddering breath and an obvious exertion of willpower, he withdrew his hand. Yet he held her gaze.

"Kaya." Desire and sadness caressed her name.

She could not tear her eyes from his. It felt as though she was engulfed in his gaze. His eyes were so like Luka's.

As she thought his brother's name, he looked away from her, stopping whatever might have happened next.

Kaylene stood, lust and the tumbling of emotions that accompanied it making her as awkward as an adolescent. "I'm going to sleep," she stammered. She all but raced from the room.

THIRTEEN

Senior Blessed Maryam looked unimpressed as Callam and Kaylene stood before her and provided the account of their spending.

"It was an indulgence to take an extra room." Her voice was weighted by the severity of her disapproval as she counted the coins they'd returned.

"I know, but you didn't hear Kaya's snores," Callam said with a graveness that Kaylene could not understand how he maintained. She had to bite the inside of her cheek to keep from laughing.

With a final harrumph, the dour-faced woman deposited the coin purse in the locked cabinet behind where she sat. The opened door offered a glimpse of coinpurses arranged in neat rows on the shelves, sitting alongside the matte sheen of leather document wallets.

With that ordeal over, Kaylene was able to turn her attention to more important matters as she settled with disconcerting ease back into the routine of Sanctuary life. It was a perverse relief to have its stone walls between her thoughts and Callam. After the intimacy of their final evening of travel, she found herself more engulfed by turbulent emotions than ever. They moved through her, twisting and changing before she could understand the raging currents of her heart. She was glad Callam was not close enough to her to hear each thought as it came. She wanted to sort through them on her own. Yet, she had become accustomed to the ease and comfort of knowing he was there at every part of the day. While she wanted to keep her confusion private, she'd been surprised at how quickly she had come to enjoy – even anticipate – having her thoughts heard and understood, her humour laughed at, her musings appreciated. During the parts of the day when they were apart, she found herself missing him and that connection.

Unsurprisingly, Merika noticed no difference in her friends, for she was too wrapped up in her delight at Lexana's calculations.

Kaylene performed her chores, undertook her study, and spent her leisure time in idle anticipation of Merika completing her calculations. The dual familiarity of routine and place had her folding back in on herself, feeling old assumptions about being Blessed slip out from where they'd been waiting at the back of her mind and claim dominance in her thoughts once more, leaving her with the sense that thoughts of life outside the Sanctuary were those of another person. Yet she could not stop from noticing the gruelling nature of the tasks assigned to her. Quiet resentment settled around her in a way it never had before as she faced the unpleasantness of scrubbing the bathing rooms, or working in the gardens with the strict instruction that she not use her Blessing. She wondered if the feeling would fade with time, and if it didn't, what that would mean. As days slipped past and Merika still had not completed her research, Kaylene felt suspended in time, as though caught at the moment of falling. Thoughts about what would happen if they got Luka back and indefinite life in the Sanctuary lurked on the edges of her mind, as if they knew she'd have to face them soon enough and were content to wait.

At last, two weeks after their return, Merika triumphantly informed them one afternoon as the four friends sat in one of the courtyards that she knew all they needed to bring Luka back.

"It's the use of energy the likes of which I've never seen before." Merika's eyes were alight with a familiar fervour.

"How did you figure it out?" Callam asked.

"Do you really want to hear about how I tracked down twelve different books?" The fierceness of Merika's question seemed almost defensive.

"Not really," Callam admitted.

"And it will work?" Kaylene asked.

Merika nodded, her gaze far away as her mind raced through the problem. "I don't see why it won't. But even it if doesn't, the mere spectacle of such a thing will be amazing."

Leshan, who had been silent up to that point, cleared her throat pointedly.

Merika glanced toward her and the two shared a brief look.

"Obviously, I hope we bring back Luka," Merika added.

Kaylene inclined her head to indicate she did not think ill of Merika's excitement about the display of power overshadowing the importance of bringing back their friend. She looked at the grass, feeling guilt curl around her. It had become impossible for her to think of Luka with clear feelings.

"We need to get to the mountain pass?" Callam asked.

Merika made a noise of affirmation.

"How do we get there?"

Merika leaned back, obviously relishing her role as architect of the scheme. "We have two choices. The first is to find a reason that the four of us would need to leave the Sanctuary. But I think we won't be able to offer one. Kaya's been away far too much, and you and me asking to go once again would arouse suspicion. Only Lesha could ask to leave and likely be granted it."

"Well, that's easy then," Leshan said. "Tell me what to do and I'll do it on my own."

Merika, normally one to be frustrated when she was interrupted in the midst of an explanation, merely threw Leshan a look of good humour and continued.

"I think more likely we'll have to steal a cart."

Astonishment flooded through Kaylene at Merika's audacity. "We'll have to do what?"

"How will we do that without being noticed?" Callam asked at the same time. No doubt was in his voice, only determination.

"We'd need to leave at night. And we'd also need to find a way to change our clothes so we're not as noticeable."

"We could buy clothes, although we'd need coin for that," Callam said.

"Can we steal some money?" Kaylene asked.

Leshan's brief expression of shock before she tucked it away was priceless.

Callam laughed quietly, no doubt having picked up on Kaylene's amusement at their friend's reaction.

Unlike Leshan, Merika seemed to be seriously considering Kaylene's suggestion. She pursed her lips, pushing a strand of russet hair back from her face. "We could do it, but it would be difficult."

Kaylene had to agree. She thought about the locked cabinet in Senior Blessed Maryam's office. The money behind those wooden doors would more than do the job, but getting to it would be a problem. They'd have to find a way to enter the office when nobody was around, to get past the lock on the office door, then to get past the lock on the cabinet door, re-lock everything, and get out unnoticed and with their theft undetected long enough to give them a chance to escape. She could only assume that Merika would know how to pick a lock – or soon would, if they needed that knowledge – but she couldn't see a way to get in and out of the room without being caught, or being quickly discovered if they somehow succeeded.

Leshan's unhappy expression conveyed her discomfort before she'd even spoken. "Is there some other way we can get money?"

Leshan's stringent morality had Kaylene biting her lip to keep from dissolving into giggles. Something about the conversation felt farcical.

"I doubt it. We'd probably be better off stealing clothes, too, to be honest. Buying them would be obviously suspicious," Merika said, as though such discussions were commonplace.

Perhaps the amusement Kaylene found in the exchange was because a part of her couldn't believe they were so close to actually reaching their goal. That every part of the instructions on the scroll had been deciphered and readied still felt unreal. After so long without him, Luka had suddenly begun to feel more like an idea to which she was clinging rather than the person she had loved so completely.

"You know that if we take this step, we can't come back?" Leshan said in a low voice, dampening their enthusiasm.

Of course, Kaylene knew, even if she didn't want to acknowledge it. She'd known from the second Ay'ash had said there was a way to bring Luka back that the Sanctuary would never stand for such an act. But that had been a problem that existed in a clouded future. Focusing on the act of chasing this seemingly impossible feat had eclipsed her capacity to consider its implications.

Callam's answer pulled her from her thoughts. "Yes."

She looked at her friend's faces and felt foolish. They'd all been aware of where this path would take them. They'd chosen to walk it with their eyes open to that truth – even Leshan. How many more times would she be confronted with the illusions she'd spun around herself before she saw what needed to be acknowledged?

"Is this..." She stopped, her throat too dry to allow words to pass. She swallowed. "Is this something you're all comfortable with?"

She looked at her friends: Merika excited, Callam calm, and Leshan determined.

A wave of love for her friends swept over her, so powerful that she found it nearly brought her to tears. Their steadfast loyalty and unquestioning help was more than she could ever repay. When she had told them about her first meeting with Ay'ash, they had not dismissed the wild story, and none of them had ever told her that what she wanted to do was too dangerous, too improbable, too selfish.

She wondered if she could really ask them to not only walk away from all they'd known, but also into danger. The Sanctuary pursued those who tried to flee – or rather, they hired Enforcers to do it. They were efficient and ruthless. The runaways were always found – even if they weren't brought back alive.

The grip with which she'd been clinging to the idea of pursuing this task faltered. The burning desire to bring back Luka had been replaced by a different motivation as she'd been forced to question so much. Perhaps Callam had flung at her a truth — Luka's significance was more a way to ease the hardship of life in the Sanctuary. Could she ask her friends to risk so much on a feeling that was no longer the basis of her entire world? Tears brimmed.

"We don't have to go immediately." Leshan's voice was kind.

Merika shifted, as though she was ready to disagree, but Leshan put a hand on her leg, and so she said nothing else.

"Ok." Kaylene's voice came out small.

The intensity of the moment dissipated with absurd rapidity.

Callam stood, brushing grass from his trousers. "I've been asked to help a youngling with her study."

"Someone else is studying anatomy?" Leshan asked with surprise. The study of the theoretical structures underlying the body was a fiddly one.

Kaylene had always assumed Callam had undertaken it with the hope that when he was released from the Sanctuary, he could work with medicines in some form. It surprised her to realise that she'd never asked him about it.

Callam's only reply to Leshan was a nod before he departed. He cast no glance toward Kaylene and she felt faint disappointment at that. She shook the emotion from herself.

"I have something I want to study," Merika announced. She clambered to her feet. Unlike Callam, she paid no attention to the grass clinging to her clothes.

"Something that will upset me?" Leshan asked, tilting her head back to look at Merika. A smile played about her lips as they regarded each other.

"Probably," Merika responded, an answering smile flashing across her face before she left.

Only Leshan and Kaylene remained.

With exaggerated slowness, Leshan turned to Kaylene. "What's wrong?"

Kaylene entertained the idea of saying nothing, or even inventing an excuse to extricate herself from Leshan's interrogation, but the truth was that she wanted too badly to speak with someone about what had transpired between her and Callam and the feelings that were at war within her. A retelling practically fell from her lips.

Leshan was a good audience, saying nothing until she was certain that Kaylene had finished. It felt good to share what had happened. Somehow the turmoil that had coiled around her chest eased as she unburdened herself.

Cautiously, Kaylene peeked at Leshan's face. She had kept her eyes averted while she spoke, too afraid of whatever judgment she may see on her friend's face. Rather than the frown she feared, she saw immense compassion. Perhaps that was worse. It made her want to lay her head down on the earth and cry into the soft soil.

"Do you still want to bring back Luka?" Leshan asked, her voice quiet.

To have the question asked so plainly was confronting. She did not reply at once, struggling to find the words. "I don't know."

"Is this why you hesitated about leaving?"

"Not exactly." Kaylene bit her lip. "But it's part of it."

The constriction around her throat was painful and she had to force the words out around it. "I don't know what I want anymore."

"Do you want Callam?"

Kaylene shook her head. "Even if I did, I would too often think of Luka around him. And he would know that."

"It would be the most exquisite of torments to be so intimate with someone," Leshan said. She idly tugged a lock of hair as she contemplated the idea. "Do you know what he wants?"

Kaylene shook her head. Strands of hair swept across her eyes, catching the sunlight and briefly streaking her vision with gold. "He said Luka protected him when they were young and he didn't understand his Blessing properly. I think he would never forgive himself if he knew he could have brought Luka back and did not. Especially given he feels he should have been the one who was killed."

Leshan sighed, her fingers working at pulling up the grass around her.

Kaylene was vaguely aware of the way the plants felt as they were uprooted, but she paid it little heed.

"If you don't want to bring back Luka, we don't have to try," Leshan said.

Kaylene gave a bitter laugh. "Merika's already halfway to the barrier. Cal's set on bringing his brother back. The only one who doesn't want to leave is you."

Leshan was silent for a long pause. When she spoke, her words held a world of sorrow to which Kaylene was not privy. "It's not that simple, Kaya."

Speaking with Leshan made Kaylene feel inordinately better. Though Callam knew exactly what was in her head, it was different for her to speak aloud about the treacherous currents of her thoughts and sentiments. While nothing had been resolved, the sense of being alone had diminished. She undertook her evening chore of helping to prepare dinner with a lightened heart. Unusually, Callam, Merika, and Leshan had not been instructed to assist her, so Kaylene was with a number of younger Blessed. Over the course of peeling and chopping vegetables, they stared at her with a mixture of fear and uncertainty. As they fried and boiled the food, they gave her a wide berth where possible. Her age may have made her an object of discomfort, but it also gave her an air of certainty and authority they did not have. In a respite from overseeing the simmering of the vegetable broth, she stole a glance at a girl with hair the pink of a soft dawn hanging across her face. Really, she should have tied it back, but something about the way she kept it as a curtain between her and the rest of the world had Kaylene staying her words to tell her as much. For so long, she had merely thought of the younger Blessed as a version of herself fortunate enough to be leaving the Sanctuary soon. In that way, she had almost considered these children superior to her. Yet, while she could remember feeling the same uncertainty of her personhood exuded by the girl, she realised she no longer felt like that. In fact, she could not recall the last time she had felt like that.

She and her friends conversed easily over dinner about trivial matters – mostly gossip about the younger students. Kaylene could not quite pinpoint the moment when they'd found comfort in being only the four of them, yet it appeared to have happened. Of course, the discussion steered carefully away from any mention of their plans. The little ears surrounding them had been known to report what they heard to the Senior Blessed. Whether out of spite or the genuine belief that they were doing the right thing, Kaylene had never been quite certain, although she was sure that she resented them for the reprimands she had received over the years for making derogatory comments about the Sanctuary, or the gratuity of the overt affection she and Luka had displayed toward one another, or Merika's mocking impressions of the Senior Blessed to what they had erroneously assumed to be a unanimously appreciative audience.

Once they had finished eating, they duly placed their crockery away and went their separate ways for the evening. Callam and Leshan had chores to perform, and Merika made a vague comment about wanting to research something. Kaylene thus found herself with time to fill. She wandered to one of the Sanctuary's courtyards. It was a warm evening and the light had not quite finished its departure from the sky. Lanlei flowers as big as her hand were blooming now that the sun had dipped below the horizon. The petals were nearly perfect circles and the plant's heady perfume suffused the air. Kaylene sat on a stone bench and leaned back on her hands and lifted her eyes to the wide expanse of night sky. The night was cloudless, offering a perfect view of the firmament, and Kaylene wondered at the vastness of the world. With a slight jolt of comprehension, she understood that what bothered her was not simply her complicated feelings for Callam, but a wonderment at what she had not seen. Seeing the skyfire trees had ignited in her a burning curiosity about what other amazing sights the world had to offer. Her thoughts turned to the day's conversation and the question of leaving the Sanctuary. Truly, departing the Sanctuary was frightening in a way she didn't want to examine – and not simply because of the suggestion that Luka had made life here bearable. In truth, something even more insidious than even the worry of being pursued kept her from contemplating escape. Her feet had been weighted by the belief that she didn't deserve to leave. But she wasn't sure she felt that anymore.

She breathed out, enjoying the stillness and warmth of the evening. From outside the Sanctuary's walls, the chirp of night insects began. Never were such insects found inside any part of the Sanctuary. She had never really thought it odd before. Now, she could not help but wonder why.

Her limbs felt pleasantly heavy. She knew she should probably leave the courtyard and find something to do, but she could not quite bestir herself. The weight of her body pressed her into the bench, and stillness settled over her.

That weight increased, becoming even more soporific. She frowned and tried to move her arm. No matter what she tried, her limb would not move. Panic replaced pleasant idleness. Something was wrong. She tried to move her legs, but they too refused to obey her wishes.

Her panic only increased when she realised that it was becoming more and more difficult to move her head. She knew that someone was using their Blessing on her, and that made it more terrifying. She could not see who her assailant was, and she did not know how to resist what they were doing to her. The frightening thought occurred to her that if this paralysis enveloped her completely, she might not even be able to breathe. It seemed a particularly awful way to die, aware of her breath stopping in her chest.

As her face ceased to move, she was flooded with relief that she continued to breathe. Her head was still tilted back and she had an unblinking view of the night sky. It meant that she could not see anything nearby. She could only hear the sound of footsteps of at least two people as they approached her.

"Is it safe?"

Kaylene recognised the brusque sound of the Senior Blessed Maryam.

"Yes."

The answering voice was that of another Senior Blessed, Thanan. He was rarely seen in the Sanctuary, attending to a business that was decidedly his own.

"Are you certain?"

There was a trace of fear in Senior Blessed Maryam's voice.

"Of course."

"Take her."

Hands seized Kaylene and lifted her. She wanted to scream, to fight like some wild animal, but she could do nothing as she was carried out of the courtyard, her limbs frozen in place.

FOURTEEN

Rough hands carried Kaylene along the Sanctuary's stone corridors. She heard nobody else nearby and wondered if that had been contrived. Because she could not close her eyes, she was forced to stare at the rough-cut ceiling. It was an utter contrast to the beautiful ceiling of Ardyn Carrow's magnificent house. The ugliness of the building was another thing about the Sanctuary she had never properly considered until recently.

Finally, she was manhandled inside what her brief glance from the outside suggested was a barren room with only a single tiny window. Those rough hands bundled her into a chair, and the sound of receding footsteps and a closing door led her to conclude she was alone in the dimly lit room. Light from some kind of flame burned behind her, providing meagre illumination. She could see only directly in front of her: an empty chair and bare stone walls and floor. As the silence settled, the sound of breathing behind her disproved her assumption that she was alone. The knowledge that someone was watching her imparted a new layer of vulnerability; it would be so easy for whoever was to strike her – even kill her. She would be powerless to stop them.

Time seemed to pass in a reluctant trickle. Fear built within Kaylene.

Finally, someone spoke, and Kaylene recognised Senior Blessed Maryam's voice. "Keep her legs still, but let everything else go."

Kaylene's head snapped forward with the suddenness of her release. She had to fight to steady herself. The enduring immobility in her legs made it difficult to feel securely balanced.

She looked around, confirming her first impression that the room was bare aside from the two chairs. Senior Blessed Maryam stood by the door with a Senior Blessed Kaylene couldn't identify. A small flame burned with the unnatural stillness of a Blessed's conjuring in Senior Blessed Maryam's open hand, but she held it a little in front of her, and angled her hand so that the light didn't clearly show the woman's face, let alone fully illuminate the room.

"Wait outside the door," Senior Blessed Maryam instructed, and the man left.

Cold fingers of fear reached into Kaylene's stomach, throat, head, as the Senior Blessed slowly circled the chair and came to stand in front of her. To be apprehended in such a manner could only suggest that her recent breaches of Sanctuary rules had been discovered. She wondered what unmerciful retribution had been selected for her. Part of what made the Sanctuary's punishment for rule breakers so terrifying was the ambiguity and rumour surrounding its exact nature.

"You and your friends have displayed remarkable determination."

Kaylene said nothing, too terrified to speak. That fear only intensified when she realised her friends were also in danger from the Sanctuary's wrath.

"Yet you have all demonstrated the highest form of foolishness."

Still, Kaylene said nothing, and Senior Blessed Maryam seemed content to observe Kaylene in silence. The weight of the woman's observation was almost too much for Kaylene to bear.

"Do you have any idea what kind of danger the four of you courted?" The softness of the woman's voice held the same quiet menace the Sanctuary promised for any defiance. It was what breathed life into the flames of Kaylene's resentment. She clung to it like she was drowning – in a way, she was. It pulled her from fear and gave her the courage to lift her chin and press her lips together. Silence was the best rebellion she could offer.

With a sigh, Senior Blessed Maryam pulled the other chair across the floor with an angry scrape. She sat. She extended the palm containing the unflickering flame in a clear offering of light so Kaylene could better see. The gesture was unexpectedly humanising.

"You must understand, none of us wanted Luka to die."

The mention of Luka's name felt like ice spinning across Kaylene's skin.

"We know how complete the bond was between you two, and we had hopes for what you both would become," Senior Blessed Maryam continued.

This confessional confidence surprised Kaylene into speaking. "I was looking forward to having children with Luka, to growing old with him. That was taken from me."

For a moment, her confused feelings for Callam receded as the enormity of the theft to which she had been victim washed across her. She had hardly dared allow herself to realise how much of her whole future, the future she had so carelessly assumed she would have with Luka, had disappeared with his death. That, as much as his absence, had been what had created such emptiness inside her. It seemed unfair that she realised it here, in this room, under these circumstances.

The Senior Blessed regarded her for a moment, pressing her lips together. "You two would never have been allowed to have children."

"What?" Kaylene realised she was clenching her jaw so tightly that her face was aching. "We would have found enough self mastery. We just needed time."

"Self mastery?" The Senior Blessed gave a snort of derision. "Surely you can understand that self-control is a byword for being controlled."

Kaylene remained silent. Fear, anger, and confusion were a potent mix inside her.

"Imagine a world in which all Blessed realised their true power. Do you really think those unBlessed would be able to resist such powers?"

There was an earnestness to Senior Blessed Maryam's tone that Kaylene had never before heard in an elder of the Sanctuary.

She shook her head.

"Of course not. And think of what tyranny our kind would wreak. If they think even for a moment that they may have the ability to gain real power, or deserve to hold positions of authority...they can't leave here if they even have the tiniest understanding of just how easy it would be for Blessed to seize control for themselves. The consequences could breed a total upheaval of everything we know here in the First Country."

The opposing sensations of weightlessness and unbearable heaviness moved across Kaylene. As much as her mind was screaming that this could not possibly be true, the Senior Blessed's words resonated with something more deeply lodged. "So...we don't learn self-control here but self-loathing?"

"It that's what you want to call it."

"Why?"

"Because it keeps the First Country safe."

"How?"

The older woman made an impatient gesture. "You read the news from the rest of the Godskissed Continent as you study your languages. Uprisings in the Third Country. Rebellion in the Queendom of the Seven Lakes. And that's not even to speak of what goes on in the Fourth Country. We removed ourselves from the rest of the land because it became apparent that they could not live with peace – could not keep their people safe."

"What does that have to do with the Blessed?"

Senior Blessed Maryam gave her a look of incomprehension. "What about us?"

The question threw Kaylene. "How are we safe?"

"Well...we are."

"We're forced to come here. We can't leave – if we do, we're hunted down. And now you're saying we've been lied to?"

"Yes. But all Blessed are safe, provided they do what we want them to. Like any other person in this country."

"But you just admitted that the Blessed are taught to see themselves as less."

"Yes."

Kaylene paused, thrown by the calm certainty of the other woman. There was a certain logic to her words, but it seemed to make sense from a perspective in which the world had tilted sideways. For as long as she had known she was Blessed, she had been told that her raging emotions made her a danger to others if she could not control herself. She had never considered that she could deliberately inflict damage, or that such deliberate damage could be used to leverage power for herself.

She stared at the woman who was one of her captors, one of her tormentors. The lines age had worn across her skin cast sinister shadows across her face. But there was an earnestness to the set of Senior Blessed Maryam's face that Kaylene could not ignore. She genuinely believed what she was saying.

Kaylene could grasp only so much. Her mind sought something simple and familiar. "What does any of this have to do with me and Luka?"

"With your skill, your intellect, you can protect so many people."

"What about Catice?" Following the episode of hysterical madness in which she had killed Luka, Catice had not been seen again. It was not difficult to deduce what had happened to her.

Obvious regret settled across the other woman's face. "What would you have us do with people like Catice? Why do you think we asked Luka to assist us with Catice? Her mind was broken beyond any fixing. No mindsmith could breach that sort of madness and maintain their own sanity."

It shocked Kaylene to realise she believed all of this.

"But Callam dealt with that boy in the library," Kaylene said uncertainly.

Heat entered Senior Blessed Maryam's voice as she replied. "And it was thanks to the many-faced god that he did not lose his mind in the process."

Grief swirled in her stomach at the blame she had laid at his feet for Luka's death, even though without even knowing it, she might have lost them both. She met the woman's dark eyes, that horror rising up in her throat and leaving her feeling as though vomit would be imminent. "Why are you telling me any of this?"

"Because there is a greater purpose for you than simply chasing the dead." Senior Blessed Maryam spoke with blunt finality. "Most Blessed are simply taught their place in the world as quickly as possible and are allowed to leave. But every few years, one of the Blessed who comes to us has more awareness of what exactly our Blessings might bring – how dangerous our kind truly can be."

"And I'm that sort of person?" Kaylene made no effort to hide her scepticism.

Maryam nodded.

"And?"

"And you would become a Senior Blessed."

Kaylene tried to imagine herself as a Senior Blessed, giving dictates like Maryam, meting out disapproval and restriction to the children who came here. She found it impossible to conceive. "Why?"

"To protect everybody else from us."

Kaylene fought the impulse to break into laughter. It was only the seriousness of Maryam's expression that restrained her from doing so. "And how do the Senior Blessed protect everybody else from us?"

"We ensure that the Blessed who come to us only ever think of their place in the First Country as to help, never to lead or to control. Everything that is taught or told to the Blessed who pass through the Sanctuary is to keep them from ever entertaining the idea of hurting someone else in pursuit of self gain."

It seemed so ridiculous, this idea that all of the Blessed in the First Country were taught, without their realising it, to curtail their ambition, to limit their very selves. How could an entire group of people believe in their own subjugation? How could she believe that she deserved less?

Her incredulity must have shown on her face.

"Very little about the wars that wracked the Godskissed Continent many generations ago is certified fact. Of course, at their conclusion, the four countries were formed. Of what we do know, the wars were waged in the names of different gods, and it is largely along religious lines that the four countries formed.

"Those who were the most ardent believers were often the most famed fighters, and the destruction for which they were responsible could only have been achieved as a result of a Blessing. Nobody knows how many died, but the wars continued for generations. The Godskissed Continent was soaked in the blood of the victims. Those who established the First Country swore that they would never allow their people to be at the mercy of Blessed in such a fashion.

"The Blessed who had fought in the wars believed the prowess in maiming and injuring bestowed upon them by their Blessings gave them the right to rule the First Country. But they knew only violence as a means to lead. They fought, among themselves and with anyone who spoke against them. And because they were Blessed, they wreaked terrible destruction."

Kaylene fought the impulse to raise her eyebrows in a display of scepticism. She was sure some of what she was being told was true, but she was also certain that it had become distorted through time and creative retellings. The wars that had divided the Godskissed Continent happened so long ago that the events of history and myth melted together and were impossible to untangle.

Maryam continued, ignoring Kaylene's expression.

"The people lived in terror of those who ruled them, and upon the death of the final Blessed warrior, Blessed and unBlessed alike agreed upon what must be done to ensure no tyranny could ever be revisited on our people. The Sanctuary was established, and all Blessed were made ineligible to vote on any matters of governance."

"Wait," Kaylene interrupted. "Do you mean to say that the Blessed agreed to this?"

"They saw what monsters our kind were. They were the ones who most strongly supported these measures."

"So," Kaylene said, drawing the single syllable out as she ordered her thoughts, "for centuries, the Senior Blessed of the Sanctuary have taught other Blessed to place themselves below the unBlessed?" Anger languidly uncoiled in her stomach.

"If you wish to word it like that, I suppose you could. It is a most noble of calling to be asked to become a Senior Blessed."

Kaylene looked at Maryam in astonishment. Her impulse was to think the woman deranged, but there was too much about what she had just been told that made a perverse form of sense.

"So you want me, and Callam, and Leshan, and Merika to become Senior Blessed?"

"Merika..." Senior Blessed Maryam hesitated, choosing her words with obvious care. "Merika's hunger to extend beyond the ends of her knowledge is something all of us have noticed at various times."

Kaylene folded her arms across her chest in defiance. "Your point?"

"It has given us pause in speaking to any of you about this. Ideally..." Again, the Senior Blessed seemed to reconsider her words. "Ideally Merika would have learned to temper this voracious thirst for knowledge. Such appetites can be dangerous."

"Why tell me now, then?" Kaylene asked. "Meri's interest in learning new things is as it ever was."

"You discovered that there might be a way to return Luka to the living."

The was an air of absurdity to the Senior Blessed's earnestness as she spoke about things that – if true – upended everything Kaylene knew.

Maryam evidently misunderstood the expression on Kaylene's face. "Really, it's amazing we didn't find out sooner, the way you four talk as though nobody nearby could hear a word that you say."

"Are we going to be punished?"

The Senior Blessed shook her head. "It was our mistake to keep this from you. We should start your training right away. Obviously, without anything to actually do, the four of you were looking for something to occupy your minds. Perhaps we should have seen that you would have fixated on Luka's death."

The anger that had quietly been prowling in Kaylene's abdomen roared through her at the offhanded manner of the woman's assumption she would want to become like her – teaching other Blessed to be ashamed of what they were, to think themselves fortunate if they were permitted to leave the

Sanctuary and live a life of restrictions and restraint. Anger such as she had never known filled her. The feeling was all-encompassing. It felt as though it was trying to split her skin from the inside out. The Senior Blessed's calm expression only fuelled her rage. All the anguish Kaylene had experienced each time she'd been told she did not possess the self control to permit her departure from the Sanctuary had been for nothing. All the times she had felt she deserved to be denied a voice had been based on lies.

Kaylene's rage roared to magnificent life. Her gaze found the other woman's eyes, turned grey by the small flame, and she extended her Blessing to the very limit of her perception. The Sanctuary was built from blocks of stone, some as thick as her arm was long. But the Sanctuary was built atop earth, rich with seeds and plants.

Kaylene's rage made her Blessing strong. Stronger than it had ever been. She had always feared using her Blessing, but the heat of her rage burned that part of her to ashes. The power roared through her and she called to every single leaf, seed, and root nestled in the ground nearby. She could feel them growing in response to her command, creeping up to the walls, finding any crack and exerting the force of their pervasive growth to break the stone apart. The growl of grinding stone came from within the walls of the building. Kaylene was certain no room within the Sanctuary was spared the sound.

Senior Blessed Maryam's face flooded with confusion. That emotion was swiftly eroded by fear. The light in her hand flickered, then extinguished, as the concentration required to summon it was lost. Darkness settled over the room.

Kaylene smiled grimly to herself, tightening her own focus and calling more urgently to the green shoots. Fuelled by her anger, they grew faster and faster.

Almost imperceptibly, the Sanctuary started to shake. As the plants made their way ever more surely through the enormous structure, the quakes became undeniable. Kaylene pitched forward as her legs suddenly unlocked. Evidently the concentration of whoever had been keeping them immobile had broken.

Crashes sounded from across the Sanctuary, followed by frightened cries. A grinding roar filled Kaylene's ears and she watched with an unexpected calm as the wall of the room crumbled. Light flooded in from the torches on the wall of the corridor outside, although the illumination guttered as the wall dissolved into a cascade of stones. The cries and crashes became louder. Had Kaylene's rage not been so all-encompassing, she might have spared a moment to pity those who had not realised that the Sanctuary was crumbling around them.

FIFTEEN

"What's happening?" Senior Blessed Maryam's scream tore across the horrible moan of grinding stone.

Kaylene ignored her and clambered to her feet. The fear and confusion on the woman's face dissolved any remaining authority which clung to her. Cold satisfaction swirled within Kaylene as she realised none of the Senior Blessed would ever be able to intimidate her again.

"What are you doing?" Maryam yelled.

Revulsion at the way the woman scrabbled to her feet filled Kaylene. She put forth a call and greenery burst through the stone floor, wrapping around the woman's ankles. Maryam yelled as the plants wound around her, climbing impossibly quickly along her body. She struggled, but the trunk of a tree had wrapped around her waist.

Kaylene looked a moment longer as the woman tried to extricate herself, then she went outside to look for her friends, leaving the Senior Blessed to her fate.

The Senior Blessed who had been with Maryam was not in sight. She could only assume he had fled in terror.

The slow pulse of her anger drove every step, every movement as she made her way down the devastated corridor. Her rage fed the rampant growth of the plants. They kept at their destructive work. She was aware of the woody stems tearing through the walls of the building Kaylene had once thought in-destructible.

"Kaya!" Callam's voice came from behind a door.

"Callam!" She ran to the door. "Are you in there?"

"Yes." His voice was muffled. "I can't open the door."

"Wait." She called to the plants nearest to her and obediently, angry green tendrils surged through the stones and ripped the heavy wooden door apart. A cloud of dust rose. A familiar figure emerged, bringing a sob to her throat. He embraced her.

"Callam," she murmured, wrapping her arms around him. It felt good to be held.

Crashes resounded at the end of the corridor. As one, Kaylene and Callam looked to the noise. An enormous section of the ceiling had fallen in. More dust and dirt swirled in the air, making it nearly impossible to see more than a little way ahead.

"Cal," she began, but he cut her off.

"I know."

Of course he knew. His connection to her thoughts meant he knew everything that had been said between her and Maryam, knew she was the cause of the Sanctuary falling down around them.

"You can't pull it back, can you?" he asked.

She shook her head. Her fury was unquenchable. That was why the leaves, branches, and stems of the plants around the Sanctuary were still tearing it apart, even though she wasn't bidding them continue with any specific thought.

Callam released her. "We need to get out."

"We need to find Lesha and Meri."

"I can do that." Callam's fingers intertwined with hers as he sent his mind out in search of their friends. Then he moved, his hand still in hers as he led her along. She clung to the reassuring warmth of his skin against hers as she followed him to a shut door. The slightest thought had plants tear it apart.

Leshan peered through the swirling cloud of dust. "What's happening?"

"No time to explain. Come on." Callam had to shout above the noise of falling stone. He moved on without waiting for a reply, tugging Kaylene to follow his uncharacteristically purposeful stride.

Leshan scrambled to follow them.

"Meri's in there," Callam roared across the increasingly loud groans of the Sanctuary, pointing at a door.

Before Kaylene could do anything, the door flew out into the corridor. Callam and Leshan jumped back. Both of them grabbed her and yanked her along with them. It was good they did, for the door would have certainly collided with her, otherwise.

Merika stepped out with an eerie calm. "They got all of you, too?" she asked, her voice raised to carry across the din.

Angry yells rang out above the noise, coming from every part of the Sanctuary.

"They're looking for us." Fear filled Callam's face at whatever he had read from the thoughts of those nearby. "We need to go."

Merika grabbed Leshan's hand and led her down the corridor. Their hands still joined, Kaylene and Callam followed.

The friends fled through the Sanctuary. Chunks of stone rained down around them, sometimes missing them by the merest fraction.

Kaylene swore she heard cries of "seize them", adding to her fear.

The floor beneath their feet rippled as roots and vines snaked their way in mindless pursuit of more space into which they could unfurl. If Kaylene had been asked to describe how she envisaged the end times, this would be how it began.

As the four threaded their way through once-familiar corridors turned foreign by the gnarled, twisted foliage, gratuitous anarchy reigned supreme. It was impossible to disentangle individual words among the screams that fed the din. Because of that slow pulsing anger she could not curb, every inhabitant of the Sanctuary was suffering this terror. They would be killed as the building fell down around them.

Kaylene slowed, dragging on Callam, intending to tell him 'we should help,', but he shook his head before she spoke even the first word.

"We can't," he yelled.

"We have to try."

"The best way to help them is to get you away from here," Callam bellowed.

Even amid the anarchy of the Sanctuary's destruction, Callam's cool logic was irrefutable. She allowed him to pull her on.

"Find them!" The voice rang over the cacophony.

They broke into a run.

The restrictive clothing made running difficult – painful. Thoughts flashed through her head too fast for her to examine. All she knew was the burning fight for breath, the discomfort of her clothes, the fear that she might fall, and the feel of Callam's hand in hers as they raced through the corridors after Merika and Leshan. She gave barely any thought to the great structure that had been her home for most of her life as it tumbled down at the hands of her unchained wrath.

A tangy smell prickled her nose.

Callam's grip around her hand turned painful. "Don't think about it."

The sound of pursuing footsteps fed Kaylene's terror. The plants greedily devouring the Sanctuary surged in response to that fear.

Someone shouted, "Stop!"

Callam pulled Kaylene forward. Her legs seized up.

"No!" Merika whirled around, one hand still clutching Leshan's, the other coming up and sweeping across in front of her in a furious motion. The immobility left Kaylene's legs.

Kaylene glanced at Merika, wondering what her friend had done. Before she could turn to look, Callam pulled her onward. They drew level with Merika and Leshan.

Near blind from the growing smoke and the intermingled terror and rage, Kaylene hurtled out of the front doors. She heaved in the fresh air, her chest eased of the pain brought by breathing smoke and dust. A few steps ahead, Merika pulled Leshan toward the stables. Kaylene and Callam followed.

The doors to the stables flew open. Merika's doing. The hearat were bellowing in alarm.

"Do we have time to hitch a cart?" Merika asked Callam. She still held fast to Leshan's hand, her dirt-streaked face set with characteristic determination.

Callam nodded. "We'll have to be really fast."

Merika directed a wagon to enter the stables, almost running over the four friends. The disturbed sounds of the hearat continued, clashing with the ominous rumbling of the Sanctuary and the smell of smoke.

Kaylene looked out the door to the main building. While the charring smell grew stronger, there was no telltale yellow or orange flicker. Callam's tug on her hand made her jump. Her friends had coaxed two hearat out of their stalls and harnessed them. Merika was already directing the animals to move as Callam helped Kaylene into the wagon bed. Her arms came around his waist and his arms folded over her as the wagon sped up to a reckless pace. She wanted the comfort of his embrace, wanted to feel him against her.

The reassurance of his solidity gave her the courage to look back as they sped off. The Sanctuary was no longer a tall, imposing structure that blocked out the silken blue of the night sky. Entire walls had disappeared. The glimmer of fire sparkled through windows and gaps. As she watched, another wall fell. The ever-increasing distance made it look almost gentle.

Merika forced the hearat to sustain the dangerous pace for a long time. The darkness made it a terrifying ride, and Kaylene worried several times that the wagon would overturn as it took a corner too quickly. As the first blush of light began to appear on the horizon, Merika gave no indication she would allow the hearat to slow.

"We need to get as far away from the Sanctuary as possible," Callam said softly when she wondered why Merika seemed determined to endanger their lives.

"They're going to come looking for us, aren't they?"

He did not reply but the way his arm tightened around her was answer enough.

"We need to get new clothes, and supplies," Kaylene murmured, allowing herself to be preoccupied by immediate practicalities instead of dwelling on the enormity of what had happened, of what she had learned, and what she had done.

"We will," Callam reassured her.

She didn't know if he was offering a baseless promise or if he genuinely believed it. In truth, she didn't really want to know.

Dawn broke tenderly, creeping up on the land until full colour returned to the world. The trees bordering the road went with shocking abruptness from being a dark conglomeration to individually distinct.

Finally, it became apparent that the beasts could go on no longer. Merika guided the exhausted animals to a heavily wooded section of roadside.

The wagon scraped between two trees and came to a halt. A glance at the hearat made it clear the beasts would go no further. Without water or fodder, Kaylene felt they may have reached the end of their willingness to go anywhere ever again.

"Kaya, is there any way you can..." Merika gestured toward the road, still visible through the trees.

Kaylene called to the trees, easily coaxing a flurry of growth so branches screened them from the road. An almost casual afterthought called the slumbering berry bushes near them to wakefulness.

"If anyone's hungry," she said as she descended the cart. Her feet hit the ground, and she swayed as fatigue crashed into her. Callam's arm came around her waist, steadying her. She leaned in to him.

Wordlessly, the four slumped to the grass, Kaylene and Callam sitting slightly apart from one another, but still close enough to reach out and touch if they wanted. Kaylene thought they probably should unhitch the hearat, but the animals seemed content enough to be still, and she was too tired to put the thought into words.

Leshan pulled a fireberry from the bush closest to her and rolled it between her fingers, offering no sign that she intended to eat it.

"What happened?" Merika asked.

Kaylene looked to Callam. He gave her a tiny nod of encouragement. She swallowed. It was clear Merika would not allow her to rest without explanation, so she closed her eyes and tried to find the strength to explain. Haltingly, she began to recount what Senior Blessed Maryam had revealed to her in that tiny cell.

When she arrived at Maryam's explanation of the Sanctuary's founding, she paused. Her throat was raw. She could not remember the last time she had drunk.

"Lesha, would you mind giving Kaya a drink?" Callam asked softly.

"Oh! Kaya, I'm so sorry," Leshan said.

A tiny torrent of rain poured down in the middle of their circle. Kaylene filled her cupped hands. It tasted almost unbearably sweet as it traced along her parched tongue. Once she had drunk her fill, the others slaked their thirst, too.

Kaylene waited until Leshan concluded by diverting the rain into a puddle near the hearat so they could drink, before continuing. It did not take long for her to conclude the story with a description of the rage that had swelled inside her, and the destruction of the Sanctuary that had been caused in answer to that anger. The rush of words ended in abrupt silence as she looked at her friends' faces. Callam, who had taken the story directly from Kaylene's mind, seemed preoccupied with thought. Kaylene wished she had his Blessing so that she could have the intimate access to what passed through his mind that he had to hers. He raised his eyes to meet hers, his expression one of obvious hurt.

She blushed and moved her gaze to Merika and Leshan. Leshan's face was pale, contorted with the shock of what Kaylene had just told them. Merika was a counterpoint to Leshan's paralysed horror. Anger came off her in such intensity that the air was thick with it. Her features were almost unrecognisable, outrage transforming her into something else entirely. While it was terrifying to see her friend so altered, Kaylene felt kinship with Merika. After all, it was exactly what she had felt. Yet while her rage had brought the Sanctuary toppling down, no thing moved at the call of Merika's fury beyond the atmosphere in the clearing. Kaylene realised how dangerous her wrath had been. Any of the rooms containing Callam, Merika, or Leshan could have crumbled and any – or all — of her three friends might have been hit or even killed by a piece of falling stone. It was a sobering thought. Almost certainly, there were people back in the Sanctuary who hadn't been so lucky. Guilt twisted inside her, dark and thorny.

"I knew it," Merika hissed. Her hands were curled into fists.

Leshan put her hand on Merika's arm. The contact seemed to draw Merika out from the very core of her rage. Her features rearranged themselves back into their familiar places.

"So what happened to the Sanctuary was you?" Merika clarified, looking intently at Kaylene. The familiar curiosity had returned, pushing everything – including her fury – aside.

Kaylene nodded, then quickly dropped her gaze to the sodden grass in front of her. She couldn't describe the tempest of feelings that surged through her at what she had done. All at once, she was unrepentant at the life her anger had adopted, yet fear lurked in her very bones at what her friends' reactions would be to what she had done.

"I think one thing's clear," Leshan said after silence had endured for a stretch. "There's no going back."

SIXTEEN

If her friends felt intimidated or frightened by her after what she had done to the Sanctuary, they did not show it. The gratitude that filled Kaylene was larger than she could find words for as the sun clawed its way into a grey sky.

Kaylene finally put voice to the question she was certain lingered in the minds of her three friends. "If we can't go back to the Sanctuary, what do we do?"

Merika said, "We go on."

"They'll be looking for us – for me," Kaylene said. "Almost certainly with Enforcers."

Enforcers were the worst kind of mercenaries. Mostly they protected ships sailing in and out of the First Country. But they were more than a mere blade. If they had an equivalent, it was the Family of Assassins from the Second Country. But the Family's kiss was rarely felt in the First Country. Enforcers were engaged to locate runaways from the Sanctuary. The cold competence of the two Kaylene had seen inspired chills. If the rumours were true, Enforcers were given the authority to kill.

"Then we go where they can't get us," Merika said. "Any of us."

Kaylene was touched by the fierce loyalty in Merika's reply, but she couldn't allow her friends to flee with her. "You three could still probably go back to the Sanctuary. Tell them you ran away because you were frightened, that you don't know where I am."

"After I now know they've been lying to us? Never," Merika said.

Almost at the same time, Leshan said, "We're not going to leave you, Kaya."

Kaylene looked to Callam. He spoke too quietly for the others to hear. "You know where I stand when it comes to you."

She fought to keep her emotions from overwhelming her. Whatever their motivations for taking part in this pursuit to bring Luka back, they'd been unhesitatingly by her side. Since Luka's death, she'd only thought about herself: *her* sadness, *her* misery, *her* overwhelming anger. She'd seen glimpses of their feelings, needs, and desires, but had turned back to her own preoccupations. That they'd never once rebuked her for it, never done anything but be there for her – she did not deserve that kind of friendship. But they'd made clear that they would stand with her.

"So what do we do?" she asked.

"Can we stay in the First Country?" The determination across Leshan's delicate features couldn't quite mask her fear.

"They'd find us." The certainty Callam's comment offered settled across them like a heavy weight.

"So we'll have to leave." Kaylene tried to make it sound as though this was the logical conclusion rather than a terrifying prospect. She failed.

Merika all but exploded. "How could we possibly want to stay in this godsforsaken country, knowing what they've done?" When none of her friends said anything, she continued. "Just think of it – there's a whole world out there. The rest of the Godskissed Continent. Aren't you the least bit curious to see it?"

That hunger to see the world, to push the limits of knowledge shone through her eyes, and Kaylene recognised its spark, so similar to the one within her.

"Well, how do we get out?"

"We can't get out through the port," Merika said. "They'll expect that."

"The port's the only way out of the First Country," Kaylene pointed out. "We could never get through the barrier across the mountain pass."

"Yes we can." Merika's expression foretold whatever she was about to say was going to be radical, insane, and probably brilliant.

"What do you mean?"

Merika chewed the fingernail of her thumb in thought. Kaylene knew she was casting about for a way to explain the complicated concept in terms easy enough for the other three to understand. "Well, to do anything – to sustain anything – we need energy, yes? Boats need wind in their sales or oarsmen; fire needs wood. We need food. So for the barrier to be maintained, it has to be drawing on something."

"Right." Leshan was either following clearly or doing a good job of pretending.

"So we need to find a way to interrupt that, and what it's drawing on, or stop the supply."

Kaylene felt a tenuous half grasp of what her friend was saying. "But if you think the supply is something like the Divine Realm, we can't stop that, can we?"

"Kind of. It draws energy from being neither in one place nor the other. So if we act on the barrier in a particular way, we can open the door between realms. But that's not where we want to go, and the second we stop acting on it, the barrier will return to the way it was. But if we force something through, that might be like—" she paused, searching for an understandable analogy "—like kicking over the fire, or making yourself sick. It...collapses."

Leshan was nodding, as was Callam.

Kaylene felt stupid for not understanding fully as they both seemed to.

Merika sped up as she found a rhythm. "I think doing that will bring down the barrier completely. We could go through the mountain pass. And we'd even have Luka with us, that way."

The silence that met her words held a multitude of flavours.

Callam spoke slowly, his words measured with caution. "Didn't we need exact measurements? I assume the plans are all still back at the Sanctuary."

"Yes. But you can get them from my mind, can't you." Merika's gaze was sharp, her mouth a hard line.

If Merika was willing to allow Callam into her mind, truly they were playing for high stakes.

"Are you certain?" he asked.

She nodded. "Not now, though."

Silence rolled between the four again, filled by the hum of insects disturbed by the unseasonal appearance of the berries. Each of the four friends was occupied with their own thoughts - and Callam with Kaylene's in addition to his own.

Leshan broke the silence. She looked terrified, yet her voice was steady. "How long will it take to get to the mountain pass?"

Merika shrugged as though she were guessing, but Kaylene would have bet her friend had researched this and knew exactly. "I think a little over three weeks. If we travel quickly."

"How can we travel quickly?" Kaylene said, hearing the edge of hysteria in her voice. "Our clothes scream who we are to anyone who even glimpses us. And the Sanctuary will be able to track us."

"Mm. It would be good if we had Luka to help us with clothes." Merika's words were thoughtless yet true. Luka's ability to change the appearance of things would have been invaluable. Guilt worked through Kaylene's limbs, accompanied by the echo of the all-encompassing grief that had clouded her being for so long.

Merika continued on, too focused on the immediate necessities to be sensitive. "If we can find a village or farmhouse, Cal can get them to give us new clothes and then to forget that they saw us."

"I'm not sure I can do all of that, Meri."

"Of course you can," Merika said. "Anyway, do we have a choice?"

Callam's silence was answer enough.

They spent the rest of the day hidden in the clearing. Kaylene tried to doze, settling herself on the grass and curling underneath the blanket of dappled green light. Yet despite the fatigue that seemed to weigh down her very being, she was unable to allow sleep to claim her. Nearby, she could hear her friends shuffling around, trying to garner a little of their own repose, and the hearat as they cropped intermittently at grass nearby. She sat up at one stage in an effort to find a different, more comfortable position. She found Callam looking fixedly at her with inscrutable intensity. The complication of the way they felt for one another should have seemed inconsequential given what she had learned in the Sanctuary, or the fact that the Sanctuary almost certainly sought them. Yet if anything, the pull Kaylene felt for Callam had increased in urgency, prickling against her skin. She could see her own desire to reach and touch him mirrored in his face. Only the sound of their friends breathing and shifting in their sleep served to restrain the impulse. She turned over, trying to sleep.

As darkness fell and the friends prepared to move, the clouds bunched closer together. Then all at once, they seemed to sigh and release, rushing out across the sky to settle across it as far as the eye could see. Kaylene could taste the possibility of rain on the air. She asked Leshan to confirm her suspicion as they clambered aboard the wagon.

Her friend pursed her lips. "I can't tell. Something about the clouds feels...unusual."

"Caused by a Blessing?" Kaylene shivered with dread.

"I can't be certain," Leshan said.

But the way she pressed her lips together gave away her suspicion that it was.

The low-hanging branches that had shielded them from view obediently retreated under Kaylene's command, allowing them exit. Merika drove again. As they turned onto the road, nobody bothered to ask if she had a plan; Merika seemed so sure of the direction in which she pointed the hearat that it seemed redundant to ask where she was taking them.

She glanced across to Callam. In the half-light she could only see his pro-file and the nervous tension in the way he held himself. She could only pre-sume that it was fear that they were being hunted eating through him. The slightest tip of his head served as validation of the theory.

The rattle of the cart's wheels seemed impossibly loud in the still even-ing. Nobody spoke. Still, the clouds threatened rain. The anticipation that seemed to rise up from the landscape crept along Kaylene's skin. She turned to look at the dark blot against the land that was Leshan, sitting on the driver's seat, gazing out across the barren fields that fell on either side of the road. Truly, the sense that the Sanctuary was built at the end of the world felt more real now than ever. It made riding through the area eerie on the few occasions Kaylene had travelled through it, but at night, with the sense of some aware-ness sweeping in a blind, groping search for them, it induced a fear that was somehow far worse than the confusion and terror that had driven them on their flight from the Sanctuary the previous evening.

The minutes seemed to stretch into an infinity. Kaylene felt she would remember the night for as long as she lived: the agony of trusting Merika to have some plan to save them from their pursuers, and the fear and uncertainty of what was to come. Rain fell. It was unusually cold and crashed down in a straight line. Almost immediately, all four were soaked.

Merika spoke, her voice sharp. "Don't do anything, Lesha. If you use your Blessing to keep us dry, they'll be able to find us."

"Don't worry, I'm not foolish enough to." Her voice had a distant quality, a certain numbness to it.

They travelled on in silence. Kaylene had never been so cold or wet. Each inhale meant she breathed in water. It felt as though she was perpetually on the verge of drowning.

After what seemed like forever, light appeared in the distance. The hearat seemed to move with an agonising slowness. The last stretch was the worst.

The hearat stayed obediently in place as the four friends finally slithered down from the wagon. The squelches of their descent were almost lost in the sound of the rain.

Merika set off toward the structure with that amazing certainty. The others followed in her wake. Through the sheet of rain, a plain structure made of sun-baked bricks and timber with a thatched roof emerged.

Its simplicity had a welcoming element about it, although that might just have been the promise of warmth and shelter. The building was a world apart from the impersonal form of the Sanctuary and Kaylene gladly followed Merika as she strode inside to where a mother and daughter sat at the kitchen table, looking at the interlopers with surprise. The scene held an old familiarity to Kaylene, from the time with her family before she had known she was Blessed, before she had been sent to the Sanctuary. Although silence had claimed the women, Kaylene would have bet they'd been exchanging idle gossip, sharing trivial pieces of information about their days, other members of the family, or mere curiosities that were meaningless in the grander scheme of things but formed a tapestry of understanding woven by kin.

Instinctively, the women moved closer together. The expressions on their faces made them look identical despite the generational gap between them.

"Callam." Merika's prompt was sharp.

An instant later, the surprise was wiped from the women's faces and replaced by blankness. Then the sound of heavy footsteps announced the impending entrance of another person.

"Callam." Merika's voice was more conversational than urgent.

Kaylene felt her knees weaken with fear.

"I know." The strain of sifting through the minds of two people made Callam's tone short.

A heavyset man entered the kitchen. His gaze swept across the benches and table, skipped over his inert wife and daughter and came to rest on the four intruders. He opened his mouth, dawning outrage on his face, but halfway through the motion, his face took on the neutrality that signalled Callam had seized his mind, too.

Callam's eyes were screwed tightly shut and he was mouthing words soundlessly. His face turned pale and Kaylene tamped down the fear that he would not be able to manipulate three minds simultaneously. Then, he relaxed. The three people in whose minds he had been enmeshed suddenly began to move again. Life and sound flooded the homely kitchen.

"My dears, you must get out of the rain." The woman practically clucked at them as she rushed forward to embrace Merika.

Merika stiffened as the woman's arms were flung about her.

"They think we're old friends," Callam explained.

Kaylene raised her eyebrows. "You can change someone's memories like that?"

Discomfort flashed across his eyes. "Not for long. I'll have to make them forget us when we leave otherwise they'll remember that we were here and weren't who they thought."

"Don't feel bad."

The look he gave her was difficult to unpick. "How else should I feel? I've violated these people's minds."

She was unable to reply as the woman seized her in a warm embrace, greeting her with false familiarity that seemed disconcertingly genuine.

"Oh my little ones, you're simply soaked. You must be famished."

Kaylene didn't know how to receive such treatment. She hadn't been spoken to like that in a very long time; she had almost forgotten what it was like.

"Sit, sit," the woman enthused, gesturing to the table. "Lerren, get out the cheese and bread."

As the younger woman prepared food, the man roughly embraced them all. He mumbled something about preparing rooms for them and stumped off.

An enormous hunk of cheese was plonked on the table with half of what would have started out its life as a truly spectacular loaf of dark bread.

Lerren – the daughter – smiled shyly at them as she carved the bread into thick slices. Kaylene wondered who these people thought they were, what lives Callam had constructed for her and her friends in their minds.

The cheese crumbled onto the bread, melting the moment it touched Kaylene's tongue. She hadn't been properly aware of the hunger that had sat inside her alongside the cold, but it flared to life as she chewed. She relished the taste of the food and the sensation of it filling her empty stomach.

The woman, Mindene, directed a series of questions at them about their journey, non-existent family members, and their general health. Once she had pressed several more slices of bread and cheese on to the friends, she declared them in dire need of dry clothes. Her lips pursed as she surveyed them, her eyes narrowed in critical appraisal.

"You're all so thin," she said. "But better you wear clothes that are a little large then stay in clothes soaked through."

Before she properly understood what was happening, Kaylene was all but shoved into a little room and sternly instructed to remove her wet clothes. She peeled off even her sudden underclothes with sudden desperation to feel dry once more and took the large square of coarse cloth given to her to use as a towel. The material scratched against her skin, but it removed the water, and the way it scoured her skin felt oddly cleansing, as if she was removing what the Sanctuary had tried to impose onto her.

Someone knocked at the door. She called for them to come in, expecting it to be one of the women. She hastily pulled the cloth around herself when Callam came in, his arms full of clothes.

She met his gaze, keenly aware of the fact that she was all but naked.

A flush crept along the arch of his cheekbones and he cleared his throat. They stared at one another for a moment, immobile, then the cloth slipped and Kaylene was forced to grab it before she gave Callam another eyeful. Her movement broke the inaction that had settled between them. He hefted the clothes. "These should hopefully fit you." The roughness to his voice said he still was recovering from the sight of her.

"Ah, thank you," Kaylene said, awkwardly keeping a grasp on the material. She cast about for a way to take the clothes from him while ensuring her modesty remained intact.

He put the clothes on a nearby chair. He straightened but did not move. He had changed into the man's clothes. The ill-fitting garb made him seem at once taller and thinner. She felt as though she was looking at someone who was Callam and yet, not Callam.

He smiled as he heard the thought. "I'd say the same about you, but..." He gestured to her uncovered state. He was close enough that he grazed her arm.

His proximity made her ask what she had been afraid to the previous night. "Are you frightened of me?"

His reply was immediate and definite. "No."

"But...what I did. That anger. I destroyed so much."

"You had cause. I didn't realise you, or any of us, could have such strength in our Blessings, but that doesn't make me afraid of you."

"What does, then?"

He hesitated, but she remained silent and expectant.

"In the Hall of Mysteries you thought about killing the Senior Blessed," he said, eventually.

His words were colder than the rain. She'd almost forgotten. But now he had reminded her, she couldn't believe she might have put such a moment from her mind. The destruction she'd wrought on the Sanctuary had been in the heat of anger, beyond her control. What she'd resolved she would do if deemed necessary in the Hall of Mysteries was out of desperation, yes, but it was a decision made before the act. It was the kind of logic and thinking she'd expect of the Senior Blessed.

"I've never heard anything like it in your mind since," he added.

"But I still thought it – would have done it," she whispered.

"We're all capable of doing despicable things. It's how we treat the knowledge of that which counts."

"And how did I treat that knowledge?" Her breath caught as she awaited his answer. The spaces between her heartbeats felt like forever.

"Like you realised you'd do anything if pushed far enough."

"Does that scare you?"

She watched his mouth as he replied. "Your thoughts are so clear that sometimes I can't tell what's your thought and what's mine. It's true for you, so it's true for me. It's not scary, it just...is."

"Is that ok?"

He moved a fraction closer. "I don't know."

She stepped forward now so they were practically touching. "Do you want me out of your head?"

His answer was a whisper. "No."

He was so close. All it would require was for the flimsy barrier of cloth between them to be removed and he could place his hands on any part of her. Desire engulfed her. She looked at his lips with hunger.

Recklessness overtook her. She let the fabric fall as she reached for him. She had all but destroyed the Sanctuary in her rage the previous evening; surely she could give in to the deep-rooted want she felt for Callam, too. It seemed so inconsequential in the face of the secrets she had learned and ruination she had wreaked.

Her lips crashed against his. His hands came to fall either side of her waist. Need for him made her giddy. Her fingers came to tangle in his hair, winding around and drawing him closer. His mouth was urgent against hers. She slipped one of her hands under the loose shirt and laid it against his torso. Hair tickled her fingers, shocking and sensual at once.

The sound of heavy footsteps in the hall outside was like a blow that drove them apart.

Callam's eyes were huge and dark in his face. She did not need to be able to hear his thoughts to know how much he wanted her. He brought a hand up to caress her cheek before wordlessly leaving the room so that she could change.

SEVENTEEN

Clothes that would be comely on Mindene's curved form hung off Kaylene. She felt absurd, like a child dressed in garments made overlarge in anticipation of future growth. It was fortunate that the trousers were secured by a tie at the waist, otherwise they would have slipped off her.

She plucked doubtfully at the loose sleeves of the blouse. After a moment of consideration, she tucked the end of the billowing top into the waistband of the trousers and knotted the tie even more firmly.

She returned to the kitchen. Every step she took was a novel experience. Rather than cling to her, the material swished about. A breeze slivered up the legs of her trousers and slid around her skin. It had been so long since she had worn clothes that did not follow the form of her body. Despite the longing she had harboured to be free from the Sanctuary's restrictive clothing, the looseness of the farm girl's clothes was disorienting.

Callam and Merika were already in the kitchen. They looked strange in the borrowed clothes.

Merika held a knife. "Come here, sit down," she ordered.

Kaylene glanced at Callam, who shrugged to indicate he had no idea what their friend had planned. Her gaze fell to the knife, but she obeyed.

Merika's hands were surprisingly gentle as she gathered the mass of blonde hair hanging down Kaylene's back. Kaylene had only a brief moment to worry about what her friend was going to do before she heard the *shick-shick* of the knife sawing through her hair. Within a few moments, Merika stepped back.

Kaylene brought a hand up to her neck, which suddenly felt unbearably vulnerable. The discovery that Merika had cut off all the hair past her nape was strange. Her fingers explored the terrain of her bare skin with trepidation. She wondered how she looked with hair so short. No woman at the Sanctuary had short hair. Long hair was easy to tie back, to keep neat, and having it free of knots, and gleaming with care was taken as yet another example of self-control. Kaylene's longing for loose-fitting clothes had been so overwhelming that she had never given her hairstyle proper consideration. Yet now that Merika had so unceremoniously lopped off the weighty locks, she could not contain a smile from breaking across her face.

"How do I look?"

Merika surveyed her handiwork with a critical eye. "Different," she said, sounding satisfied.

Kaylene turned to Callam. Heat flooded through her as their eyes locked. The desire and heat of their shared moment, and of what had nearly transpired between them, still lingered underneath her skin.

"You look good, Kaya," he said, his voice quiet.

Merika evicted Kaylene from the chair and handed her the knife. She shook out her damp, dark tresses and waited expectantly.

Fighting the tremble in her fingers, Kaylene lifted her friend's hair and began to cut. Leshan came in as Kaylene was halfway through. She, too, looked almost unrecognisable in the farmer's clothes. She stopped and stared. It must have been quite a sight, one of her friends brandishing a knife at the head of the other. Then she realised what was actually happening, and she mutely waited until Kaylene had finished cutting Merika's hair before she took her place in the chair.

It was mid-morning before they were ready to leave, a freshly baked loaf of bread and an enormous wheel of cheese thrust upon them by Mindene. Her husband, the taciturn Luch, had tended to the hearat the previous evening and Kaylene had to admit that the beasts did look far more content. Although they'd only grasped a few hours of sleep, they all seemed refreshed. Perhaps the ersatz kindness of Mindene, Luch and Lerren had been an unexpected balm for their shattered nerves. Luch mumbled something about wanting to have had more time to tinker with the wagon so the ride was smoother as he saw them off. Kaylene was struck by the goodhearted nature of the man. Guilt assaulted her at the knowledge she and her friends had used these people. She understood Callam's remorse at having reached into their minds. That he would have to intrude once more to compel them to forget the travellers had ever been there inspired a queasy discomfort that refused to dissipate.

Merika took the reins but did not signal the hearat into motion. She twisted in the seat and glanced meaningfully at Callam.

Kaylene glanced at him, hoping guilt – both his and hers – wasn't affecting him too deeply. He was frowning, but not with concentration. Puzzlement clouded the blue of his eyes. Then fear replaced his confusion. He masked it quickly and leaned over the cart's side.

"Thank you so much for having us," he said warmly to the family who had all gathered to see them off.

Mindene stepped forward to place her hand atop his with that maternal warmth so alien to Kaylene. "You're such a good young man."

"Come on, let's go," Callam said, his voice clipped.

Kaylene looked questioningly. The tiny shake of his head indicated she shouldn't ask anything.

An anticipatory silence descended upon them until they were on the road.

"What happened?" Kaylene demanded when she could bear it no longer.

"I couldn't reach their minds."

"But you managed last night."

"I know." He leaned close to her. His proximity offered her a thrill as she remembered the way they had been tangled together the previous evening. "I can't hear your mind either," he said softly enough so that only she could hear.

Her eyes widened in surprise. "What?"

He nodded, then raised his voice so Merika and Leshan could hear. "It would be like if someone stuffed your ears with cloth. Everything's muffled."

Merika had a particular way of holding herself as she chewed over a problem, a slight rounding of the shoulders and tilt of her head. Despite the foreignness layered over her by the short hair and different clothes, the pose was wholly familiar, and Kaylene's worry eased as she watched her friend contemplate what Callam had just announced.

"If someone was searching for Leshan's use of her Blessing yesterday, this could be a way of trying to find you, Cal," she said eventually.

"Can a mindsmith even do whatever Cal's experiencing?" Kaylene asked.

Merika shrugged. "We don't really know what we can or can't do. None of us." She glanced back over her shoulder to emphasise her comment, the I-told-you-so pasted across her face. "How hard did you try to reach their minds, Cal?"

In the space between her question and his answer, Kaylene held onto the comfort her friend's familiar tone of argument offered.

"Quite," he said.

There was a distinct note of worry that lurked underneath Merika's characteristic brusqueness. "They likely felt you."

A chill coursed through Kaylene. "They know where we are?"

"Perhaps," Merika replied evasively. She said no more, but the pace of the hearat increased to a fast clip.

Callam stared unseeingly in front of him, eyes wide and frightened. Kaylene wanted to say something to him, but found herself unable to put into words anything that felt right. She missed that he would have heard the unarticulated sentiment, looked over and smiled with tight gratitude. Only with its absence did she realise how accustomed she had grown to the comfort of knowing she was not alone so long as he was nearby.

The landscape was indifferent to the grim mood of the four. Blue-grey crops rose up on thin stalks from the fields. A light breeze rippled across the fields and the sunlight shone in stark contrast to the omnipresent rain and gloom of the previous day.

The unexpected serenity was shattered by the sound of urgent travel. A few moments later, a closed carriage came speeding up behind them. The tension across the friends built to a feverish pitch, and Kaylene knew that the other three, like her, were readying themselves to fight. Driven by four hearat whose reins were in the hands of a fierce-looking woman, the carriage was large enough to accommodate at least three other people. Kaylene realised the pressure in her chest was from holding her breath and she forced herself to inhale as the carriage drew level with them but showed no sign of slowing, let alone stopping. As it passed, she thought she glimpsed the Sanctuary's distinct clothing on one of the occupants, but they were gone too quickly for her to properly see.

The four let out a collective breath. The new clothes and hairstyles had shielded them from notice, it seemed.

"We'll have to get a new cart." Merika sounded as confident as ever and impossibly calm.

Kaylene couldn't understand her friend's demeanour – she expected to hear the carriage coming back for them at any second.

Worry hung over her as the day wore on, yet they saw no other travellers. Again, they drove in silence, worry, fear, and preoccupation effectively isolating each of them from the other.

They arrived at a busy inn at a crossroads just after dark.

"Is it safe to stay here?" Leshan asked as Merika pulled the cart to a halt. Her voice sounded creaky from the day's disuse.

"Safe enough."

The other three had yielded control of decisions to her by unspoken consent. It was comforting to have somebody else take control.

"They'll know what we look like soon enough from the family." Callam's voice sounded strained rather than customarily soft.

"Yes, but we'd draw even more attention to ourselves if we stay in the open," Merika pointed out. "Here, we can get a new cart and new clothes."

"Meri, we don't have any money," Kaylene said.

Merika threw an amused look over her shoulder. "I'll take care of it, trust me."

And because she was tired and afraid, and she did not have the first clue as to how she could produce money or get shelter or food, Kaylene did.

This inn was very different to the genteel Sanctuary-approved institutions Kaylene had stayed at on previous journeys. The establishment was not a modest affair with private rooms that accommodated at most two or three people; the rooms housed a minimum of four. The guests were different, too. These women and men were a rough, bawdy lot who seemed to extract particular delight from making as much noise as possible.

The experience of being so unnoticed was strange. Kaylene hadn't realised just how accustomed she had become to drawing stares and of being treated with only the thinnest veneer of courtesy until she was confronted with the absence of that treatment. The gazes of the others in the room skipped over Kaylene and her friends – if they even turned to them in the first instance. To be unremarkable made her feel like she belonged, in a way she'd never been.

Merika contrived to acquire a four-person room for them – a luxury by the inn's standards. After her negotiation with the proprietor she returned to their tiny table, her face flushed with success. While the three others hunched amid the hubbub, Merika was at ease, calling to the staff to bring food, joking with the person who brought the assortment of hard cheeses, coarse bread, and fruits, and cheerfully munching on the simple food.

Kaylene gingerly bit into the cheese and bread. She revised her initial assessment of the food from "simple" to "rough". Food in the Sanctuary was plain but of high quality. Most of the ingredients were cultivated in the Sanctuary's gardens. Any other necessities were brought in twice a week by merchants. She had never considered the food there to be particularly good. The places where the Blessed were allowed to stay when they left the Sanctuary served food of a similar standard. Kaylene felt the dawning suspicion that the food to which she was accustomed was better than what most people enjoyed. That suspicion was reflected on the faces of Callam and Leshan, who were nibbling at their own food and wore near-identical expressions of poorly concealed distaste.

"You seem very comfortable here," Leshan said after she had suffered a few more delicate bites of the unpleasantly sharp cheese.

Merika shrugged, popping another piece of the tasteless, chewy bread in her mouth. "I grew up in a place like this."

Three sets of eyes came to regard her with keen interest. Merika had never spoken of her childhood, never volunteered even the smallest scrap of information about the life from which she had been plucked. She nodded with a nonchalance that seemed all too contrived.

"My parents owned an inn like this, but nearer the Kerl region." The region, known for its livestock, was almost a month's journey from the Sanctuary. "I used to sit and watch people from all over the First Country come and go. The occasional foreigner came in, too, and most knew how to wrangle free meals and ale with stories of their homelands."

Merika smiled, a rare unguarded smile, at the memory.

"Were you going to take over the inn?" Callam asked.

Merika shook her head, reaching across to take another piece of cheese. "I was going to travel to the lands I'd heard so much about. But then my Blessing was discovered." Her mouth twisted into a bitter line.

"You hid it?" Leshan was making no effort to disguise her fascination.

Merika nodded. "For years. But someone saw me use my Blessing to catch a pitcher of ale I was carrying, contents and all, and told my parents."

"Your parents didn't know?"

"I knew what would happen if they found out. They sent me to the Sanctuary to avoid any trouble."

The bitter twist to her mouth distorted her face. Resentment sat on her features. Merika did not speak of disappointments such as these, and Kaylene suspected it was because they ran so deep that if she allowed herself to dwell on them, they would consume her. She understood that feeling all too well. The multitude of intervening years had turned her family and life with them into hazy memories. But it had done nothing to render any less clear the expression of horror on her parents' faces when they had seen the cinnabon flowers blooming outside their house despite it being far out of season. The flowers could only be the work of a Blessed and from there, Kaylene's Blessing had been quickly discovered. Despite the way her family's behaviour had so immediately changed – all but her grandfather, whose wife had been Blessed – Kaylene had still missed them fiercely during the first few years at the Sanctuary. Then one day, she realised how long it had been since she had thought of any of them. Time had slipped along in its unnoticeable fashion, and her longing for the familiarity of home became replaced by a dull resentment of her family's rejection of her for something she could not control.

Habit had her looking over to gauge Callam's reaction to her thoughts. But he was looking at Merika with a total concentration that forcefully reminded her that her thoughts were only her own. Loneliness swept through her.

Merika and Leshan went up to the room first, both claiming fatigue from the day. Despite Kaylene's discomfort in the environment, the inn intrigued her and she wanted to observe it for a little longer. Callam did not volunteer a reason for staying with her, but she hoped it was because he wanted to be with her. They exchanged no words. She was still so accustomed to him being able to hear her thoughts. She couldn't stop herself from looking for his responses to what she thought rather than said. The way he watched her more carefully, as though trying to hear something she'd whispered, was a constant reminder that a distance had been imposed between them. As she thoughtlessly continued to graze at the remains of the uninspiring food, she realised that despite her disquiet at Callam being unable to hear her, there was an unexpected contentment in being lost amid the crowded room's hubbub. She felt safe in the lack of notice they had received all evening.

Abruptly, the noise reached a pitch that was too overwhelming thanks to a group breaking into song, and it forced Kaylene to retreat to their room. Callam wordlessly followed. It seemed he was slipping back into being the quiet, unassuming boy she had incorrectly assumed he was for far too long.

As she pushed the door open, she was greeted with the sight of Merika and Leshan entwined in an embrace that undulated with passion. They hadn't noticed her entrance, and for several seconds, Kaylene stood staring at them in surprise.

Callam's hand on her arm made her jump. An amused smile lit his face at the shock she assumed was scrawled across her features as he gently pulled her away and guided her through the inn.

"Did you know?" she asked once they were outside, sitting on a bench at the edge of the meadow onto which the inn backed.

He nodded.

"For how long?"

He shrugged. "Perhaps a little over a year."

"And they never told us? Why not?" Hurt coloured her voice. She could believe that Merika would keep something like this to herself, but it felt like a betrayal that Leshan had not confided in her.

"It was theirs."

Kaylene looked down at the fabric of her stolen trousers. She wished she had the insight into others that Callam did. The nuances of the heart, the complex rush of feelings, and the layered meaning of words and gestures seemed such an impossible maze in which she was so lost.

"Can you still not hear me?" she asked, her voice tiny.

It was too dark to see his expression, but she saw his nod.

"It must be a relief in some ways. You've said before how hard it is to have to hear every thought that passes through my mind."

"At times. But it's disorienting to have you near and not feel your mind, actually."

"Really?" She knew she shouldn't want to hear him say he missed the intimacy of her mind, but she did.

"Really." He had turned his head away but she could hear the smile in his voice.

"You said you couldn't tell my thoughts from yours sometimes..." She wasn't sure where the sentence was going, but knew, had he been able to hear her thoughts, he would have been able to complete it for her.

"Yes."

"It must be nice to not have to wonder."

"I like the sound of your thoughts, even if I sometimes can't tell them from mine."

"Really?"

"Really." He was silent for a moment, then words rushed out of him. "It's strange, being so alone with my thoughts. I thought I'd be able to sort out what were my ideas and what were yours and what were Luka's if I couldn't hear you. But instead, all I can think about is how much I *like* knowing what you think about the landscape, or the discomfort of the cart, or the taste of that horrible food." He paused and took a huge gasp, panic obviously overwhelming him. She put a hand on his leg, the comfort of touch the only thing she could offer.

Finally, he recovered enough to keep speaking. The anguish in his voice tore into her heart. "And I thought I could understand what I feel for you, whether it's some part of my brother's mind that I heard for so long that it became true for me, too, and whether the way your thoughts bring up those parts of him in me. But I still don't know and all I want to do is kiss you again."

His head fell to her shoulder and he began to weep. Since she had become so acutely aware of her powerlessness, the sensation of impotence had become unbearable. It bore down on her as she found no way to offer respite to this person beside her.

Gradually, his breath evened out.

Almost of its own volition, her hand reached for him. Her fingers enfolded his, and they sat in silence like that for a long time.

EIGHTEEN

Callam still could not hear others' thoughts the next day. The moment Kaylene saw how he searched her face, she knew her mind was as closed to him as his was to her. All she could offer was the lightest touch on his arm and an expression of sympathy, both of which she knew were woefully inadequate.

Their breakfast was more of the coarse dark bread from the previous evening, although it was freshly baked, which made it marginally more palatable. Gluggy porridge was also offered, but Kaylene could not bring herself to even contemplate putting such a thing in her mouth. It seemed a wholly different type of food to the porridge of the Sanctuary topped with fresh, seasonal fruit and, occasionally, cream. The four ate in silence.

When Callam and Kaylene had returned to the little room the previous evening, Merika and Leshan were both asleep on separate bundles of bedding as though nothing lay between them. No indication of the desperate passion that had suffused their embrace was evident at the breakfast table, either. Kaylene had to restrain herself from continuously glancing between the two of them in an effort to discern whether there was some furtive interaction between them she had overlooked.

Almost before she had crammed the last of her bread into her mouth, Merika stood up and crossed the room to confer with the proprietor. He was an impressively large man, although if he ate only the offerings that Kaylene had consumed during their stay, she couldn't understand how he had attained such a girth. Merika's hands waved about as she spoke with the man, the slender line of her form making her seem comically small against him. Yet while he placed his hands on his hips and frowned at various intervals, he seemed to be listening intently to everything she said. Finally, they shook hands, and Merika strode back to her three waiting friends. A satisfied smile stretched across her face.

"We have a new cart."

"He's agreed to trade the old one?" Kaylene asked.

Merika nodded. "What we'll get is smaller and less sturdy, but it's different to ours, which is more important."

"You've seen this cart?" Callam asked.

"I looked at it earlier this morning," Merika replied.

She reached across for another slice of bread, dragging her sleeve in a bowl of porridge. She swore with vicious abandon, trying to remove as much of the gelatinous mess as possible. "These sleeves are impossible."

The other three valiantly tried to maintain straight faces, but the sight of Merika so ignominiously picking the food off her clothes so soon after her smugness at making the trade was too amusing. Kaylene was the first to break into snickers, followed by Leshan and finally Callam. Merika suffered their laughter with offended dignity and pursed lips.

Kaylene found it much less funny when, a few minutes later, her own sleeve fell victim to the porridge bowl. Her curses weren't quite as imaginative as Merika's, but then, she hadn't grown up in an inn patronised by people from every corner of the First Country – and even beyond. Leshan and Callam sniggered, and Merika looked triumphant.

They left while morning was still breaking. The new cart was indeed smaller and far less sturdy than their previous wagon, but it was of a different shape, and Merika exuded confidence that it would allow them to slip underneath the search being conducted for them. Certainly, among the exodus of wagons piled high with goods and passengers, their little vehicle was an unremarkable footnote. For a while, they followed a convoy of wagons laden with diverse stock from grain to bolts of undyed cloth. The drivers and a few of the passengers seemed to loosely know one another. They made amicable conversation, shouting gossip, idle observation, and stories. It amazed Kaylene that the same kind of conversation that took place within the confined world of the Sanctuary existed in almost the same state among the free world of traders and travellers.

Kaylene might have revelled in the lingering sense of liberation were it not for the vague unease on Callam's face that signalled his Blessing was still being blocked. It was a constant reminder that the search for them was ongoing. She did not wish to contemplate what punishment was being planned for them – for her – because of her destruction of the Sanctuary and their subsequent flight.

As the morning passed, Kaylene found her anxiety subsiding into a low sense of boredom. She leaned back in the cramped confines of the rear of the cart she shared with Callam. She glanced at him and for a moment, her mind played a trick on her and she thought she was looking at Luka. She looked more closely and he was once again unmistakably Callam. But in the way he leaned back tilting his face skyward, she could see Luka. The fact that Merika's plan required them to proceed with Luka's resurrection made an anxiety entirely unrelated to the sense of being pursued writhe in the pit of her stomach. It was a luxury to be able to examine this thought knowing Callam was not privy to it. Since it had been first mentioned as part of Merika's plan, she had focused on the immediate need to find shelter and know how they would evade the Sanctuary's search. But the flight upon which they were now embarking was unexpectedly boring, and she had time for her mind to wander.

It was with a sense of curiosity that she realised she could remember Luka without the acute ache that had accompanied her recollection for so very long. Relief mingled with guilt at that knowledge.

She could remember Luka's gentle smile – so like and yet unlike Callam's – the unexpectedly wicked sense of humour, his kindness toward everyone. Her thoughts took her back along their history to secluded hours spent together, talking quietly, content with each other's presence. Nights in which they were curled into one another, so close that it seemed their dreams intertwined. She had never thought it possible that two people could ever be so intimate, such a fulfilment of one another. But she'd also never thought she would be able to walk back through those memories without feeling like a knife was being slowly pushed through her chest.

Leshan's laughter was a golden cascade of sound that danced across her thoughts. Kaylene turned to observe Leshan and Merika sitting side by side. Is she facing backwards? Now that she was looking for it, she could see the way their bodies curved toward one another. Because she was behind them she could see only the slightest part of their faces as they spoke to one other in voices so quiet that only the occasional word drifted back to her. Obligingly, Merika turned her head to say something to Leshan. A smile played about her mouth, and lines fanned down from the corner of her eyes in answer to the smile. The affection between them all but screamed itself in proclamation.

Kaylene could not understand how blind she had been to it before.

"It is very subtle," Callam commented, his voice so quiet she almost didn't catch every word.

She stared at him in incomprehension, then realised he had answered her thought. "You can hear me?"

He nodded. "It came back just now." The expression of relief that flowed across his face went some way to loosening the knot of worry within Kaylene. Even though she knew it would be folly to think that the removal of whatever had been prohibiting Callam from using his Blessing meant the search for the four friends had been concluded, the tension that had gripped Callam had been deeply unsettling to witness.

He tapped Merika on the shoulder.

She twisted around and looked down inquiringly.

"I can use my Blessing again."

"Excellent." The brusqueness to her tone seemed totally at odds with the warmth and gentle smile she had given Leshan. "We should stop in one or two hours. You can get the information about the measurements from me then."

"I can probably get it now, if you want."

Merika seemed agitated at the suggestion. "No."

Kaylene supposed she had become so accustomed to Callam knowing every thought that other people's discomfort at the idea seemed strange. Still, she thought Merika could have been less brusque.

Callam caught her eye and smiled as he settled back against the uncomfortable side of the cart. He seemed unoffended, so she contented herself by returning her attention to the passing countryside.

Merika consented for Callam to search her mind for the information about opening the doorway to the Divine Realm when they stopped to ease their aching backsides in the middle of the afternoon. The shade of the tree under which they stopped made it obvious that all four were sunburned. Kaylene hadn't put much thought to the way her skin had begun to feel uncomfortably tight over the previous hours. She had merely assumed it was the accrued discomfort of spending so long in the heat in the uncomfortable cart. After all, she'd been travelling with Merika and Callam, and hadn't suffered any ill-effects. But it was now closer to summer, and – in fairness to the Sanctuary – they'd given them hats to wear, which none of them had even thought of in their heedless flight, let alone had time to get. Gingerly, she put a hand to her nose and winced as even the slight pressure from her fingers elicited pain. The three girls quickly discovered they had it worse than Callam; the tender skin on the back of their necks that had previously been covered by hair was a shade of red that seemed to exude anger. Kaylene wished her Blessing was the capacity to heal. While most Blessed with the ability didn't have particularly strong control of it, a sunburn would have been easily manageable.

"It hurts," Merika said grumpily.

"Yet it didn't for the hours we were all burning," Leshan said.

"Yes, that's because I wasn't thinking about it," Merika retorted.

"Kaya, can you feel for nearby plants?" Callam asked.

In response to her thought of query, he rattled off the names of several plants.

"I'm not sure I know any of them." Kaylene had never found herself fascinated by plants in the way that she was by language. Her Blessing did not define her interests, nor what studies she pursued. From the corner of her eye, she saw Merika's expression of incomprehension that Kaylene could lack interest in plant lore.

Unlike Merika's, Callam's expression bore no sign of judgment. He briefly described what the plants should look like, and Kaylene sent out her senses to the surrounding soil for the plants. One seemed to fit his description, so she called it forth. He stooped to pluck it as the bush sprouted and grew before their eyes. She felt the brief anguish of its displacement, if the way plants felt things could even be called that. He snapped the stem and thick white sap oozed out.

"Come here," Callam said as he dabbed some of the sap on his finger.

She stepped closer to him and turned to present the raw skin on the back of her neck. The sudden coolness as his finger applied the salve, as much as the intimacy of his touch, made her jump.

"Better?"

Merika's question startled Kaylene from her focus of Callam's fingers still moving along her skin.

"Much," she said, mustering her thoughts away from more intimate places.

Once the immediate problem of the sunburn's pain was dealt with, Callam and Merika faced one another.

Merika's expression made clear she felt she was about to undergo a very unpleasant ordeal. "Only the figures."

He nodded. "Don't worry, I won't look at anything else. Try to clear your thoughts."

It was over in a matter of moments. Callam recited the figures he had plucked from Merika's mind, and Leshan scribbled them down on a scrap of linen paper.

"Don't worry, she'll remember everything," Callam told Leshan.

Merika's eyes sharpened. "What did you do?"

Kaylene thought the suspicion in Merika's voice not particularly fair. Callam was just trying to help. However, where she may have snapped back at Merika, Callam's reply came in an even, calm voice. "I simply fixed it in your mind – not just the measurements, but everything about what we'll need to do."

Merika fixed him with her gaze. Her eyes were angry, but she eventually nodded. "That's a good idea."

They set off almost immediately, the lunch of more unpalatable cheese and chewy bread consumed with little enjoyment. Once back on the road, they were in the full glare of the sun again. Kaylene put a worried hand to her burned face.

A cloud formed out of nowhere and hovered in front of the sun, offering respite from the burning rays.

Kaylene tapped Leshan on the shoulder. "Was that your doing?"

Her friend twisted around from the driver's seat she shared with Merika and offered her a smile. "Yes."

"Thank the many-faced god for you."

"It's not going to stop the sun completely," Leshan warned. "But it will make it less strong."

"When we stop tonight, we should see if we can get some hats," Merika added. "I forgot that none of us are outside often." A hint of bashfulness entered her voice at the admission she had overlooked something. It amused Kaylene, and in the look she still shared with Leshan, she saw that amusement reflected in her friend's dawn-coloured eyes.

The day passed with little of note except for the continuing sense that they were being sought. Despite the lifting of whatever had stopped Callam from hearing others' thoughts, the fact that it had followed the dismal rain conjured by a weather-working Blessing worried Kaylene. To fling that kind of power across such a great distance could not be achieved by one person alone. That inspired a particular kind of terror, because it meant the effort to locate the four was coordinated and unlikely to be dropped.

Callam reached across the cart to take her hand. She knew she should have pulled away but she took too much comfort in the reassurance of his touch. Their hands remained intertwined as the cart continued on.

They reached a wayside inn after darkness had fallen. This one had a resident minstrel who played through the evening in search of the appreciative coin of the inn's patrons. He wasn't without talent, and had Kaylene any coin to give, she would have handed it over.

Once more, Leshan and Merika claimed fatigue and retired early. Callam reclined in his seat as they left. "I think we should give them a while."

"Aren't they worried one of us will walk in?"

"Probably. But I'd imagine they think it's worth the risk."

"I don't understand why Meri's so unwilling to let you in her mind," Kaylene said.

Callam shrugged. "It's an intimate thing, being in someone's mind."

"I know," Kaylene said dryly.

He laughed. "Not everybody is as comfortable with it as you are. And much of the time, even you aren't that comfortable with it."

She sighed, hating that he had a point. "Gods, can you imagine two mindsmiths together? You would not be able to tell where you began and ended. That would be an entirely new level of intimacy."

"It is."

She looked at him with surprise. She hadn't known Callam had ever had any romantic encounters. Amusement twirled across his eyes as he heard her thought.

"It was a while ago. He wasn't at the Sanctuary for very long."

"What was it like, being with him?" Kaylene asked, fighting something that felt very much like jealousy.

Callam's eyes went distant as he delved into the memory. "I felt completely understood. There was no part of me that he couldn't see, but that was fine, because I knew every part of him. To know that someone else has the same petty concerns and regrets, even that they can feel the same depths of happiness and love as me...it was the most complete I've ever felt."

His words and the expression across his features made her feel as though she'd been hit. She stood in an abrupt movement. "It's too warm, I want some fresh air," she said, even as she knew he could hear her thoughts screaming a different truth.

The cool night air and the anonymity of the darkness were a relief. She unleashed her thoughts, berating herself as foolish for thinking Callam inexperienced in love. She felt stupid for thinking she and Callam shared something uniquely intimate. She had allayed her guilt over developing feelings for Luka's brother with the belief in that special bond, but it seemed that uniqueness was illusory. Did she and Callam really have something that intimate when she could not share his mind as he did hers?

Such thoughts led to ones of Luka. She no longer thought of him with the acute, desperate ache that had driven her discovery of the way to bring him back and now offered escape from the First Country. The only thing about Luka about which she was certain was that she was completely uncertain whether she wanted to see him again. Life had somehow settled without him, and she was not sure where he fitted anymore. Would he find her anywhere close to the same person she'd been, and would that be a good or bad thing? Thurien's comment danced across her mind, the movements of the thought disturbing and strange. The Kaylene who Luka had known had flowed through her existence with a certain lightness. Now, the revelations of how the Sanctuary taught Blessed to see themselves as worthy of less, and of what her Blessing-driven anger could do weighed on her.

What pressed that weight into her very bones, though, was the question of whether the Sanctuary was right, and her destruction of it had proved it. Even as she ran from pursuit, she wondered whether she should turn herself in and face what she'd done. What stayed the impulse, aside from an ironically newly awakened sense of self-preservation, was the fact that her friends were implicated, and they'd never let her take sole accountability. The sense of being buried by all these worries surely had etched new lines across her face. She was in no way someone Luka would recognise. But it didn't really matter how she felt about him. His return was necessary for their escape, and if she had harboured any doubts about the imperative for the four friends to leave the First Country, the way Leshan and Callam's Blessings had been worked against them had dispelled those uncertainties. And if they managed to resurrect him, that was a problem she would address once they were across the border of the First Country.

A particularly raucous song drifted out from the inn. It felt so discordant with the anguish that seemed to entomb Kaylene. The question of Callam returned, unresolved and painful. The expression on his face as he spoke of the completion he had found in that other mindsmith was unforgettable. Kaylene could give him all of herself but she could never see him in reply. That would leave her forever feeling inadequate, as though she was denying him something. She could not do that to him – or to herself. Regret swirled around her, tugging at her with insistent hands. But the decision had been made. At least she could be certain about something.

NINETEEN

The further inland they went, the more monotonous the food became. Kaylene had never thought she could possibly miss the food of her childhood, which had relied heavily on fish straight from the ocean. Even though she had hated the diet, its freshness now was a wistful memory.

The sense of being pursued was inescapable, yet the edge of urgency faded; the days of flight were surprisingly boring, even as Kaylene found herself relaxing into an unexpected contentment that she'd never before experienced. It was only when they entered the inns for the night that the sense of pursuit returned, banishing the sense of freedom that the travel brought. The rumours of what had transpired at the Sanctuary had outstripped them in its spread across the First Country and by the fourth evening of travel, the news of the Sanctuary's destruction was the subject of conversation across the common room.

As with all sensational stories, depending on who was doing the telling, the details varied wildly. Within the one room, people who had never met before bonded over the argument about whether the Sanctuary was a pile of rubble or if it was untouched save a fire in one of the stables. Similarly, people argued about what had befallen the seemingly infallible institution. The more mundane explanations such as an out-of-control kitchen fire were shouted down in favour of tales that involved an array of antagonists ranging from bandits to the many-faced god taking on corporeal form and turning on the Sanctuary in a fit of pique. It would have been a relief to know that the truth had been so distorted in the minds of most people were it not also very well publicised that four people – three women and one man – were being sought across the First Country for their involvement.

Once again, the inclination of people to create a tale that was most interesting offered some protection.

"They're likely just runaways," a swarthy woman declared on the fifth evening. Yet this was countered by the assertion of a farmer who claimed they were probably foreign spies who had deliberately sabotaged the Sanctuary.

The four friends listened to all of this mutely, trying to be as inconspicuous as possible.

On the seventh night, Merika suggested Kaylene should dress as a boy, whispering, as the debate about their motives raged on about them.

Kaylene gave her friend a look of surprise. "Why?"

"They're looking for three women and one man."

"I understood that. But why me?"

"You're the least endowed of us."

Merika's matter-of-fact delivery had Callam spraying the mouthful of ale he'd just taken all over the table. His performance earned him a round of applause from those in the room who noticed.

"Thanks," Kaylene said dryly.

"You're still pretty," Leshan said with an earnestness that managed to make Merika's declaration even worse.

Yet Merika was correct, and when taken with the sunburn that had turned into a tan thanks to the salving plants Kaylene procured at Callam's direction, it certainly meant they no longer fitted the descriptions of them.

They skirted the edge of the skyfire district. The blooms were long gone; the two weeks across which they had graced the countryside were only a memory. Their route took them along fields where the lysellum plants were being harvested. Kaylene watched from the back of the cart as workers cut the long stems. As far as she knew, the drug forget-me-not, which was made from the lysellum, was not used very widely in the First Country. Yet there was a near-insatiable demand for it in the Fourth Country. She wondered what would drive someone to lose themselves in the oblivion of any drug. She liked her mind the way it was. Anything from which she may be seeking escape would still be there once her mind was returned from its altered state.

On the eighth day, they departed the skyfire district. The inn at which they stopped was particularly weathered, despite the low standards set by the previous ones. Now they were truly entering the less auspicious areas of the First Country, where practicalities took precedence over aesthetics or comfort.

The food that evening was especially offensive. Kaylene ate the distasteful stew, wondering whether there was some sort of agreement among innkeepers to serve the least palatable food possible. She supposed she shouldn't be so ungrateful. The food at least was nourishing. She hoped. At very least, it was sustaining.

Late in the evening, Kaylene woke suddenly. For one moment she thought she had been woken by some instinct of danger, but she realised it was simply the incessant demand from the large quantity of ale she had drunk in an effort to wash down her dinner. She slipped out of the room in which Callam, Leshan, and Merika still slumbered and padded down the stairs of the silent inn. She made her way to the privy out the back – all inns seemed to share a similar layout as well as poor culinary offerings. On her way back along the corridor that passed by the common room, the low sound of conversation arrested her. It was so out of place amid the blanket of sleep that otherwise covered the building that the inbuilt human impulse to snoop had her listening.

"...certain it's three women and a man?" one voice was saying. It sounded like the innkeeper, a painfully thin man who had the air of one who would brook no dispute under his roof. "We've two parties of four tonight, but one's all men, the other's two men two women."

"I'm certain that the Sanctuary seeks three women and one man." The voice that replied was silken. Kaylene had no doubt that the woman to whom it belonged was competent and ruthless. She took a step back and flattened herself against the wall.

The innkeeper replied, but his voice was too low for Kaylene to hear any more than an indistinct murmur.

"Well, if they come in, use this parchment to inform me," the cool voice instructed. Every syllable reached Kaylene's ears without any impediment. If someone had the proper Blessing, they could command a single sheet of parchment cut in two to mirror the writing placed on one of the halves. The parchment halves fetched an exorbitant price, as they were outrageously useful for communication across large distances both quickly and reliably.

Kaylene heard the innkeeper's tone of query even if she couldn't make out the exact words. She did, however, hear the response.

"The Sanctuary's Blessings are many." There was a ripple of impatience in the smooth voice.

The scrape of chairs spoke to the finality of the conference. Footsteps made the floor underneath Kaylene's feet vibrate. Fortunately, they were heading away from her, toward the inn's main door.

"My pardon for waking you so late," the smooth voice said.

"No matter. I don't need much sleep most nights, anyway." The innkeeper's voice, now audible, carried relief mingled with obsequiousness.

As the creak of the door opening resounded through the otherwise empty lower floor, Kaylene crept up the stairs, shaking so hard she could barely open the door to their room. She woke the others and in a trembling whisper told them what she had overheard. In the darkness, she could see only the shape of her friends, but she knew them so well that their postures told her what they were feeling. Merika was lost in thought, Leshan was caught somewhere between fear and worry, and Callam was reaching out to see if he could sense the mind of whoever had been asking the innkeeper about them.

He was the first to stir, shaking his head slightly to let Kaylene know he was unable to find the woman with the smooth voice.

"The innkeeper?" she asked softly.

"I'm too far to hear anything clear." Then he stiffened. "Wait. He's afraid. She wasn't from the Sanctuary."

Merika's question was sharp. "What?"

"I can't hear anything more than that."

"But you're certain she wasn't from the Sanctuary," Merika said.

"Yes."

She hissed through her teeth. "I think it was an Enforcer."

After the attempts to locate them via Callam and Leshan's Blessings, there had been no signs of pursuit. Kaylene hadn't relaxed, exactly, but the monotony of the days had taken the edge off the sense of omnipresent danger. That an Enforcer was so close was an unwelcome reminder of just what they faced.

"What do we do?" Leshan asked.

"Keep going," Merika replied.

Dawn set the sky aflame. The four friends were already well on the road by the time the sun graced the land with its glow. They had spent a few more hours attempting to sleep then left as soon as the sound of others stirring began to spread through the inn. Although it was still summer, as they ascended toward the mountain pass the air grew cold – especially without the warmth of the sun. Kaylene shivered as an otherwise gentle breeze swished across the land.

Merika assured them that if they maintained a fast pace, they would be able to reach the pass within a few days. The appearance of the Enforcer had worried Merika more than she let on. It was obvious in the hard pace she set and the tension that had settled across her shoulders. Even the low conversation between Merika and Leshan had lost its playful tone. That Merika was worried struck true fear into Kaylene. Merika wasn't afraid of anything. If she was, it meant they were at very real risk of being found.

The next days of travel were hard. They were in the cart with virtually no break. Adding to the discomfort was the fact that, since the night Callam had told Kaylene about his past relationship, she tried to keep away from him. It was so hard to not try to catch his eye as a humorous thought occurred to her or look to see if he agreed with some observation. Of course, he respected that decision with his customary courtesy and she hadn't even needed to endure a painful conversation with him. In some ways, that hurt, too, knowing he wasn't fighting to change her mind. Perhaps her realisation was one at which he had arrived some time ago. The fact that she had no way of knowing this without asking him aloud, while he could simply pluck it from her mind, made her all the more resolute. She wondered how she could interact with him when he could hear the regret and desire that filled her every time she looked at him. It made their conversation awkward, when it did take place. Fortunately, Merika and Leshan seemed too wrapped up in their own worry – and their own conversation – to notice, especially as they were at the driver's seat, not looking back to their friends sitting behind in awkward silence.

Kaylene could not help but resent her friends for failing to see their discomfort, even as she knew it was petty of her, given the scope of their other worries. But across the next three days of travel, she could not dispel that little resentment. It was only as she looked at Leshan, the person she'd rushed to tell when she and Luka had first kissed, the person who'd shared her exuberance as the relationship developed, the person who'd stayed by her side in the days when grief had claimed her completely, that she realised she had no idea what to say to her at all. So much had happened – the revelations about the Sanctuary and Kaylene's destruction of it, and her discovery of Leshan and

Merika's relationship, had placed distance between them that Kaylene was unable to broach. If Leshan kept something as significant as a relationship from her, perhaps she also kept how she truly felt about the Sanctuary's lies and Kaylene's reaction to it.

Perhaps she also kept from Kaylene the true motivation for going along with the mad quest to bring Luka back. After all, Leshan wasn't one to break rules – she of them all had imbibed most fully how the Sanctuary wanted them to see themselves.

"Sore?" her friend asked as Kaylene rolled her neck out during a brief comfort stop to rest the hearat.

"Everywhere," Kaylene admitted. "You?"

Leshan put a hand to her own neck. "Same. The driver's bench is precarious to lean back against, and I'm constantly worried I'll fall off, given the way Meri drives."

Kaylene laughed, some of the awkwardness and darker thoughts she'd been harbouring sliding away at the familiarity of her friend's wry humour. "She's not really focusing on comfort, is she?"

Leshan's smile lit her eyes like sunrise. "I see where she steers. Sometimes it's like she drives toward every rut and hole in the road."

It felt good to laugh like this with Leshan. The sense of distance that had only a moment ago seemed unfathomable contracted. But still Kaylene wondered why her friend kept her relationship with Merika secret, almost as much as she wondered at her own blindness for failing to see it. Leshan glowed at the mention of Merika, smiled irrepressibly whenever she was around. This was more than mere infatuation; it was love. And just like that, Kaylene understood why her friend had acted so entirely against her nature all this time.

Over dinner that night, Merika announced she had accepted the offer to transport sacks of spice to a roadhouse a day's ride away, claiming that it made their story different to the description of four travellers.

"I've told a different story about us at every place we've stopped," she said casually as they ate their dinner – another unpalatable dish. "People are more likely to remember us by what we claim we're doing rather than our appearance."

Kaylene wondered how much of this sneakiness Merika had picked up from her time in her parents' inn. Her friend's thirst for knowledge certainly seemed to be useful in keeping them away from notice. Of them all, Merika had always been the quickest with lies to explain away any behaviour that might have earned a reprimand from the Senior Blessed. It was a talent Kaylene had never really thought would be put to such use.

The spice sacks squashed Kaylene and Callam together. The spent the first few hours of the ride trying to remain as separate as possible, but it was exhausting. She relaxed as the hours wore on and her body gradually turned to face him. It was a shock to realise that her thoughts were more preoccupied with Callam than his brother, but, while guilt threaded through her, the horrible misery that had seemed to characterise life in the Sanctuary had disappeared, and for that, she was grateful.

The next day, the friends passed the open salt mine, which was one of the First Country's most famous human-made wonders. Comprised of shallow pools cut into the side of a mountain, the mine was the source of one of the First Country's most in-demand exports. Streams trickled along tiny gullies that connected the enormous network of pools.

Kaylene watched people moving along the tracks between the pools, their tiny size the only indication of how vast the entire thing was and how far it crawled up the mountainside.

It was a truly magnificent sight, and for a moment the fear of pursuit slipped away as she took in the spectacle.

There was something unexpectedly timeless about the mine. Nobody quite knew when it had been built, or who had built it, but its place in the First Country's commerce and history was taught to every child. It was another sight Kaylene thought she would never see in person. The sunlight glinted off the pools, turning the water in them to fiery golden mirrors. The tang of the minerals and salt collected in the open air, which was reminiscent of Curnith, but without the sea breeze, the scent hung heavily in the air.

Merika cheerfully explained how the pools, once filled, were blocked so that the water dried, leaving only the salt behind. Once the salt was collected, the block was removed so that the pool could fill once more.

"Why do you know this?" Callam asked.

"It's interesting," she replied offhandedly.

"And I told you about it," Leshan added with a laugh.

"Well, yes," Merika conceded, warmth to rival the sun in her tone.

Leshan's area of study was history; she'd occasionally told them snippets of information about the regions and towns through which they passed.

Kaylene shielded her eyes against the sun's glare as she regarded the terraced rows of shallow pools. She couldn't fathom how clever the person who came up with the mine must have been. Her eyes slid across to Merika who was explaining the intricacies of the salt mine to Leshan, who was either an interested audience or doing a good job of impersonating one. Beside her, Callam shook with silent mirth as he heard the thought.

It took them a good two hours to pass the mine. Kaylene drank in the sight, wondering if she would ever again see something so spectacular. The warmth of the sun was captured by the mountainside, inciting a certain drowsiness.

"How long will it take to travel through the pass to the Third Country, once we've taken down the barrier?" Kaylene asked Merika in the early afternoon as they left the last of the pools behind.

"I don't know."

"But you know everything," she said.

The comment earned her an amused glance from Callam.

"Thank you for your faith in me, but I really don't know how I'm supposed to know how long it takes to cross a pass that nobody has been able to traverse for centuries," Merika called back over her shoulder.

"Surely there's some old text that makes some reference to it," Kaylene persisted.

"If it makes you feel better, I did try to find information on the length of the pass, but there's not even a hint in any of the texts I read. I know how we can bring the barrier down, but I don't know much about how it was made or what really keeps it up. It's infuriating, really. Not even a hint...not one book, scroll, or manuscript mentions such things."

"Surely Meri's allowed to have one thing that she doesn't know," Callam said, his eyes teasing as he looked at Kaylene.

She smiled back at him. It felt as though a hand squeezed her heart.

Her feelings for him had not disappeared. If anything, she was more uncomfortably aware of them than ever.

Yet, Kaylene found herself able to forget the bitter depths of her sorrow and fear for a while as she thought of the gleaming salt pools. The enormous sight made her problems feel so small that they were ultimately inconsequential. The mine would exist long after she died, as it had existed long before her birth. In the face of that kind of knowledge, her feelings seemed distant and unimportant. It was a curious sort of comfort.

The calm gifted by the magnificence of the salt mine stayed with them as darkness fell and they reached the inn. Merika, as usual, did the talking as the others heaved the sacks of spice to the appreciative innkeeper. As her hands screamed in protest at the heavy, coarse sack, Kaylene wished Merika could use her Blessing to move them.

Discussion across the evening was limited as a players' troupe staying in the inn had started a bawdy performance of *Ronan the Red-faced*, a comedic play beloved by much of the First Country,

The four settled down to watch the play and were swiftly carried away by the farcical lunacy of the plot. Kaylene glanced over at the innkeeper and saw the woman regarding her with a speculative expression.

Callam, from his seat behind her, put his hand on her shoulder. His lips near her ear, he whispered, "I'll read her." That he took her observation so seriously brought back the sense of fear and pursuit that had been banished by the sight of the salt mine. It took all of her focus to keep her eyes on the players as one of them delivered a monologue containing several filthy double entendres. The audience was in fits of laughter, but Kaylene could only feel the pressure of imminent danger. How the innkeeper might have identified them, she did not know, but as Callam searched delicately through the woman's mind, she became ever more certain that her suspicion was correct. Callam's hand tightening on her shoulder confirmed what she already knew. She could hear the urgency in his voice as he leaned across to Merika and said at a volume just loud enough to carry across to their friend, "We have to leave. Now."

TWENTY

In the dark, the rattle of the cart on the road was unforgivably loud. It seemed to fill the vastness of the night, announcing their location to everybody nearby. They had left with the crowd once the players had finished their performance. Callam confirmed that the innkeeper had sent a message to an Enforcer through the same kind of parchment Kaylene had seen a few evenings previously. The innkeeper did not know how far away the Enforcer was, but none of them wished to find out.

"How far until the pass?" Leshan's question made Kaylene jump.

"At this pace, midmorning. Maybe early afternoon." Merika sounded terse, but not as worried as Kaylene felt.

"Do you think we'll make it?" Leshan asked.

"I think we will," Kaylene said.

Callam gave a hum of agreement, though it was hard to read his expression in the dark, with only the tilt of his head as a guide.

"But once we bring down the barrier, then what?" The smallness of Leshan's voice screamed out her fear.

"Then we'll cross the pass." The strength in Kaylene's voice surprised her, but her friend's uncertainty called forth her own determination.

"How will we survive?"

Merika answered without turning her attention from the road. "You can ensure we have enough water to drink, Kaya can get food for us. Then we'll go into the Third Country, and we can find a place there."

"Won't the Enforcers follow us to the Third Country?"

Even in the dark, Kaylene could clearly picture the way Leshan's face was creased with concern.

Merika's sigh was like a rush of wind. "They might. But Lesha, there are four of us – five if you count Luka. Between us, we can fend off the Enforcers."

Leshan's silence indicated that she was yet to be fully convinced that they would be safe.

Kaylene bit her lip. Leshan had finally said what they'd all chosen to ignore: the tenuousness of their plan. In the way she'd refused to consider anything beyond what it would take to bring Luka back, she'd somehow thought that bringing down the barrier and stepping into the Third Country would make their pursuers vanish. She shook her head at her foolishness, wondering why she continued to fall into this way of thinking.

Callam leaned across the tray of the cart. His voice was so soft that only she could hear it. "Do we have any other choice than to continue?"

His words drew her raging thoughts to a halt. In the end, it didn't really matter how she felt or what worries were harboured in her heart. This was the path on which they had been inextricably set since she had destroyed the Sanctuary. Whatever happened was inevitably going to unfold.

A golden dawn broke across the sky. Beams of light ran across the earth, turning grey to yellow-gold. The little cart was being laboriously drawn across grass rather than a road and had been for some time. They almost missed the point where the needed to leave the road. It was only indicated by a small marker which made mention of the barrier nearby, but that was all – there was no point in building a road, or drawing attention to, what was effectively a wall, especially when the First Country's government didn't want to encourage its citizens to cultivate any interest in the world beyond its borders. The wheels were coping poorly with the soft earth rather than the packed dirt of the road. It was fortunate there had been no recent rain, or the hearat would have struggled to pull the cart anywhere.

Hours passed. The sun rose, bathing the land in hot rays. Kaylene pulled her hat across to shade her face, fearing another uncomfortable sunburn. She was hungry; there'd been no thought to ensuring they had food with them as they fled the inn, and even if they had, there was no guarantee they could have gotten anything without arousing even more suspicion, or even an attempt to seize them. They all were, but it was clear Merika would not allow them to stop even for a moment.

Suddenly, Merika jerked in the driver's seat. "Can you feel it?"

Kaylene shared a glance with Callam. He shook his head. But a few moments later she could feel something out of kilter with the world. It was far off, more a tickle in the mind, but she was certain it was the barrier.

"I can feel something now," Leshan said.

"What does it feel like to you?" Merika asked, customary zeal for information infecting her voice.

"As though the air around it – the weather — around it is being disrupted." Leshan's voice contained awe and confusion. "I've never felt anything like it."

"It's like that with the ground," Kaylene said.

"What about you, Cal?" Merika asked.

"It's like there are so many thoughts tightly packed together that I can't separate one from the other. So many thoughts that it sounds like there are no thoughts," he replied after a moment.

"Interesting," Merika said. "Whoever placed the barrier must have been brilliant." She received no reply.

As they forged on, Kaylene's sense of disruption intensified, as if the plants around them were being pulled into frantic growth and yet somehow kept in order. Her stomach began to churn in a way unrelated to hunger.

Eventually, Merika pulled the carriage to a halt. As she descended from the carriage, Kaylene's backside made a vociferous protest at the effect of the hours of sitting rigid in fear.

The three followed Merika as she strode across the summer-yellowed grass, her hands stretched out in front of her. She would have looked comical but for the determined set to her face. After a few steps she paused, her hands apparently meeting an obstruction. "All right, this is it." She picked up a stick from the ground and began to draw an oblong-shaped space. The stick's point carved a thin but deliberate scar in the ground, turning the yellow-green to sharp brown. "Good idea to fix the measurements in my mind, Cal," she added, in a rare acknowledgment that she had been wrong.

"So how will this exactly work?" Callam asked, ignoring the compliment.

Merika paused. "Whoever made the barrier needed to find a way to keep it in place. Any Blessing that makes some impact on the world has a limit, but the barrier across the pass has been in place for generations. We think that's because it's drawing on the power of the Divine Realm somehow, almost like it exists in the two worlds."

"'We?'" Kaylene interrupted.

Something like guilt flashed across Merika's face, highlighted by the morning light.

"What do you mean 'we', Meri?" Callam's voice was sharp. He'd either noticed the expression on their friend's face or heard the concern in Kaylene's mind.

Merika looked down, her lips pursed. Kaylene knew that face. It was the face Merika made when she was about to confess something she knew was not going to be well received. This was the only time when Merika chose her words with care, knowing that she would need the most precise of phrasing to evade ire.

"Meri," Leshan murmured.

Merika's words came out in a rush. "I spoke with Ay'ash. There wasn't enough information on what we needed to do, so I went to find her."

Cold prickled across Kaylene's skin. The Old One's manner had been most discomforting. Kaylene had been glad she would never need to see the woman again once Thurien had translated the scroll. He, too, had left Kaylene feeling uneasy. They had seemed too delighted with the torrent of anguish that had taken root inside her.

"You went to the Old One?" Callam's voice was uncharacteristically pointed.

Merika lifted her chin defiantly. "I told you, I needed help. If you suspect me of something else, go searching in my head. You'll find I'm telling the truth."

Merika's offer was a bluff and they all knew it. If Callam accepted her proposal, he would be saying better than any words could that he did not trust her. It was not something he could do without shattering their friendship.

Leshan placed a hand on Merika's arm. "He's not saying he suspects you of anything."

"Why didn't you tell us you'd been to visit the Old One?" Callam asked. The sharpness had left his voice, but his usual gentle tone had yet to return.

"I was embarrassed. I didn't want to admit I couldn't do this without help." Contrition and defiance alternated on Merika's features as she faced them.

Merika did not apologise, nor was she at all self-conscious. That she admitted her weakness to the three now, even under the duress of their scrutiny, made Kaylene uncomfortable. She saw that discomfort shared in Callam and Leshan's expressions.

Leshan cleared her throat and the moment passed. Merika straightened. The stick with which she was measuring resumed its work.

"I think I'm best able to act on the barrier," she said as she worked, her eyes fixed on the ground, safely away from the scrutiny of her friends.

"Good thing we have your Blessing," Callam said, his tone conciliatory.

"Oh, any of us could do it, really," Merika replied, still looking down. "Whoever's opening the divide must feel the presence of the barrier and literally open it however their Blessing would allow them to do so. Kaya could try to pry it open with a plant; I imagine Lesha would strike it open with a lightning bolt. You, Cal, you'd think it open. Perhaps it might be a little easier for me given I can just open it like a door."

"I'm very happy to let you do it." It was clear Callam was offering peace.

Merika glanced up, her smile as thin as a blade of grass. "Kaya, remember I need you to actually bring Luka back."

"We definitely need to bring Luka back to take down the barrier?" Kaylene asked.

Merika raised an eyebrow, but did not offer any comment on the question. "Yes. I mean, I suppose we could bring anything across from the Divine Realm, but it's best if we know what we're bringing across. That's what will disrupt everything in a way that brings the barrier down"

Kaylene nodded.

"You need to focus on Luka as you remember him," Merika instructed. "After that, all you need to do is use your Blessing to build a shell for him from the earth."

"What?" Kaylene yelped.

Merika nodded, seemingly unconcerned by the precision she'd requested.

"How?"

Kaylene's question earned her a look that was tinged with scorn. She supposed it should have occurred to her to ask about this earlier. It was her own fault that she was being blindsided by this now. "You can grow anything, Kaya. Grow Luka's body and when we bring him back, it will change from plants into flesh. And if it doesn't, he can change himself with his Blessing."

"You do know what you're doing, don't you?" Callam asked.

Merika raised her chin in that defiant gesture once more. "Of course I do. I had to be creative with a few elements, but I know this will work."

"This is my brother you're talking about growing from nothing more than grass seeds." Anger burned in Callam's words.

Merika's voice lifted into a scream. "Trust me, don't trust me, it doesn't matter anymore!" Colour burned in her cheeks and her eyes blazed. "We're being pursued by the Sanctuary and its hired thugs, our life there was a lie. Either you go back to them and whatever they've got planned for you, or we leave this godsforsaken country now."

Merika stilled. She was prone to snapping, to outbursts of quick temper, but this uncontrolled flash of pure rage was something none of them had ever seen in her. She took a deep breath, then the controlled, sharp-witted Merika was back in front of them as though she had never lost control of herself.

"Are we ready?"

She received mute nods in reply.

"Good." Merika returned to double-checking her measurements as a brittle silence stretched between the four friends.

Kaylene allowed herself to be steered to a spot right next to the barrier. The sensation of something she couldn't see pressing against her was an uncomfortable one. She could feel each heartbeat thudding against her chest, as though it was trying to escape the confines of her flesh. The inside of her mouth suddenly felt dry.

"I'm starting now," Merika said. Her eyes sparkled with excitement. She appeared to have forgotten her outburst and the awkwardness it had wrought.

Kaylene couldn't understand how her friend could be thrilled by what they were doing. It was terrifying. They were trying to bring down a centuries-old barrier, retrieve someone who had died almost a year previously, and evade people who, it was a fair bet, were not overly interested in preserving their good health.

She tried to swallow but her tongue felt overlarge and her throat was constricted so tightly that the movement was painful. She closed her eyes and tried to bring a picture of Luka into her mind. But she couldn't remember exactly what he looked like. True, she could envisage him mid-laugh, and she was able to picture the way his eyes crinkled when he was amused but didn't want to show it, but she couldn't quite remember how much taller than her he was, or what his hands looked like, or whether his shoulders were actually broad or not. Panic unrelated to the task at hand filled her. Was this what it truly meant to die? To become slowly and unnoticeably erased from the minds of those left behind? Was that the fate that awaited them all, if they were unable to get into the Third Country – or even if they succeeded?

A hand on her shoulder had her looking up into Callam's eyes – those eyes that were like his brother's but not. "Can I help?" He was asking her permission.

She didn't need to nod; he heard her think the assent.

His hand tightened briefly as he skimmed through her mind. Kaylene knew Callam's work was done as an image of Luka came to her mind so clear that it was as though he was standing in front of her.

Really, Kaylene had no idea how she was supposed to complete the task that Merika had set out for her. She had never crafted something as complex as a person's body from plants. She suspected it was why Merika had only told her about this part at the last moment – because she knew Kaylene would have proclaimed herself unable to do it. She inwardly cursed Merika for keeping this to herself. Yet the urgency of their task seemed to fill the air itself, so she pushed aside her doubts and focused. She called upon the grasses and tiny wildflowers that grew inside the shape Merika had drawn on the ground. They eagerly reached upward in reply. Drawing on the memory of Luka, she offered it to the plants as the shape they should become. Tiny blades of grass twined together, slowly thickening, creating something that could be mistaken for the form of a person. Certainty eclipsed the nerves and fear that had threatened to dominate her. At her command, flowers had bloomed in singular profusion. Her rage had roused vines and grasses to tear down the Sanctuary. Now, love fuelled the creation of a person from nothing more than her memory and the plants surrounding her – and the love of a brother who had helped her remember. She understood how Merika could become so excited about pushing the limits of her knowledge and ability. This was truly phenomenal – a feat straight from legend.

"Good, Kaya," Merika said.

Kaylene dared not look away from her task but she could hear the strain in Merika's voice as she used her own Blessing on the barrier.

The form was taking on the appearance of a solid entity when Callam gave a soft cry of alarm. Still Kaylene didn't look up, her focus intent. The effort and strength it required was enormous. Then Callam spoke, and his words were like hooks grabbing her attention. "Enforcers are nearby. They're following our tracks. We only have one or two minutes at most before they get here."

TWENTY ONE

"Don't stop!" Merika barked the command before Kaylene even had time to react.

The order had the opposite effect to its intention. Kaylene immediately raised her head to look back the way they had come.

"Lesha, Cal!" Urgency lashed across the three syllables from Merika.

Callam's hand landed on Kaylene's shoulder once more. He spoke quickly in her ear. "Merika's using all of herself to force open the divide between our world and the Divine Realm. We have to bring Luka back as quickly as possible otherwise she's likely to lose herself in the process."

Kaylene focused her attention back to the form she was creating. It looked nothing like Luka. There was much work to be done before it was a proper simulacrum of a human being.

"Lesha, are you able to handle whoever comes?" Callam's voice was so calm.

Kaylene glanced up, saw Leshan nod, her friend's face tight with some combination of fear and determination. Briefly, Kaylene wondered how the sweet, gentle Leshan, who had always striven to avoid confrontation, felt about going to keep the Enforcers at bay. But like Kaylene's feelings for Luka, Leshan's feelings were ultimately irrelevant. They had come too far to look back.

"Luka," Callam said, to bring Kaylene's distracted thoughts back to heel.

The pressure of his hand on her shoulder vanished. Her eyes flicked back up to watch him walking over to Merika.

"You need my help."

"No I don't." Merika's snarl was a contrast to his measured tone.

"Meri, I can feel you coming apart at the edges. This is too much for one person to do. Either you let me help or we all fail."

"I can do this alone!" Merika's voice raised to a shriek to be heard over the wind that had suddenly leapt up, signalling that Leshan was already at work against the Enforcers.

"I'm helping whether you like it or not. Lesha will only buy us so much time." Callam's voice was so forceful.

Merika did not reply, which spoke volumes to the nature of her assent.

The wind increased in strength. It picked up tendrils of Kaylene's hair and whipped them around her head. She ignored the distraction, focusing all her attention on the mental image of Luka that Callam had set in her mind. Even with his help, she had to focus with more effort and precision than she'd ever needed to when using her Blessing. Now was the part that required true finesse — the delicate sculpting of detail. The plants at Kaylene's call seemed to move with agonising slowness. Somewhere in the near distance a clap of thunder sounded – Leshan's doing. She pushed aside worry about what was transpiring between Leshan and the Enforcers and concentrated on directing a tiny creeper vine as it formed the arch of Luka's cheekbones.

The precise detail of the task was more than anything Kaylene ever envisaged she could accomplish. It was incredible. Despite the sudden fall in temperature, sweat trickled along her skin.

Another clap of thunder cracked across the land, this time in hot pursuit of a flicker of lightning. Kaylene ignored it, her attention locked on the formation of Luka's mouth, the way his bottom lip curved up then swept down into the cleft of his chin. Now what was in front of her was not simply a human-like form, but a living sculpture that, startlingly, resembled Luka.

"Are you ready, Kaya?" Callam yelled. The strain of whatever he and Merika were doing to pry open the divide between realms was heavy in his voice.

"Nearly." She threw the word out, her attention still intent on the formation of the detailed, delicate body before her. It truly felt as though she was creating life. Exhilaration raced along her as she realised that they may actually succeed in doing something god-like.

The wind sounded as though it held tormented voices. Flickers of lightning heralded the arrival of thunderclaps that seemed to shake the sky itself. The near-continuous thunder was disquietingly similar to the sound of the Sanctuary as Kaylene's rage had torn it apart. Yet as the thoughts entered her mind, she thrust them aside. The intensity of her concentration, the exertion of her will upon the plants, was starting to wear her down. A headache was building in the back of her skull. It constricted her head in time with the thunderclaps.

The body was nearly complete. Kaylene added tiny details her memory provided: a ridge of grass across the back of his hand for a scar Luka had acquired from a sharp rock, the oblong shape of his fingernails. A wave of tiny leaves crested across his forehead in the way Luka's hair fell when he hadn't transformed it. They were the tiny things noticed by nobody other than someone who knew him with a profound intimacy. Someone who loved him.

She cajoled and bullied the plants through the final details, instructing them to weave together in a surface that was nothing like skin, but was at least something that Luka could transform into flesh. It was exhausting. Nothing she had ever done required plants to work with such intricacy, to meld together where they otherwise would not. This was where the true force of Kaylene's will needed to be exerted: to push the shrubs, weeds, flowers and grasses to go where they naturally shirked – close to one another, bending back in on themselves, and to ensure they stayed there once she relinquished the pressure of her command.

Time could have galloped past or barely moved at all. Only when she finally released the grasp on her Blessing did she notice that days had not passed, that night had not taken over the land, but perhaps only a few minutes had elapsed while she had constructed the form into which Luka would go.

Exhausted, Kaylene sat back next to the intricate twining of plants that looked eerily like Luka. She felt totally drained of any capacity to move. It took almost all of her remaining energy to call across to Callam and Merika that her work was completed.

For a time that lasted both an infinity and only a few breaths, there was complete silence. It was pierced by the whistle of the wind Leshan commanded. Kaylene pushed one hand deep into the earth to ensure she did not fall sideways. Her breath sounded earth-shatteringly loud in her ears. Then the plant-figure that she had created stirred and turned toward her. Hands made of leaves and grass woven together with nothing more than her will reached for her. The mouth opened, but no sound came out – Kaylene had not given her creation a tongue or throat with which to speak.

"You need to use your Blessing to transform to flesh." Kaylene had to force the words out, past her fatigue, past the pain that encircled her head. For a moment, she feared the wind had snatched them from her lips and ensured they did not reach the plant-man, but then she saw him nod.

She slumped onto the ground and the world tilted. From this vantage, she saw the wind race across the land. The sound of thunder washed across her anew.

Leshan came into view, running toward them with something beyond panic across her face. Kaylene's head upon the earth distorted her vantage, lending an even more sinister perspective to the sight. Three Enforcers followed her friend. Unlike Leshan's desperate run, there was a fluidity to their movements that made them seen unencumbered by the wind and thunder.

The green and brown of the plant-Luka took on a pinkish hue. The leaves and stems slowly fused together and become more smooth, more consistent. Kaylene barely had the strength to wonder what would happen to him if the Enforcers overpowered them all. Her work and effort would have been for nothing. Worry and fear tried to make themselves known, but she could not find the energy to notice them. It was difficult enough to keep her eyes open to see what was going on in front of her.

As the entirety of Luka's body took on the hue of skin, the Enforcers drew closer. Their faces were blank, a counterpoint to Leshan's obvious fear. Had Kaylene possessed the strength to be afraid, terror would have overtaken her. As it was, she just observed them as they neared. The menace of competence was imbued in each stride that brought them closer and closer, catching up to Leshan. Soon they would be level with her. She wondered if they would kill them all. They were no ordinary runaways, after all. She was so tired that the question was not accompanied by any emotion.

The Enforcers gained ground on Leshan. As her friend drew closer, the wind became even more intense. Any soil not firmly in the embrace of grasses or plants was picked up and swirled around.

If this was to be her end, Kaylene thought sluggishly as she watched the Enforcers draw near, she should probably feel something other than the deep-rooted fatigue dragging her toward unconsciousness. If she died, she hoped it would be quick and painless.

"No!" Callam's desperate yell speared through the wind. "Meri, stop!"

Kaylene did not see what happened. She could not have moved her head even if she wanted to.

A few heartbeats after Callam's cry, a tendril of bright, violet light whipped across Kaylene's field of vision. For a second it seemed as though it would hit Leshan. Kaylene didn't know what would happen if it touched her friend, but she could only assume it would be bad. But the light reached past Leshan and disappeared.

"Merika stop."

Another tendril of light flickered across Kaylene's eyes, this one thicker. It extended out nearly to the Enforcers.

Leshan reached Kaylene and skidded to a halt, falling heavily onto the ground next to her. Her dawn-coloured eyes flicked down to the increasingly human form before them. Her mouth dropped into a perfect "o" of amazement. Then her eyes went to something behind Kaylene, and her face became a frieze of horror. Suddenly, the pressure of the barrier that had been insistently pressing upon a corner of Kaylene's mind was gone. Whatever Callam and Merika had been doing was completed. Kaylene could do nothing other than watch as the Enforcers took the final steps to reach them. It seemed a shame that they had come so far – brought Luka back, removed the barrier – only to be stopped now. The Enforcers carried the kind of short swords that looked as though they could end life with a single, well-placed blow.

But they stopped before they could even raise their blades. They looked behind Kaylene, the same sort of confusion and fear that had stolen across Leshan's face now on theirs.

Another tendril of violet light whipped into Kaylene's sight. This time it made contact with one of the Enforcers. The woman – perhaps the same woman with the silken voice on whom Kaylene had eavesdropped those nights ago – screamed in agony. The light greedily dived into the woman's open mouth, making the sound of her scream take on an inhuman quality. Kaylene's skin prickled in animal response to such an awful noise. She wanted to close her eyes and save herself from the terrible sight of this woman, immobilised by the light that clung to her like a living second skin. But when she did shut her eyes, the scream continued and Kaylene's mind demanded to know what was transpiring before her.

She opened her eyes to see Merika striding to the Enforcers. She, too, was covered with crawling tendrils of that malevolent violet light. But Merika did not seem to be suffering at all. The Enforcer's scream continued to roll around, carried by the wind, despite the fact that she long since should have needed to pause for breath. Light flashed, bright enough to obscure everything. When Kaylene's vision cleared, the Enforcer had vanished. Merika raised an arm and pointed at the second Enforcer who seemed rooted to the spot in shock. The man tried to run, but he had only half turned before a tendril of light uncoiled from Merika's arm and snaked across the distance between them. It eagerly wrapped around him. The rictus of agony that fell across his face was terrible.

"Meri, stop!" Callam ran past Kaylene toward Merika. The earth pounded against Kaylene's temple in time with his footsteps.

It was like a nightmare to watch Merika wave casually at Callam and see him fall to the ground, unmoving. Merika turned her attention back to the Enforcers. A flick of her fingers made the crawling bolts of light constrict, and suddenly the terrible scream of the woman ceased as the two glowing bodies seemed to disappear into nothingness. The light returned to Merika's outstretched arms. She smiled as she turned back to her friends, but that smile faded as she found Leshan standing, her posture clearly one of defiance. From her vantage, Kaylene could only see her friends' profiles. But the wind dropped suddenly, and every word they exchanged was crisp.

"Meri, what are you doing?"

"They would have killed us." Merika's voice sounded different, thicker, and as though it was coming simultaneously from a distance and up close.

"I'm not talking about them. Did something go wrong when you brought down the barrier?" Leshan took a step toward Merika, but only one.

"No. Everything went exactly as it should have." An almost dreamy note brushed Merika's words.

"What's that light all over you?"

"Oh." Merika glanced down. Cords of the violet light she had used to kill the Enforcers wound slowly around her skin with a terrifying beauty.

"You used it to kill two people."

"What it can do... what I can do with it...it's incredible, Lesha."

"Meri, you're scaring me."

"You don't need to be scared. I told you, everything's fine." The detached way in which Merika spoke made words of comfort disturbing.

"You killed two people."

"And?" Merika tilted her head. The violet cords moved like living things, some with the slowness of a lover, others racing around her limbs, tangling in her hair and sliding across her skin.

"You killed two people," Leshan repeated.

Merika waved her hand dismissively.

"Something's wrong, Meri. That light's dangerous." Leshan took another step forward.

Merika laughed. The sound seemed to tear itself free of her throat. "Don't be ridiculous. It's fine. Here." She reached out a hand and a cord of violet light flashed across to encircle Leshan's waist. She screamed.

Kaylene's breath froze, but Leshan spoke, and while she seemed afraid, she did not appear to be hurt.

"What is it?"

"It's magnificent."

"Just answer me. What is it? What happened?" The sudden burst of anger that ignited her voice sounded odd coming from gentle Leshan.

Merika cocked her head and regarded Leshan. "You're going to try to stop me."

"Stop you from what?"

Merika didn't answer. Instead, a crack seemed to tear the sky in two. A brilliant flash of light blinded Kaylene. When her vision cleared, Leshan was still standing in the same place, staring uncomprehendingly at the space where Merika had been only seconds before.

Movement in front of her drew Kaylene's attention and she dragged her gaze with aching slowness to look at its source. Before her lay Luka. Not a version of him formed from vines and grasses, not a memory. Luka. He looked as exhausted as she felt.

"Kaya?" Luka reached for her, confusion in his eyes that were so like Callam's, but not like Callam's at all. "What just happened?"

Kaylene tried to speak, but even had she the strength to piece together a full sentence, she had no way to explain what had just transpired. The Enforcers were gone, the barrier was gone, and Merika was gone.

TWENTY TWO

Exhaustion robbed them of all impetus to move. As true night claimed the land, the four lay in the embrace of the earth as fatigue and disbelief left them immobile.

At some point Kaylene must have slept for she opened her eyes and the stars in the sky above her had moved. She was cold, but she had insufficient will to address the problem. Luka lay near her, clothed in the garments Leshan had found for him before she too had succumbed to the catatonic state that had seeped across all of them.

Eventually, energy returned to her body and she began to feel as though she would be able to move. Slowly, and with limbs aching at every movement, she sat upright. Luka lay near her. She could see the night sky reflected in his open eyes. He did not turn his head to regard her as she struggled to sit. She wondered what he was thinking.

She pulled herself over to him.

"Did I die?" he asked.

"Yes." She hesitated, wondering if she should ask her next question. She forged on. "What's the last thing you remember?"

His voice was soft. "Pain." His pause had the taste of thought. "How did I come to be here?"

Words refused to resolve themselves into an explanation. "It's a long story," she said finally.

"Was it really that bad?"

Tears stung her eyes. She felt self-conscious, even though he once had been one of the few people she was comfortable crying in front of. Silence was carried by the wind which blew gently across the land for a long time as Kaylene worked to keep her tears at bay.

"We're not going back to the Sanctuary."

Evidently realising that she was unable to speak about what she had undergone to get to this point, Luka changed the subject. "Your hair's short."

A brief smile graced her lips. "Yes, we all had to cut our hair. At Meri's insistence." The smile vanished as she remembered what Merika had done. She still didn't quite understand, but she knew that any explanation would only tear yet another hole through her.

"Merika?" Luka's voice was cautious. "What happened?"

"I don't know." The inadequacy of the response made her feel even more hollow.

A groan announced that Callam was waking.

Kaylene dragged herself over to him. In the dark, it was hard to see his expression.

"Are you all right?"

With obvious discomfort, he heaved himself up to a sitting position. He rubbed his face and raked his fingers through his hair. "She's gone."

"Yes."

His sigh was world-weary. "Luka?"

"I'm here, Cal."

Callam shot upright. He stared at the dark mass on the ground that was his brother. Then, with as much haste as he could manage – which wasn't much at all – he crawled to his brother.

Their silhouettes blended into one as Luka sat up to embrace his brother. Callam's sobs were almost melodic. He held Luka for a long time, then the single dark form became two once more.

"I can't believe we did it." He whispered it more to himself than anything, but the stillness of the evening carried his words to Kaylene's ears.

The depth of his emotion had tears burning in her eyes.

Luka held out a hand toward her and she moved over so she was sitting beside the brothers. She was grateful to be near them; the heat from their bodies was a bulwark against the chill of the night.

"What happened to Merika? Did something go wrong?" she asked Callam. Her voice was low but she was certain Leshan was listening.

She knew Callam's silences well enough to know he was choosing his words carefully, trying to find the best way to break whatever news he had.

"I didn't mean to, but I went inside her mind as we levered open the barrier to break through and get Luka. I could see every thought as it passed through her head. She–" he hesitated, clearly unwilling to say what came next "—she had planned all along to do this. I mean, Meri – she's always wanted to test the limits of her Blessing, to attain more skill, more power. She went to Ay'ash after you told us about her, not to get help with the scroll but to find out what exactly she could do if we managed to open the way to the Divine Realm. The Old One told her that pulling people through from the Divine Realm is only one thing that can be done. She...she told Merika that it is possible to take some of the power that's in there as well.

"Meri claimed whatever was in there as her own, but it changed her. I couldn't stay in her thoughts once she had that light at her command, but I know it wasn't what she expected. The way her thoughts felt...they changed as soon as she grasped that power. Like there was a second set of thoughts, a second identity there."

"She lied to us?" Dismay seemed far too insignificant a word to describe what was in Leshan's voice as it floated across.

"She kept it from us," Callam replied.

"It's the same thing." Leshan's bitterness resonated within Kaylene's heart.

"Did...did Ay'ash trick her somehow?" Kaylene remembered the smiling sadism Ay'ash and Thurien seemed to share, and the sense that they knew far more than they were revealing. She wondered if this had all been part of some greater plan, and if she and her friends had unwittingly done something truly disastrous. As much as she hated to admit it, she could see how Merika's ravenous appetite for knowledge and new experience could have been used against her.

"I don't know. She thought it was possible, but thought it was a risk worth taking." Callam sounded tired. Old. Far older than his age.

"So what happened? Where did she go?" Kaylene asked.

"Like I said, I was thrown out of her mind, so I only glimpsed a little. I know she did want to protect us from the Enforcers. But it was like there was an impulse to leave us. Perhaps that took precedence at the end."

"Where did she go?" Luka asked.

"I don't know."

Into the desolate silence that followed, Luka voiced a question, awe filling his voice. "You opened a way to the Divine Realm to bring me back?"

"Once Kaya found out it was possible to bring you back, there wasn't anything we wouldn't have done to see it through," Callam answered.

Luka took Kaylene's hand. "You did all that for me?"

"Of course." Guilt over her uncertainty about her feelings for him stabbed her as his hand squeezed hers, especially in the face of how obvious it was that Callam had never given up on Luka in the way that she had.

"So what do we do now?" The question seemed to take on a physical presence that floated on the cool night air.

Leshan answered, her voice harsh in a way Kaylene had never before heard. "We go through the pass."

Nobody pursued them. In the mountains, the summer heat was soft and it made for pleasant travel. Yet the party of four was subdued as they trekked into the Third Country. The hearat, having bolted during what had unfolded in front of the barrier and been reharnessed, reluctantly pulled the cart.

Merika's betrayal felt no less unreal with each passing day. Her absence was all too noticeable. Her vivacity and determination had given them all a sense of purpose that was sorely lacking without her. Leshan was the most affected, for obvious reasons. Kaylene tried several times to speak with her about Merika, but could never find the right way to open such a sensitive discussion. They all pretended not to hear Leshan's muffled sobs late in the evenings or the way her golden-orange eyes would suddenly fill with tears at intervals during the day.

They gave Luka the story in pieces of how they came to bring him back from the Divine Realm. Kaylene could not face telling in one sitting the enormity of what she had faced over the past months. She assumed Callam and Leshan felt the same way.

He listened with the same seriousness he offered to everyone, eyes that she had spent so many years loving clouded as he listened. He was the same Luka as ever: kind, caring, and predisposed to a humour that was unique in its gentleness. But the space he occupied among the group of friends felt odd where once it had felt natural. Some of that was Merika's absence, but not entirely.

After two days, Luka finally approached Kaylene alone. His expression was transparently one of worry. She had forgotten that about him. He had changed his hair to a vibrant orange, adjusting the tone of his skin so that the flaming locks looked almost natural. Even changing his features – something he had done for as long as Kaylene had known him – was an unexpected note. It felt flippant in the face of all that had happened. But, as she reminded herself, he had not experienced any of what she had.

"Is everything all right?" he asked as they were settling down for the evening. Kaylene was calling forth a dinner of wild berries and fruits. With no provisions, her Blessing was keeping them nourished. She was coming to long for even the inns' unpalatable bread.

She said as much, easily drawing a chuckle from him.

"That's not really what I meant."

She paused in picking berries off a bush. "Do you remember anything from when you were..." She didn't want to say the word "dead".

He shook his head, inclining it in the manner so familiar it was almost painful. "Honestly, it's like no time has passed at all."

She chewed her lower lip as she thought how best to express what she wanted to say next. The weighing of her words was a habit that she had refined from being so close to Callam. Even that change in her, she observed Luka noticing.

"Time did pass for me," she said eventually. "And I suppose I still can't believe that you're really here."

He reached for her, placing his hands under hers, cupping a handful of bright pink berries.

"You've changed. It's like you're Kaylene, but not."

She turned away to conceal a sardonic twist of her lips. It was so simple to conceal such darting thoughts from Luka. Guilt stabbed at her for her deception and her thought. Her eyes, of their own accord, flicked to Callam a little distance away. He was looking away from her, but she knew he had heard all her thoughts.

She turned back to Luka, the man who she had once loved so completely that there was nothing else in the world of any importance aside from him, and made herself smile. It was not his fault that his compassion had seen him killed. It was not his fault that she had been so empty that she'd set in motion all that had transpired. Had he not died, the horror and sorrow at her understanding of the world being peeled away to reveal unpleasantness and deceit would never have taken root within her heart. Better to hold herself responsible for being so entombed in love for him that she heedlessly sought to tear the world asunder to bring him back.

Perhaps some of those thoughts were ill-concealed after all, because concern shadowed Luka's face.

"I didn't mean that you've changed in a bad way."

That elicited a genuine smile from her. There was nothing as completely Luka as his desire to soothe.

"I know," she said. "I suppose I hadn't realised it until you said it."

"I think I like your hair like this." Luka offered her the observation along with a smile that contained as much love for her as it ever had. She still hadn't found a way to tell him that her feelings for him, which once she had thought as unchanging as mountains, were perhaps not the same as they once were.

There was something very childish about that belief, now that she considered it.

The shadow that haunted Leshan's eyes did not depart. If anything, it became more prominent in the next two days of travel. Finally, Kaylene could take her friend's self-contained despair no longer. She approached Leshan in the morning, while the chill of the mountain air still stung the edges of the air.

"It hurts me too, what Merika did." Kaylene spoke bluntly because she knew no way to cushion the sentiment.

Leshan looked as though she had been pulled from a dream. From the corner of her eye, Kaylene saw Callam pull Luka aside, presumably to give Kaylene time to speak with their friend.

"What?" Leshan asked.

"What Merika did. It hurts every time I think about it," Kaylene repeated.

"There's something you don't know, though."

"I do know," Kaylene said before Leshan could go on. She didn't want to put her friend through the discomfort of explicitly revealing her romance with Merika.

Leshan's surprise was obvious, as was her embarrassment. Kaylene gave her friend a moment to collect herself by lifting her gaze to the surrounding landscape. The plants around them had gradually changed as they moved into the warmer climate of the Third Country and began to descend the mountain. They were unfamiliar to her. If she reached out to them, she could sense just how different they were. She realised that the skill she had cultivated – the languages she had learned in the Sanctuary – could finally be put to practical use. It offered a tendril of excitement, even if that excitement was dulled by the pain of Merika's betrayal.

She returned her attention to Leshan. Her friend's eyes were dulled with sadness, but her face was as composed as ever.

"Did you love her?" The question escaped Kaylene's mouth before she could stop it.

An attempt at a smile draped itself across Leshan's mouth. "I suppose I did. Do."

"And she—"

"Let me think she cared about me," Leshan said.

"I'm sorry." It was the most insufficient platitude that Kaylene could offer her friend, but she said it nevertheless, trying with that inadequacy to let Leshan know that she was there, and would be there, for her.

"It seems foolish that I believed she wanted to find a new world with me." Those dawn-coloured eyes closed and a solitary tear slipped from underneath one lid.

"You can't know how whatever she took from the Divine Realm changed her."

"But she still lied about what she was planning. She'd been lying to us for weeks."

To that, Kaylene had no reply. The weight of Merika's deception was unavoidably suffocating. Rather than see Leshan's grief, she looked back to the landscape. The vegetation was unexpectedly beautiful in its novelty, each new tree and flower a delight. The joy of discovery refused to be barred from Kaylene's heart, and she could not contain the amazement and budding excitement at being in a part of the world that was wholly new to her. Soon they would be in the Third Country. All information about it was filtered through the few merchants who travelled outside the First Country to hawk their wares, so it was sparse and pertained only to what the merchants themselves found useful. Now, she would see everything for herself. Her sorrow at Merika's deception could not contain the thrill at exploring a new place, as well as the prospect of finding a place for herself within it that was not contained by the dictates of the Sanctuary.

She took Leshan's hands. "Nothing that I say can possibly make what Merika did less hurtful. But if we keep going, it may become less painful. And while we wait for the hurt to become manageable, there's so much for us."

"What could possibly be left for us?" Leshan asked. Despair and hurt infused her voice.

Kaylene looked up at the new landscape before them. "The whole world."

ACKNOWLEDGEMENTS

Wow.

This book was written in 2017-2018, but I only came back to edit it at the beginning of 2020, after several significant losses and disappointments. I realised then that the core of the story was about grief, and how we incorporate loss into our lives. Then Covid-19 hit. Living in Melbourne, Australia, we weathered the storm with reasonable ease, all things considered. Although, in the sliver of time between the two major lockdowns, my grandfather passed away. Coming from a small, tightly-knit family, it was devastating, and as I came back for the major pass at *Deliverance*, the work took on even more meaning. I edited it amid the still winter days locked inside, while I wrestled with the way my world had changed in so many ways. I like to think it means it gave the book an emotional trueness. First and foremost, my thanks to my wonderful psychologist, Vera, whose guidance is always invaluable. At the beginning of 2020, I said to her, "I just wonder what's going to happen next, how can I possibly cope with it?" (I just had to ask, didn't I). She said, "but you thought that the last time something happened, and the time before that. And you didn't break." It's a piece of wisdom I hope people reading this can take for themselves.

Of course, thanks to my family; my stronger-than-steel grandmother, my stronger-than-stronger-than-steel mother, my father, my sister, my partner, and my friends, who are also family. I have always known how lucky I am to have you all. Thank you for your support, interest, patience, and love – and in the instance of my parents; beta reads, formatting, helping me refine the title, and just general encouragement.

As always, I must extend my appreciation to the team who help take this to an actual book. My editor, Jason, who is the absolute best, Marcus, who brings these beautiful covers to realisation – all the way from Austria, Ellen, who very patiently took my myriad of reference pictures and made her best map yet, and Nicole who is a superb cover illustrator.

Perhaps my most effusive thanks must go to the Bookstagram community, because without their support, I would not be publishing my seventh (!) fiction book. It's also how I connected with the amazing Katherine from *Debut Books*, which published the non-fiction *Mirror, Mirror*. Kat was also the first person to read *Deliverance* and reassure me it wasn't a flaming dumpster fire of a manuscript but instead, possibly, quite a good book. Kat, you're a true marvel.

Final thanks – of all people – go to Taylor Swift. I often have a 'centering song' that I listen to in order to get into the mood for specific projects. 'Delicate' was that song during the first draft (largely because I felt it captured the uncertainty of the relationship between Kaylene and Callam), and 'the 1' and 'cardigan' helped me get through the final push of editing.

ABOUT THE AUTHOR

Alice Boér-Endacott is a Melbourne-based author whose passions include nerding out over literary theory, playing videogames, and – when there isn't a global pandemic occurring – leaving her house.

When she isn't writing, she's either thinking about writing, or eating, and very occasionally performing the role of Secretary for LoveOzYA (an organisation which seeks to champion Australian Young Adult literature).

You can find out more by visiting her website, **www.abendacott.com**, or following her on Instagram (@alicejaneboere), or Twitter (@ajendacott).

If you enjoyed *Deliverance of the Blessed*, please consider leaving a review on Goodreads, Amazon, or the Storygraph. Reviews are vital to ensuring the success of any book, and even one review can make a significant difference.

COMING

Kaylene's story doesn't end; she'll return, along with some other familiar voices:

Strange forces are moving across the Godskissed Continent, and the world is changing.

Four exceptional women are brought together by these events:

A healer and councilwoman,

An exiled heiress,

A fugitive,

And an assassin.

What they witness will be the stuff of legend.

During the wait, why not catch up on the other series in the Godskissed Continent...

If you were interested in the tale hinted at when Kaylene met Lexa, then read about it in *The Ruthless Land*...

To outsiders, the Fourth Country is an unforgiving place. Under the leadership of ruthless women, powerful families regularly wage brutal campaigns against one another to increase their land and wealth, and men live in a state of complete subjugation.

Lexana, heiress to the Farwan family, is sent to the Academy, an elite institution where the daughters of powerful families learn and refine techniques to maintain and gain power. There, she finds herself attracted to Jaxen, one of the teachers who defies convention and goes about unveiled. His apparent disregard for what is expected of him leaves her both uneasy and fascinated.

Then the impossible comes to pass, and disaster befalls the Farwan family. Lexa must leave the Academy to find her mother and help restore her family to power. Jaxen insists upon accompanying her, arguing that she cannot survive without his help. Lexa can't be certain that she can trust Jaxen, but he is right; she needs his help if she is to succeed.

Set after the events of Queendom and King of the Seven Lakes comes a standalone book set in the Godskissed Continent which explores questions of family, equality, love, and betrayal.

Curious about the recent history of the country to where Kaylene and her friends flee? Read about its recent history in *Dark Intent*.

Many years after the brutal Kade takeover of the Third Country, healer Freya Kuch has succeeded when many Pious have failed: she is a perfect Kade citizen. However, this life of willing subjugation is torn apart when she is caught in an attack perpetrated by the anarchic followers of the Dark Gods and is assigned to care for Zarech, their captured leader. Contrary to her expectations, he is not a raving madman but charismatic and rational. As she unwillingly becomes closer to Zarech and he reveals knowledge the Kade has deliberately repressed, she begins to reconsider everything.

Her obedience to the strict Kade regime is further complicated by her attraction to Ashtyn, whose bold comments against the Kade frighten and compel her in equal measure. She tries to ignore her feelings knowing full well the brutal punishments for adultery and dissidence. But soon, she is forced to decide: will she maintain her life of careful safety, or give in to her heart's dark desires and fight against the Kade's regime?

Or read about the book which introduced the world to the Godskissed Continent, *Queendom of the Seven Lakes*

No man has ever ruled the Second Country. Until Now.

When the Family of Assassins is engaged to protect the first male heir to the throne, Elen-ai reluctantly takes the contract.

But dissidence brews in the Queendom of the Seven Lakes, and she is quickly entangled in it, willing or not.

CPSIA information can be obtained
at www.ICGtesting.com
Printed in the USA
BVHW071014180121
598050BV00010B/231